**Other Jane Jameson adventures
available from Pocket Star Books**

Nice Girls Don't Have Fangs

Nice Girls Don't Date Dead Men

NICE
GIRLS
DON'T LIVE
FOREVER

MOLLY HARPER

Pocket **STAR** Books
New York   London   Toronto   Sydney

Pocket Star Books
A Division of Simon & Schuster, Inc.
1230 Avenue of the Americas
New York, NY 10020

This book is a work of fiction. Names, characters, places, and incidents either are products of the author's imagination or are used fictitiously. Any resemblance to actual events or locales or persons, living or dead, is entirely coincidental.

First Pocket Star Books paperback edition January 2010

POCKET STAR BOOKS and colophon are registered trademarks of Simon & Schuster, Inc.

For information about special discounts for bulk purchases, please contact Simon & Schuster Special Sales at 1-866-506-1949 or business@simonandschuster.com

The Simon & Schuster Speakers Bureau can bring authors to your live event. For more information or to book an event contact the Simon & Schuster Speakers Bureau at 1-866-248-3049 or visit our website at www.simonspeakers.com.

Cover design by John Vairo Jr.

Manufactured in the United States of America

10 9 8 7 6 5 4 3 2 1

ISBN 978-1-4165-8944-0
ISBN 978-1-4391-6669-7 (ebook)

Acknowledgments

Many thanks to my husband, David, for putting up with a sleep-deprived and occasionally cranky spouse who has conversations with people that don't really exist. To my mom, the one-woman maternal marketing machine: I would not be here without you. To my dad: many fathers wouldn't know what to with a daughter who writes this sort of thing, so thanks for showing me how proud you are every day. To Russ and Nancy, who probably didn't expect nearly this many vampire-related family dinner conversations when I married your son: thank you for all of your support.

And finally, the Jane Jameson books would not have seen the light of day without the enthusiasm, patience, and subtle prodding of my agent, Stephany Evans. My endless gratitude, darlin'.

The worst thing you can do in a relationship, vampire or otherwise, is actually telling your partner that you don't trust him. Even if it's true.

—Love Bites: A Female Vampire's Guide to Less Destructive Relationships

My life didn't begin until I died.

Pre-vampire Jane worked Saturdays and holidays and any other days that no one else on the library staff wanted to work. I had never done anything for myself. I'd never traveled. And now, I was my own boss. I'd had the opportunity to kiss foreign soil. Actually, it was the tile in Heathrow Airport's Sunproof Lounge on the very first stop of our trip—London. I think my worship of solid ground embarrassed my sire/boyfriend, Gabriel Nightengale. And the pickpockets were able to peg me as a tourist right away. But I was really, really happy to be off that plane.

I have claustrophobia issues.

I'd never had a healthy adult relationship as a live girl. Then again, I'd just abandoned my 150-year-old boyfriend in a hotel room in Brussels, so maybe this one didn't count, either.

I'm pretty sure it was Brussels. We'd made quite a few stops since London.

My 'round-the-world romantic getaway with Gabriel turned sour early on, right after we checked into our first hotel in London. There was a note waiting for Gabriel at the front desk, fancy linen paper addressed in spidery black ink. Whatever it said, it put him in a very foul mood. The minute we'd settled into the exceedingly posh room, he put his flowy black coat back on, said he had to make some phone calls, and disappeared for most of the night. My newly purchased trunkload of lacy underthings took this very personally. When he returned, he gave me a cursory kiss good night and collapsed into sleep. I managed to say, "What the hell?" in about fourteen languages.

You know how after you've hung around a person for a while, you can tell when they're *trying* to have a good time? Well, this phenomenon was just frightening in Gabriel. He was like a Carlson Wagonlit agent on crack, manically planning all-night excursions to museums, the opera, beer gardens, fancy intimidating parties with his fancy intimidating friends—anything that would keep us out of the hotel room from dusk till dawn. Gabriel's credit-card company put a fraud watch on his accounts as we switched hotels on a whim, two or three times per city. Each time we checked in, a creamy linen envelope was waiting for him at the front desk. And each time, his eyes got just a little more Manson-ish. Charles or Marilyn, take your pick.

His cell phone rang incessantly, and every time it did, he either let it go to voicemail or whispered, "Business," and took the call outside. I tried to ignore the warning signs. I tried to give Gabriel the benefit of the doubt, but a girl can only bury her head so deep in the sand. He had told me months before that he was having issues he couldn't tell me about. There were frequent business trips during which I couldn't reach him by phone. And I'd found out that on several occasions, he'd lied about where he'd been. He'd assured me that it wasn't another woman, despite the fact that the name "Jeanine" had popped up on his cell phone several times. Never had I wished so much that my stupid, inconsistent mind-reading powers worked on my sire.

Even though I still had (raging, screaming) doubts, I had chosen to believe him. And now, I was starting to feel like one of those women at whom people yell, "How stupid can you be?" when they inevitably appear on *Dr. Phil*.

I suppose one should expect a certain amount of drama in a relationship that started with one party dying in a muddy ditch off a dark country road. I don't like talking about the night I was turned. All young vampires eventually get drunk with their buddies and share war stories about how they became undead. I do not partake in such revelries. Why?

The short version is this: I was (unfairly, unceremoniously) fired from the library and replaced by my supervisor's barely literate firebug stepdaughter. But instead of getting a severance check, I got just enough of a gift certificate to get rip-snorting drunk at Shenanigans. I met Gabriel, flirtation ensued. I sobered enough to drive, but as a result of unfortunate circumstances, my ancient car, Big Bertha, died halfway home. I was spotted walking down the road by the town drunk, Bud McElray, who mistook me for a deer and shot me. I was left in the ditch to die, only to be found and turned by Gabriel.

You don't become a vampire just by being bitten. Vampirism isn't a germ or a curse or karmic justice for overtanners. To make a childe, a vampire will feed on a human until he or she reaches the point of death, then feed the initiate as much undead blood as he or she can take. The process takes a lot out of the sire, which is why a vampire will only turn a handful of "children" in his or her lifetime.

Gabriel being my sire *and* my boyfriend caused some complications in our relationship. It was his job to lead me through the transition to vampirism, but since I rarely listened to him, that didn't work out so well. And confrontations between the two of us tended to get sort of violent . . . and naked. So, instead of indulging in accusations of infidelity and undead Johnny Depp hotel theatrics, I bit my tongue. Hell, I bit a hole through my tongue. Fortunately, I had vampire healing, so it grew right back. But then we checked into the Mandarin Oriental Hotel in Munich, and a linen envelope was waiting.

The look on Gabriel's face made a bellboy cry.

Our itinerary became even more packed. I was frequently left alone with Gabriel's strange Euro-vampire friends as he held urgent "business meetings." I occasionally woke up at dusk and couldn't figure out where Gabriel was. Of course, we switched locations so often, a few times I woke up and couldn't figure out where *I* was. But that didn't make me feel any better when Gabriel crept into the room with lame excuses about running out for a newspaper or a fresh bottle of blood. Even my "white lie acceptance" level has limits.

When Gabriel was in the shower one night, I happened to peek into the wastebasket, where he'd left the torn remnants of his latest note. I saw words like "bloodmate" and "love you."

I swear, it wasn't my fault that the basket tipped over and those little bits of paper somehow managed to reassemble themselves perfectly into their original order. OK, fine, I abused my jigsaw-puzzle skills. But if Gabriel didn't want me reading the note, he probably should have burned it. My vision tinged red as I made out phrases like "Remember what we are to each other," "Remember what we have," "The woman you're with can't satisfy you like I do."

Satisfy you like I *do*? In the present tense? Gabriel had recently been satisfied by this woman? I fell on my knees, stunned by an explosion of pain in my chest. If my heart beat, I would have sworn I'd blown an aorta. He'd promised. He'd sworn that he was faithful to me. And, like an idiot, I'd believed him.

The phone rang. With numbed fingers, I knocked the phone off its cradle and heard the voice of my best friend, Zeb. I launched into a paranoid diatribe on cheating boyfriends. I ignored all attempts on his part to make me think like a normal person or believe that all of this could be a very complicated coincidence.

"Whose side are you on?" I hissed, listening for the sound of Gabriel's shower running. I swiped the little bits of paper back into the wastebasket.

"Um, logic and reason?" Zeb suggested. "And as much as I enjoy paying ten dollars a minute to listen to you rant hysterically, I called to let you know there was a burglary at the shop last night."

After my masterful string of profanity, Zeb explained that two nights before, someone had thrown a brick through the front window and ransacked the stock. Oddly enough, some of the more valuable items—figurines and crystals and ceremonial objects—had been ignored in favor of tearing through boxes of books. Books were thrown aside, their spines cracked and damaged, Zeb's descriptions of which were enough to make me produce distressed sounds in several different languages.

Zeb said in a soothing voice, "Fortunately, they didn't know how valuable some of the books were, because they didn't take anything."

"What kind of underachieving burglars don't take anything?" I asked, grasping at any excuse not to think about the nauseating ripple of pain shredding through my body. I could do this. I could get through this. I just had to focus on what Zeb was saying.

"I don't know. Mr. Wainwright was out on the town with your aunt Jettie, so he was no help. It's my theory that one of the adult-video store's old clients just got confused and was searching for his recommended daily allowance of visual stimuli," Zeb said as I pulled my suit-case out of the closet. "Dick thinks it was someone look-ing for something specific, who couldn't understand your weird shelving system."

"Yeah, alphabetical order is revolutionary." I snorted. "So, how much damage are we talking about here?"

"Not much. Other than the window being broken and the books being tossed around, nothing. Which, to me, says the thieves were over thirty. No angry teenager could pass up the chance to mess up newly painted walls and a shiny new espresso machine."

"Look, I'm coming home on the next flight," I said, randomly tossing clothes into my bag.

"What? No, Jane, there's no reason to do that. Dick and Andrea can take care of everything. Andrea's almost as anal-retentive as you are. She's doing a great job."

"I'm coming home, Zeb," I repeated.

"Jane, don't turn this into a— You're hanging up on me now, aren't you? Dang it, Jane!" he cried as I snapped the phone back into the cradle.

Gabriel emerged from the bathroom, his hips swathed in a huge white towel. His deep gray eyes tracked warily from my packed bag to the phone. "Who were you talk-ing to?"

My head snapped up, and it took everything in me not to throw the nightstand across the room at him. I wanted to scream, to strike at him until he hurt as much as I did. But I couldn't. I had become numb. Empty. I took a few deep breaths, unlocked my jaw, and concen-trated on keeping my tone even, unaffected.

"There's been a break-in at the shop. I need to go home and take care of it," I said, clicking the suitcase shut. "If you could send the rest of my stuff home, I'd appreciate it."

I looked up, hoping to see some response from Gabriel, something to show that he wanted me to stay. But he seemed relieved. He blew out a breath and slid into a pair of black jeans. "Well, if you have to go, you have to go. It's probably better this way."

And then he helped me pack.

It was like being slapped with indifference. He honestly did not care whether I was there or not. I could have just announced that I was going to take a flying leap off the roof, and he would have just nodded obligingly.

"Well, OK, then," I muttered, throwing my jacket on. "I'll see you when you get home. After you've finished your business."

"I'll see you soon," he promised as gave me a sterile peck on the forehead. It was a dismissive and fatherly sort of kiss. "This is really for the best. I think we can both agree that this trip hasn't quite worked out as we'd hoped. I'll call you."

As the door literally hit me in the butt on my way out, I was struck by the realization that Gabriel had just used classic brush-off platitudes on me. Did he just break up with me and not even have the decency to tell me? Now well and truly pissed, I carted my luggage to the front desk.

You know those French movies, where a weary lover climbs into a taxi wearing an oversized shawl and Jackie O sunglasses as Paris slowly fades away? And as she's driven to the airport, they might show a single glistening tear sliding down her cheek? Yes, the image is dramatic and glamorous, but living it just plain sucks.

If one is undead and hell-bent on travel, I must suggest Virgin Airlines' Vamp Air. Trust Richard Branson to find a niche market involving carefully shaded windows and a selection of blood constantly warmed to exactly 98.6 degrees. Plus, few parents are willing to bring crying babies onto a plane full of vampires, so it's blissfully quiet. I dragged my sunscreened, jet-lagged carcass through the Nashville International baggage claim at four A.M. to find Zeb waiting for me, holding a sign that said, "Undead Tourism Bureau."

I propped my sunglasses on top of my head and smirked. "What were you going to do if someone else fit the bill?"

"What'd you bring me? What'd you bring me?" he asked, hopping up and down.

"Tiny liquor bottles from the minibar," I said, holding up my suitcase proudly and thumping it into his chest.

"Sadly, that's the same thing my uncle Ron gave me for Christmas." He snorted, taking my little carry-on bag onto his shoulder.

"I wrapped them in hotel towels from four different countries," I added.

He grinned. "Excellent."

I actually had gotten him and Jolene fancy 500-thread-count sheets and some very expensive snacks from Harrods. The hotel towels were for me.

We reached Zeb's car, threw my luggage into the back-seat, and took our places up front. Zeb started the car and paid the exorbitant parking fee. "So, tell me every-thing. Where did you go? What did you see?"

"Went to some parties, met strange and snotty people. Saw some great museums and restaurants, but being in France and not being able to eat chocolate is downright masochistic. Oh, we saw *Carmen* performed in Vienna. Did you know the whole first song is about cigarette smoke?"

"I didn't know that," Zeb admitted. "But I'm surprised *you* didn't know that."

"Oh, ha-ha. So, where's your lovely wife?" I asked as we pulled onto the interstate. "What's she doing letting you take off for Nashville after midnight? Doesn't she know you get lost?"

Zeb grimaced. Things between Jolene and Zeb had been tense lately. They were still trying to build a home on the land I'd given them as a wedding present. The house was slow to finish because Jolene's family was pressur-ing them to move back onto the McClaine family com-pound. Werewolves are notoriously territorial, and Jolene was the first McClaine to live "off-site" since they'd settled in the Hollow two hundred years before. The family owns multiple businesses in the Hollow, including several con-struction firms. And what they don't own they could in-fluence with scary male werewolf dominance. So, to say that it was difficult for Zeb and Jolene to get contractors to show up—risking pissing off Jolene's kin—much less finish their work, was an understatement.

To top it off, the brand-newish trailer they'd been offered as an incentive to live on McClaine land had mysteriously evaporated when Zeb and Jolene announced they were building their own home, leaving the newly-weds with the camper recently vacated by Jolene's stoner cousin, Larry. And one could live in the close quarters of a cannabis-saturated camper for only so long before one's marriage began feeling like the last half of *The Shining*.

I would say that Zeb was a saint to put up with such interference from his in-laws, but his family's no prize herd, either. Let's just say that one of the Lavelle family's favorite Christmas activities is to gather around the TV and watch their highlight reel from the "Rowdy Rural Towns" episode of *COPS*.

Zeb's mother, Ginger Lavelle, had a number of reasons to shun me lately, the least of which was that I refused to let her ruin Zeb's honeymoon. To bastardize Harry Potter, I was Zeb's "Secret Keeper" for his honeymoon destination. Zeb told his family that he and Jolene were going to the mountain retreats of Gatlinburg, when he, in fact, took his blushing bride to Biloxi, for a week of Gulf shrimp, putt-putt, and blessed silence. Their hotel information was sealed in an envelope and given to me with the instructions that it was to be opened only if someone was dead or incapacitated . . . well, more incapacitated than usual.

While contrite over her wacky antiwedding antics, Mama Ginger could remain chastised for only so long. Incensed that she could not locate her son after calling every hotel in Gatlinburg, Mama Ginger called me to demand that I give her the location and phone number *right now*, because she was having chest pains and was being taken to the hospital. Used to this ploy, I refused. She switched tactics and said that she needed the number because Zeb's father, Floyd, had dropped an automatic cigarette lighter into his lap while driving and was being treated for several third-degree burns in sensitive areas.

While that scenario was far more plausible, I still withheld the number, which prompted Mama Ginger to announce that she would never speak to me again. I was not properly devastated by this announcement, which just made Mama Ginger angrier. Mama Ginger had long held out hope that Zeb and I would one day wed, but now that she knew about my "unfortunate condition," she was slightly ashamed to have wanted a vampire as an in-law. She was still less than civil to Jolene. But she now preferred her daughter-in-law to me, because at least Jolene wasn't a vampire. Of course, Zeb hadn't yet broken the news about his new bride being a werewolf, but that was neither here nor there.

I'd promised myself that I was going to back off and stop interfering in Jolene and Zeb's relationship, but it was so much healthier than talking about my own relationship. So, I think I earned a pass just this once. "Tell me you haven't been watching *The Howling* again," I groaned. "You know it's just a movie."

Zeb gave me a distinctly not-amused look, then sighed. "Marriage is a little harder than I thought it would be. Just normal stuff, you know. Things that get on each other's nerves." He began ticking off Jolene's numerous faults on his fingers. "She chews her fingernails *and* her toenails. She cannot stop herself from answering the questions from *Jeopardy* out loud, even when she knows she's wrong. She sheds. She puts ketchup on her egg rolls."

"Blasphemy." I shuddered. "And as much as it would be in my own personal interest to interfere with your marriage and reclaim your full attention, you do realize that you are married to arguably one of the most beautiful women on the planet. And you are a male kindergarten teacher who collects dolls."

"Action figures," he corrected.

"And she stuck with you, despite the fact that your mother tried to make wedding-party casting changes during the rehearsal and had you hypnotized by a five-dollar psychic so you'd dump Jolene at the altar."

"Her family put out a bear trap for me!" he huffed.

"Well, that just means that your families cancel each other out."

He snickered, his expression softening. "She's pregnant."

My jaw actually hit the middle of my chest. "Well, that explains the egg rolls and ketchup."

My throat tightened at the thought of Zeb having a baby. This was so huge, the last step toward Zeb really growing up. I'll admit I was a little jealous. I was being left behind again. Zeb was doing something I would never do. But, as I'd discovered last year when Zeb's mom dumped an infant on my doorstep in an attempt to jump-start my biological clock, I am not cut out to nurture. And because I no longer have a pulse, I can't have children—which works out nicely.

"But this is a good thing, right?" I shook his shoulder. "I'm going to be an honorary aunt."

"It's a great thing, except the idea of being responsible for a whole family sort of scares the crap out of me. We wanted to have kids right away, and given how fertile her family is, we knew there was no contraception on earth that would work. But that's not really our problem. Her mother comes over every single day. Her aunts are always bringing over food, or they're putting up curtains that they made, or they're moving our dishes around in the cabinets without asking. And Jolene just lets them. And the men! If they don't back off and let a contractor come out to finish the house, we're going to be raising their grandchild in a pot-soaked RV. Is that what they want? I'm just frustrated and feel . . . impotent."

"Well, obviously, that's not the case. When is she due?"

"In about four months," he said.

"What? You guys were pregnant before the wedding? And you didn't tell me!"

Zeb rolled his eyes. "No. It's a werewolf thing. The average wolf pregnancy is only about sixty days. Werewolves sort of split the difference with five months."

"Wow. So, you have very little time to get ready for this baby—babies? How many kids is Jolene going to have? Is it going to be like a litter?"

Zeb looked horror-struck.

"Seriously, you hadn't thought of that before?" I asked him as little beads of sweat popped out on his forehead.

"There are four sets of twins just among Jolene's first cousins."

"I'm still processing everything!" Zeb shouted.

"Maybe I should drive," I suggested.

"No, let's talk about why you think Gabriel would suddenly start cheating on you. That will keep me awake."

"Let's not," I told him. "I don't want to rehash the whole thing. I just want to pretend it didn't happen."

"Because denial usually works so well for you."

"I'm going to deny that I just heard that. Should we stop by the shop? I'd like to see the damages, know what I'm getting into," I said.

"Your internal clock must be off, world traveler. The sun's going to rise soon." He nodded to the lightening blue-gray sky on the horizon. "We'll have just enough time to get you home."

As the sky turned toward lilac, I snuggled under a blanket and dozed the last hour or so before we reached the family manse, River Oaks. More English country cottage than sprawling Georgian plantation, River Oaks is at its heart just an old family farm home that happened to be built before the Civil War. Despite my having spent the last few weeks in buildings that were much older and far more elegant, my house had never seemed so beautiful.

I kissed Zeb's cheeks, mumbled a good night, and dashed for the door with the blanket over my head. In my room, on sheets that were weeks old and slightly musty, I lay down and, for reasons I hadn't quite processed yet, cried.

2

Successful relationships are about compromise. If you agree not to bring up his undead ex-girlfriends during arguments, he should agree not to seek out your old human boyfriends and kill them.

—Love Bites: A Female Vampire's Guide to Less
Destructive Relationships

The problem with sleeping during the day is that people tend to overestimate the joys of early-morning visits.

It started about an hour after I finally fell asleep, when Aunt Jettie sauntered into the house and discovered my carry-on by the door.

"Baby doll, you're back!" she cried, materializing at my bedside.

"Gah!" I screamed, leaping off the bed and clinging to the ceiling. "Knocking! Aunt Jettie! We have a rule about knocking!"

My ghostly favorite aunt/roommate placed her transparent hands on her hips. "Oh, get down from the ceiling and let me look at you. I haven't seen you in weeks. Don't make me float up there, it makes me dizzy."

Jettie Belle Early, sister to my grandma Ruthie, took me under her wing when I was around age six and when Ruthie and I both figured out that we were basically incompatible. (Grandma Ruthie wanted to give me a home perm and enter me in the Little Miss Half-Moon Hollow Pageant. I hid in her attic all day to avoid the perm, pretending that I was Anne Frank.) I spent entire summers with Jettie at River Oaks, which she inherited after spending her formative years caring for her elderly father. This was a great shock to Grandma Ruthie, who had already made plans to overhaul the house in time for the local historical society's annual tour of historic homes.

Aunt Jettie was a linchpin in every major moment in my life. It was Aunt Jettie who helped me fill out financial-aid paperwork for college. It was Aunt Jettie who persuaded me to stay in school and get my master's in library science so the local public library would have no choice but to hire me. It was Aunt Jettie who helped me through that first night as a vampire. It was Aunt Jettie whose upside-down face was now smiling up at me expectantly.

"I missed you, too, Aunt Jettie," I grunted as I disengaged my fingernails from the plaster and hopped down to the bed. "Is Mr. Wainwright here?"

She smiled as she thought of her beau, who also happened to be my recently deceased boss. "No, he's really beating himself up over this break-in, so he's standing guard at the shop. I told Zeb not to bother you with it, but he insisted you'd want to. Why are your eyes all puffy?"

"Oh, it's just the French," I said, wiping at the oh-so-attractive bloody tear tracks drying on my cheeks. "They were so damn rude."

"I thought you were in Brussels," Jettie said as I climbed back into bed. Outside my bedroom window, creeping fingers of sunlight were flirting with the edges of my blackout curtains. My internal clock told me it was almost six A.M., and I was so tired I could actually feel the drag on my limbs. Aunt Jettie pulled the covers up to my chin as she asked, "Where's Gabriel?"

"Still in Brussels," I said. "He had some things to take care of."

Jettie studied my face in that unnerving X-ray method of hers. Fortunately, any penetrating wisdom on her part was cut short by my mother's sudden appearance at my bedroom door.

"Hi, baby!" Mama cried. "Thank goodness you're back!"

"What the hell is wrong with you people?" I howled, chucking a pillow at her. "What are you doing here so early?"

"Oh, I've been coming by every day to check on the place," she said, throwing her arms around me. "Let me look at you! Oh, don't ever go away for that long again, honey. I got so nervous not being able to see you or check in on you."

Mama's idea of a good vacation spot was the Blue Pineapple Motel in Panama City Beach, Florida. She did not see why it was necessary for me to see the world or why it was necessary to run off "God knows where" and share hotel rooms with a man I was not married to. She insisted that the hoteliers would know that we were not a married couple and we would give people a bad impression of America. I told her that if American tourists hadn't already done that by eating string cheese while they toured the Louvre, I doubted my premarital sleeping habits would bother them all that much. She didn't laugh.

Mama's predictions of travel tragedy included my getting mugged. (I have superpowers, so it wasn't likely.) Or developing food poisoning. (I don't eat, so that was even less likely.) Or getting a rash from hotel soap. (OK, that actually happened, but it cleared right up.) But I doubt she foresaw me getting dumped in such a halfhearted, half-assed way. She definitely would have warned me.

Wait a minute. My brain finally caught up to what she'd just said.

"You come by the house when I'm not home?" I asked.

Mama gave me her patented "Well, of course, I'm invading your privacy, silly!" expression. "You gave us a key for emergencies. Someone has to keep your plants watered."

"I don't have any plants." I pressed the pillow over my head and muttered, "I'm getting a moat."

Mama pretended not to hear me, instead dropping a pile of envelopes onto my lap. "Here, honey, I got your mail while you were away."

"Touch that curtain, and I won't give you your present." I didn't bother looking up as Mama approached the window. Mama considered for a moment and then backed away.

In general terms, Mama had stopped trying to reha- bilitate me out of being a vampire. This was good, be- cause I was out of the coffin to most of the community. I was one of a few vampires in the Hollow who chose to live out in the open and maintain relationships with the living. Studies showed that most vampires turned since tax consultant/vampire Arnie Frink outed us with his right-to-work lawsuit dropped out of sight and moved to big cities like New York or New Orleans. They assimilated into the large populations of vampires and learned how to adjust to their new lifestyles . . . or their neighbors claimed to have no idea how they managed to fall into a puddle of gasoline, then trip into a burn- ing leaf pile.

Thanks in no small part to my former supervisor, Mrs. Stubblefield, the news of my vampirism had offi- cially made the beauty-parlor and kitchen circuit. Mama said people had stopped talking whenever she walked into the pre-church coffees on Sunday mornings, which meant the congregation of Half-Moon Hollow Baptist Church was aware as well. She took to her bed for a few days. But ever since a well-known member of the cast of *All My Children* came out as the parent of a vampire and Oprah did a show featuring Friends and Family of the Undead, Mama figures my being a vampire makes her "current." She now introduces me as her "vampire daughter," even to people I've known since I was a kid. She's got a little bumper sticker with two inverted white triangles on a black background, the international symbol of support for vampire rights. She's even insisted on attending a meeting of the Friends and Family of the Undead, which, fortunately, had suspended activities after the foreclosure of the Traveler's Bowl, the hippie restaurant that hosted our meetings.

Of course, Mama still stocked my freezer with homemade pot pies to tempt me off my liquid diet. She showed up while I was sleeping and opened windows, hoping that I would slowly build up a tolerance to sunlight. As much as she loved me and being *en vogue,* Mama was determined to have a normal daughter. Even if it killed me.

I sifted through the alarming pile of mail while Mama bustled about my room, gathering dirty clothes. I'd been approved for an obscenely high-limit credit card that I hadn't applied for. I'd been accepted as the newest member of the Half-Moon Hollow Chamber of Commerce, which I had applied for. My letter to the editor for the American Library Association newsletter regarding the nationwide need for more vamp-friendly resources and hours was rejected. The fancy linen envelope stuck out like a sore thumb among the cheap, glossy promotions. My hands shook a little as I turned it over in my hands. Had Gabriel's mysterious pen pal finally decided to contact me? Imagine my horror when I saw the neat printed label addressed to "Miss Jame Janeson" from the Half-Moon Hollow High Alumni Committee instead. "Miss" was underlined. Twice.

"Oh, no."

"What is it, hon?" Mama asked, folding my jeans with sharp creases.

I opened the overtly elegant invitation decorated with a palm tree. "My tenth high school reunion is this year. Ugh. And SueAnn Caldwell is our class president. I would rather face a den full of zombies than go to this thing."

"Well, why on earth would you say that?" Mama cried. "You had such a good time in high school."

"No, that was Jenny, the cheerleader. I was the one with the braces and the tuba."

Mama winced at the venom in my voice when I said Jenny's name. My older, perfect sister was not speaking to me for various reasons, including the dismissal of her lawsuit against me. The judge had this wacky idea that property that was willed to me in a legal and binding last testament should remain mine, even though I was no longer technically living. This, combined with her overall disgust with how I handled the outing of our potential step-grandfather as a ghoul, had prompted her to tell Mama that I was officially dead to her. Even Mama saw the lack of logic in that statement, but she declined to comment on it.

Crafty, blond, and born with a naturally disdainful curl to her lip, Jenny was the twin-setted, Martha-worshipping yin to my never-even-considered-baking-from-scratch yang. She was the undisputed "good daughter" between the two of us. She rarely disagreed with Mama. She enjoyed most of the things Mama loved: quilting, reading inspirational romance novels about Amish girls, actually ironing clothes instead of just throwing them in the dryer for a few minutes. And she'd done her duty to the family by bearing two obnoxious spawn, Andrew and Whatshisface.

Life was oddly quiet and stale without Jenny's needling and disapproval. I'd always thought I would be so much better off as an only child, but now, I sort of missed her. Of course, I would never admit this, even under pain of death and/or a threatened *Baywatch* marathon.

Mama rolled her eyes in a gesture that was somehow both dismissive and loving. "Oh, you have to go. Jenny went to her tenth reunion, and she had a wonderful time."

I scanned the invitation. "Jenny organized her high school reunion. I'm sure she had a great time. Oh, come on. Our reunion theme is 'Enchanted Paradise,' which was our senior prom theme. They haven't had an original idea since then!"

"I just think it would be good for you to go back and see that some of the people you went to school with weren't as scary as you made them out to be. You gave them a lot of power over you. Maybe it would do you some good."

"Hmph."

"When I went to my tenth reunion, everybody had gotten bald and fat. The Prom Queen was married to the Septic Tank King."

"That makes it slightly more tempting," I admitted.

"I'm going downstairs to get your laundry started up. You get your rest."

"That's not necessary, Mama, really."

"Oh, don't be silly. I'm sure you didn't have time to find a laundromat when you were gallivanting around God knows where."

"Actually, the hotels had very nice laundry services. I didn't even know hotels did that."

"You let a stranger wash your clothes, but you don't want me to?" Mama gasped.

"If it will make you happy and let me get back to sleep, wash away," I told her.

"No problem, honey." Mama grabbed the freshly folded *dirty* clothes and walked out. She popped her head back into the bedroom doorway. "You were just teasing about the zombies, right? They're not real?"

I pulled a sleep mask over my eyes and did not answer.

My mother ironed my jeans. With starch.

And because I am obviously incapable of washing my own clothes properly, Mama gathered all of my clean clothes out of my closet and washed those while I slept. So, without other pants options, I was basically moseying into the shop, John Wayne-style.

On the drive to Specialty Books, I worked on a self-improvement plan, a personal to-do list, if you will. I had taken way too much time adjusting to my new vampire lifestyle, using it as an excuse for just floating along, reacting to problems as they came up. It wasn't surprising, really, when you considered that if there was a "Most Likely to Be Paralyzed by Fear of Change" award, a picture of me cringing would have been prominently featured in my high school yearbook. I had to get pro-active. I had to demand things from the universe. I had to start kicking some ass . . . though not in the physical sense, because I'd basically lost or nearly lost every fight I'd gotten into since being turned.

Moving on.

My plan to become a Brave New Jane went a little something like this:

(1) Develop a healthy, normal romantic relationship, preferably with Gabriel.
(2) Create a fulfilling career for myself.
(3) Demand that my family love me without judg-ment. Even if it means I have to rent a new family over the Internet.
(4) Find a solution for world peace.

I can live without that last one, though I know it's far more likely than the other three.

Considering that I was estranged from a sibling and a boyfriend, so far I'd failed miserably at the list—with the exception of the shop. It was barely recognizable, and not just because we'd torn down a wall and expanded into the porn store next door. Other than the plywood Dick had nailed over the broken window, there were no signs of a break-in. Books that might have been dam-aged by the hands of thieves were laid out carefully on the bar. The rest were piled haphazardly under heavy plastic drop cloths.

The space had been realigned, expanded. The front counter, still the same antique leaded glass and maple affair Mr. Wainwright had left behind, had been moved closer to the door. New beige carpet had been installed and was prepared for the bolts needed for the new shelving system, a shelving system that would actually allow customers to find what they want and navigate their way back out of the store, neither of which was encouraged by the previous system. While I planned on offering general-interest books and classic literature, the inventory would focus on vampire needs: cookbooks, history, finance, investment advice. I had already ordered two hundred copies of *The Guide for the Newly Undead.*

The walls were painted a cheerful midnight blue with a sprinkle of twinkling silver stars—Andrea's suggestion, to keep the place from being "too serious." I could have gone with the stereotypical blood-red walls and black-lacquered surfaces, but I didn't think that would be very restful for the customers. If not for the blood warmer next to the espresso machine and the chalkboard advertising a "Half-Caf Fat-Free Type A Mocha Latte" (Dick's attempt at bonding with our yuppier customers), the store would look like any intentionally whimsical small-town bookstore. It was remarkable progress, considering that the first time I'd come into the store, I narrowly missed having a shelf collapse on top of me.

Despite my wandering into the shop one night and rearranging stacks without permission, the former owner, Mr. Wainwright, had hired me on the spot for my organizational skills and rabid love of books. He became a surrogate grandparent, a mentor, and a close friend. Even though he'd died the previous year, he was the happiest he'd ever been, quite content to haunt the Hollow and pursue a logic-boggling relationship with my aunt Jettie. When he left me the shop in his will, I'd considered closing it. But, aside from the library, Specialty Books was the only place where I'd felt at home. I loved the smell of the books, the odd and nonsensical variety of titles. I loved the memories I had of Mr. Wainwright, his quirks, his stories of a lifetime searching the globe for paranormal creatures. I could just imagine him, standing at the end of the counter, giving me that fond, slightly befuddled smile.

It was at that moment that I realized I was not imagining Mr. Wainwright. He was standing at the end of the counter, giving me that fond, slightly befuddled smile.

"Mr. Wainwright." I sighed at the apparition and, forgetting that he was noncorporeal, tried to throw my arms around him. I ended up falling through him, a clammy got-in-the-shower-too-early sensation that set even my teeth on edge.

"Where have you been?" I asked. "I haven't seen you since I got back. I've missed you."

"To be honest, I've been rather ashamed to face you," he said, twisting his hands. "I spent less and less time at the shop while you were gone. I have been ever since . . ."

"You started enjoying my great-aunt's company."

"Yes, thank you." He cleared his throat. "And as it turned out, the shop being in such upheaval, well, it upset me more than I anticipated, and I haven't wanted to spend as much time here."

"Oh, no." I was stricken. When Mr. Wainwright had given me his blessing to burn the shop for insurance money if necessary, I charged ahead with the renovations, thinking that if he was onboard for arson for hire, surely a little remodeling wouldn't bother him. I was an ass. A complete and utter ass.

"I just didn't realize how much change you would deem necessary. I don't take it as a personal insult, dear. I didn't expect so much to happen so fast."

"I'm so sorry, Mr. Wainwright—"

He waved away my apologies. "The point is that I told you I'd keep an eye on the shop while you were gone, and it was my fault that someone broke in. I wasn't here."

"Hey, do not play the self-blame game with the world champion, OK? It's not as if they did a lot of damage, Mr. Wainwright. It's not a big deal. Besides, you're not tethered to the place. You're allowed to have a life . . . or not, as the case may." I cringed. It took Mr. Wainwright a beat to grasp the insensitivity of what I had just said, but then he hooted. I laughed, and then it turned into an all-out ghostly giggle fest, which was a fabulous emotional icebreaker.

I wiped at my eyes, trying to compose myself. "Any idea who might have broken into the shop? Have there been suspicious characters hanging around? More suspicious than the characters we normally get?"

"No. If there had been, I would have given them what your aunt Jettie calls the usual."

Cold chills, goose bumps, a vague feeling of unease as if they've left the iron on?" I asked. Mr. Wainwright nodded. "Why don't you go visit Aunt Jettie?" I suggested. "I'll be here for a while."

"Well, we did get rather used to having the house to ourselves while you were gone—"

"No details, please," I said, holding my hands up. "Just go and enjoy yourselves, in a way that I never have to think about."

"Thank you," he said, fading slightly. "And Jane?" I looked up, and he smiled at me. "I missed you, too, dear."

Mr. Wainwright winked at me and dissolved into thin air.

Outside the shop, I heard the motor of Dick's El Camino roaring to a stop. I laughed and ran to the door. Richard Cheney, who, for reasons I didn't understand, insists on being called Dick, had enjoyed annoying the hell out of Gabriel since they were children in the pre-Civil War Hollow. In their last human years, Dick had developed a bit of a gambling problem and lost his family plantation house to Gabriel in a card game. Gabriel's guilt over winning against an incredibly drunk Dick and Dick's pride-fueled refusal to take the house back led to a rift that lasted long after they were both turned into vampires. Immortality had just given Dick a lot more time to think up insulting nicknames and juvenile practical jokes.

A mystifying mix of fierce loyalty and moral flexibility, Dick was the local go-to guy for under-the-table commerce. And he had fallen hard for Andrea, the first woman to turn him down in about a century. Andrea didn't put up with much in the way of bullshit from Dick, which, apparently, was what he was looking for all along. She was the only woman he was willing (intentionally) to make a fool of himself over.

They were now shacking up in a big way. He slowly but surely had moved his vaguely obscene T-shirts and *Dukes of Hazzard* memorabilia into her swanky condo. Before she realized it, they were cohabitating. It's by far the sneakiest thing I've ever seen him do, and that's saying something.

For her part, Andrea didn't seem to mind. They didn't seem to have the adjustment problems that Gabriel and I had. Neither of them had really changed. Andrea was still the same classy, ethereally beautiful redhead with the elegant wardrobe. Dick was still the same guy you wouldn't want to take home to Mom. But he spent a lot more time at the shop and way less time in back alleys negotiating for counterfeit concert tickets. That's progress, right?

To be fair, Andrea had more experience that I did at dating the undead. When she was in college, her rare blood type caught the attention of a vampire professor, who convinced her to drop out, move in with him, and be his personal human wine cellar. A few years later, Andrea was unceremoniously booted by her fickle vampire lover, leaving her with no education, no job, and a family that refused to speak to her. She'd moved to the Hollow, where she worked part-time as a blood surrogate and, now, full-time as an employee of Specialty Books and a part-time dog-sitter.

In addition to her clerk duties, Dick and Andrea kept

Fitz for me while I was out of town. As much as Jolene and Fitz loved to play, it can be confusing for weres to spend a lot of time with dogs. There are food-competition issues.

Fitz bounded into the store and nearly knocked me down with the weight of his hello kisses. Fitz is a pound find, the apparent result of a night of reckless passion between Scooby-Doo and a bean-bag chair. The only thing remotely dignified about him is that I named him after Mr. Fitzwilliam Darcy from *Pride and Prejudice.*

Despite being the size of a small tank, Fitz wasn't much of a daytime guard. Now that I'd had one of those "shock collar" invisible fences installed around the property to keep Fitz from bothering Jolene and Zeb, he mostly just enjoyed loping around the acreage, protecting the perimeter from roving bands of squirrels.

"Hello!" I squealed, scratching behind Fitz's ears. "Oh, who's a good boy? Did you miss me?"

Andrea and Dick stepped through the front door. A huge smile stretched across Andrea's face. Dick usually greeted me with a wildly inappropriate single entendre, but today he had an agenda. "That dog," he informed me as Fitz licked my neck, "is a menace."

"Oh, he wasn't a bother, were you?" Andrea cooed as Fitz rolled over for a belly rub. "Were you, buddy? No."

"Are you wearing a golf shirt?" I asked, fingering the light blue material of Dick's collared attire.

Dick seethed a moment before slapping my hand away. "He ate my favorite T-shirt!" He kissed Andrea's temple and stalked off. "I'm going to go steal something."

"Sorry," I called after Dick, who continued to sulk as he went about gathering boxes for the trash. "The shirt will probably pass in a few days." I turned to Andrea, who threw her arms around my neck. "He seems really pissed. When he said he was going to steal something, did he mean from me?"

"Don't worry about it," she said. "Dick loves Fitz. He would ignore Fitz and scold him for getting up on the couch, but the minute I left the room, Dick was scratching his ears and baby-talking to him worse than I do."

"Dick was using baby talk?" I said, limping as I rounded the counter. "You've neutered him. What's next? Sweater vests?"

"So, what are you doing back?" she asked, squeezing me tight. "I told Zeb not to call you. The break-in wasn't that bad."

"Yes, I'm very glad to be back, and I missed you, too," I responded in a flat voice, avoiding the question. "Keep this barrage of homecoming welcome going, and I won't give you your presents."

"Presents!" Andrea cried, clapping and hopping up and down.

"From the snottiest personal *parfumerie* in France." I paused to hand her a little lavender gift bag. "I have to tell you that the chemist was slightly unnerved that I was able to describe your natural scent in so much detail, but it was important to get the blend that would complement you."

"*I'm* a little unnerved that you could describe my natural scent in such detail," she admitted. "Did you get Dick what he asked for?"

"Yes, I got him shot glasses from every country we visited. And in every gift shop I entered, I was glared at and called a 'horrible American,'" I said, rolling my eyes as I handed her the tinkling box of extremely embarrassing trinkets. "And I got him this!"

She squinted to read the wrinkled red T-shirt I was holding up. "It's in Italian."

"It says, 'My friend went to Italy, and all I got was this stupid T-shirt,'" I said. "I thought I'd add some class to Dick's T-shirt collection."

"I just got rid of most of the tackier ones." Andrea groaned.

"So . . . you framed my dog for T-shirt theft, huh?" I narrowed my eyes at her.

"If you were laundering a "Federal Bikini Inspector" T-shirt what would you do?"

"I would not use an innocent dog to mask my attempts at giving my boyfriend a makeover," I told her.

"I'm not trying to change all of him," she whispered, eyeing the back of the shop, where Dick was working. "Just the tackier T-shirts. And the ones with crusty armpits."

Andrea eyed my hesitant gait as I rounded the counter. "Did you get a rash while you were traveling?"

"Mom, jeans, starch. I don't want to talk about it." I shuddered as I climbed onto one of the high, cushioned bar stools I'd ordered in a deep eggplant. "How do you guys do it? You make it look so easy. You've only been dating for a little while, and your personalities are so different. Frankly, your googly-eyed happiness is starting to piss me off."

"Well, to be honest, we had a little outside help," she said, her tone a bit sheepish. She disappeared to the self-help section, then came back with a large pink book with pouty fang-puckered lips from the cover.

"*Love Bites: A Female Vampire's Guide to Less Destructive Relationships.*" I read the title aloud. My eyes narrowed at her. "You read this crap?"

"We sell this crap, you hypocrite," she said, her lips pinched into an expression that would have made Jenny proud. "Besides, there aren't a lot of books out there for mortal women dating vampires. I think the psychiatric world at large believes that if you're dating a vampire, you have other issues that need to be addressed before your relationship problems. But this was really helpful. It's written for women who have recently been turned and are having a hard time adjusting to dating their undead peers. There's lots of stuff about healthy expectations and boundaries and violent tendencies. So, do you want to talk about it?"

"No."

Andrea walked to the coffee bar. A few seconds later, the espresso machine roared to life. "Right, because what would I know about being in a relationship with a much older vampire you may or may not be able to trust?"

"Dang you and your logic." I pressed the heels of my hands into my eyes and took a deep, unnecessary breath. Andrea was the first human I'd ever fed from. It tends to bond gals for life. Andrea helped me bridge the gap from semi-social-phobic closet vampire to respectable undead citizen. Thrilled finally to have someone to take classes with after years of an empty social calendar, she enrolled us in yoga classes, ceramics classes, jewelry-making classes, even cake decorating, which we agreed later was a mistake. She'd basically become the girlfriend I'd always tried to make Zeb into. If I couldn't talk to her about this, whom could I talk to?

I sighed. "He's probably cheating on me. And I think he might have broken up with me . . . but without saying the actual words."

Andrea chewed her plump bottom lip. "Gabriel is a pretty direct person. I'm sure he would have—"

"He said, 'If you have to go, you have to go.' And then he said, 'This is for the best. This trip didn't exactly work out as we'd hoped. I'll call you.'" I caught the flash of horror cross her features. "See? You flinched! I knew it!"

"Let's go back to the beginning. Why did you think Gabriel might be cheating on you? Not impressions or feelings, actual facts."

I ticked the offenses off with my fingers. "Weird phone calls that he refused to take around me, manic behavior, constant changes in our hotel plans, notes at our hotels that he wouldn't let me read. And what I could read wasn't good. Lots of present-tense words. But I'm just being paranoid, right? I mean, there's probably a rational explanation for all this, right? Like he's an undead secret agent? That's plausible, right?"

Andrea winced as she poured me an espresso in a tiny white demitasse. "Well . . . probably not. That's all pretty suspicious stuff. When Mattias cheated on me, he had a lot of late 'faculty meetings.' He took calls from his 'teaching assistant' in another room."

"Please stop using the quotation marks, I need this life lesson to be unvarnished and without ironic subtext." Andrea pushed the fancy cup at me again. I considered claiming some sort of vampire aversion to the high-octane concoction, but Andrea was well aware that while we lack the digestive enzymes to digest solid food, we have no problems with most liquids. Sometimes it's a pain that Andrea is so well informed.

I was not a big coffee drinker in life. Iced frappuccinos from Dairy Queen were about as adventurous as I got. But Andrea insisted that if I was going to sell coffee, I had to know what I was talking about. And now that the machinery was up and running, she was my self-appointed caffeine pusher.

"Do I have to?" Andrea shoved the cup at me with more force. I took a sip. "Gah! That's awful! My cousin Muriel isn't that bitter, and she has two gay ex-husbands . . . who now live together. Is that how it's supposed to taste?"

"Sadly, yes. It's an acquired taste," Andrea admitted as she sipped her own coffee without making Edward G. Robinson faces. "So, invisible quotation marks aside, when Mattias cheated on me, he stopped taking me to familiar restaurants, because he'd started taking her to our places. It was new restaurants all the time. He was on edge. He accused me of being paranoid when I asked legitimate questions like 'Why did you change your e-mail password?' or 'Where did you sleep yesterday?'"

I groaned. "I'm going to be miserable and alone for the rest of my long, long life."

She shrugged. "Oh, it's not so bad. We still have yoga on Thursday nights."

"Oh, yeah, that will make up for the loss of companionship and sexual gratification."

Andrea grinned salaciously. "Well, you never know what you might *learn* in yoga."

"Perv." I chucked a coffee filter at her.

Andrea finally gave me the full report on the break-in. She'd arrived early a few evenings back, expecting a delivery of comfy chairs for the reading nook, and found the front window bashed in. She called the cops, who were sadly familiar with the neighborhood, and they chalked it up to drug addicts, teenagers, or drug-addicted teenagers. Proving precisely why I hired her in the first place, Andrea had already filed the insurance paperwork, arranged for an antiques appraiser from Louisville to come by to estimate the damage to the books, and contacted a glass repairman to replace the front window the following afternoon.

"So, really, there was no reason for me to come home," I said, awkwardly stuffing my hands into my pockets.

Andrea arched an eyebrow at me. "Yeah, I wish someone had thought to tell you that."

3

In an undead relationship, it's best not to focus on the "nots." Not being able to have children. Not being able to legally marry. Instead, focus on what you can have, true long-term commitment.

—*Love Bites: A Female Vampire's Guide to Less Destructive Relationships*

I could smell that Jolene was pregnant, a new, soft, green sort of scent that hit me the moment she opened the creaking trailer door.

I put on my "ignoring my surroundings" smile, the one that said, "I do not see the huge streaks of rust lapping down the pink wall panels or the carpeting that may be Astroturf." Zeb was overseeing a PTA meeting that night and had asked me to check in on his bride. She'd missed me, he said, and was a little put out that it had taken me three days to make it over to their place. Fortunately, I was carrying two recently reheated pot pies to win my way back into her good graces.

"Hey!" She beamed until she saw what I was holding. "Oh, no."

"What?" Jolene loved Mama's pot pies. For the last year, they were the only thing that kept her enormous appetite at bay when she visited my house. Since she and Zeb became my neighbors, I brought them over regularly for Jolene to snack on. And now, the mere presence of my foil-wrapped gift seemed to be turning Jolene a delightful shade of "bleh."

"I'll be fine," she whimpered. "I'm just a little sensitive to smells right now. Hormones combined with werewolf nose make it so much worse. Zeb was brownin' hamburger the other night, and I had to run out of the room to throw up twice. And I can't eat the foods I usually love. I couldn't get enough of your mama's pot pies a few months ago, and now, just the thought of breakin' the crust—" Jolene took a deep breath and pursed her lips.

"I'll leave it outside," I said. "You sit down."

I went to the kitchen and managed to smack myself in the face with a half-attached cupboard door while I poured Jolene a glass of water. The trailer was snug, to say the least. The kitchen was what Jolene's mother, Mimi, called a "two-butt model," meaning no more than two butts could fit side by side between the stained faux-wood-grain counters at any one time.

"You're out of Saltines, so I grabbed some Ritz crackers," I said.

"Thanks," she said, the color of her cheeks returning ever so slightly as she opened the wax-paper tube. "So, how was your trip?"

I launched into what was now the standard, heavily edited description. Lovely hotels, rude people, beautiful museums. Jolene paused mid-chew and clapped a hand over her mouth. With an "Oh, God," she ran for the bathroom door and retched pitifully.

Like a doofus, I followed her into the tiny bathroom. "Are you OK?"

I pressed my hand over my nose as Jolene's sick smell smacked me in the face.

"This is as close to pregnancy as I ever want to get." I handed her the water glass. "I thought morning sickness was just supposed to be, well, in the morning."

"My ass. It's around-the clock- 'no-warnin' sickness,'" she wheezed. "One minute, I'm a perfectly fine, functioning human being, and the next, I'm tossin' up everything I've ever eaten."

"And that's saying something," I marveled. She glared at me. "Not helping, sorry."

"I threw up in the parkin' lot at the Piggly Wiggly the other day. I had to tell Bitty Tate I was pregnant, because I didn't want her telling everybody I've got a drinkin' problem. Everything makes me sick. I ate a salad the other day, a salad, without any meat at all. I'm gonna waste away to nothin'."

I eyed her belly paunch, which made her look about four months along in human terms. "I wouldn't worry about that."

She glared up at me. "I'm gonna hit you, just as soon as I can stand up."

"Fair warning."

"I'm so miserable," she said, tears welling up in her eyes. "And I should be grateful that we made a baby so easily. Some mixed couples can't, you know. And I can't complain to my mama, because she'll camp out here in the living room and refuse to leave until the baby is in college. And I can't complain to Zeb, because he gets this weird, frightened-rabbit look in his eyes if I imply that I'm anythin' but one-hundred-percent awesome. I'm just—I'm glad you're here, Jane."

"Well, you look great," I told her, pushing her hair back from her sweaty forehead. And it was true in an infuriating way. Even the sweaty glow and water retention of early pregnancy only bumped Jolene down to what would be considered gorgeous for most humans. It just wasn't fair to the four billion or so other women on the planet. My only consolation was that eating a Ritz cracker had just made her throw up.

"So, how's your family?" I asked, helping her back into her chair.

"Well, Mama's overjoyed. Calls me six or seven times a day. She says hi, by the way. Daddy's sort of torn between pride and the horror of knowin' what his little girl's been up to. I think up until now, he'd been tellin' himself that Zeb and I were sleepin' in bunk beds. My cousins are sort of holdin' their breath, I think, because they know my aunts are gonna make a huge fuss because it's my first baby. And my cousin Vance has run away with a carnival."

I shuddered, picturing the none-too-bright cousin with unnatural feelings for Jolene operating a Tilt-A-Whirl. "Is this one of those things where I hope that you're kidding but assume that you're not?" She nodded.

I tried to use a nonchalant tone as I asked, "How are you and Zeb doing?"

She sighed again. "Weird. He's so quiet. He's never quiet, except for when, you know, under a whammy. Oh, man, you don't think Mama Ginger scrambled his brain again, do you?"

"No. You know what I think?"

"Obviously not, or we wouldn't be havin' this conversation," she muttered.

"I think Zeb's just scared. Scared of growing up. Scared of not being able to take care of you and the . . . litter." Jolene got it together enough to smack my arm. I winced, glad that bruises didn't last long on me. "OK, think about what happens to married people with children in Zeb's family. They end up drunk and angry and living in matching trailers in their relatives' backyards. He's terrified of ending up like Mama Ginger and Floyd. I think he convinced himself that he could handle the transition to husband pretty well, but what I will only refer to as his spontaneity and your superabsorbent eggs came back to bite both of you on the butt."

"What do I do?"

"Stop putting ketchup on your egg rolls, for one thing. That's gross. And maybe your family could spend less time rearranging your cabinets. Other than that, hell, I've never been married or pregnant. What do I know?"

She huffed. "Well, you're a big help."

"I do what I can. Or don't, as the case may be. Now, tell me, how is Mama Ginger? Is she still all skittish and sorry? Or has she returned to her deranged, yet strangely effective, ways?"

"No, thank the Lord." Jolene rolled her eyes. "She seems to feel just bad enough to stick to snippy comments when Zeb's not around and then pretendin' not to know why I'm upset."

My brows lifted. "Comments about?"

"About having everythin' handed to me. How it must be nice to have a family that will give you a trailer, friends that will give you land and money to build a house. About how I need to cut the apron strings and stop letting my family boss me around. I guess, 'cause she wants to be the one bossin' me around. Then she'll start makin' suggestions on how I could make her son happier. And then I just mention how you might be droppin' by, and she gets really quiet."

"She knew I was out of the country, right?" I asked. Jolene nodded. "Well, it's not as if I can teleport home."

"She doesn't know that."

"Have you told Mama Ginger about the baby yet?"

"No," she said emphatically. "I was thinking we would wait for the baby to be a year old or so. Maybe in kindergarten."

"That is not unwise," I said, picturing what Mama Ginger might consider appropriate boundaries and advice for an expectant mother. "So, how does this whole werewolf pregnancy work? Zeb already told me about the shorter-gestation thing. But what else is different? I mean, can you still transform? Are werewolf babies born able to transform? Do you give birth in a big cardboard box with towels in it?"

"That's not funny," Jolene said, glaring at me.

I held up my thumb and forefinger, measuring "a little bit funny."

"I can phase for about another month. After that, it can be stressful for me and for the baby," she said, rubbing her belly. "Pups can't phase until they're at least five. Their little bodies can't handle it until then. Mama always said it was God's way of keepin' them from runnin' off and never being seen again," she said. "I'm going to have a perfectly normal human birth with a perfectly normal baby. And even though the women in my pack have given birth at home for the last twenty generations, I'll be givin' birth in a hospital. Zeb's sort of insistin' on it. I think the idea of not havin' doctors, expensive machines, and high-test drugs—for him, not me—makes him a little panicky."

"Well, you can't really blame him."

"Oh, no, I'm sort of relieved to have an excuse to go to a hospital," she admitted. "I've always hated attendin' the births on the farm. I mean, I know I don't exactly have modesty issues, but the idea of being laid out like that and, you know, all that stuff coming out while my aunts and cousins come runnin' in and out of the room, takin' pictures and smokin' and describin' their own horrible births. No, thank you. Mama's a little disappointed, and I think it hurts the aunts' feelin's. But to be honest, I think everybody else is sort of interested in what it's gonna be like to wait around in the hospital for a baby. It will be a McClaine family first."

"But what about prenatal care? Ultrasounds? Won't a

doctor notice that you gave birth to a full-term baby four months early?"

"There's a midwife in town who's been takin' care of the family for years. She helps with the births and pre-natal care. She helps us fake the medical records and the birth certificates so they appear normal. The humans will just assume I was pregnant before the wedding, which I can live with," she said, toying with her glass. "But I have a favor to ask you."

"If this involves the words 'birthing coach,' my answer is 'I'm touched, but no thank you,'" I told her.

"No." She laughed. "I was hopin' you would come be there at the hospital, as sort of a referee/bouncer. Keep my family from invadin' the labor room and Zeb's family from killin' each other."

"And I don't have to see anything or hear anything or, again, see anything?"

"Nope."

"Then I'm your girl."

I should have suspected something was wrong with the Half-Moon Hollow Chamber of Commerce as soon as I saw the chamber seal was pink.

It had been a while since I'd attended a chamber meeting—ten years, to be exact, since I was awarded a $1,500 Chamber of Commerce good citizen's scholar-ship for writing an essay on "Patriotism: What Living in Half-Moon Hollow Means to Me." It was May 1995. I was a senior. I was $1,000 short on tuition and faced living at home and attending the local community college. I would have written it in limerick form if they'd asked.

That dinner was unremarkable, the main difference being that the chamber seal was still navy blue and gold. I was served bland chicken while the chamber president gave a speech on the perils of youth and supporting good, decent young people where they could find them. I was handed a check and dismissed so the chamber could discuss the possibility of attracting a rubber-band manufacturer to the Hollow.

The present-day chamber office had moved to a swankier part of downtown, to a restored Victorian townhouse with a dizzying amount of gingerbread. With the pink and white seal proudly presented on the lawn, the place looked more like a sorority house than the place where our community's collective business interests met.

To be honest, joining the chamber was sort of a test. Reopening the shop and trying to attract a larger clientele meant I was going to have face the living public with much more regularity. I'd managed to operate on the fringes of polite society for the past year or so. And frankly, I had no confidence that I wasn't going to get staked by a random customer in a disagreement over a senior discount. I wanted to see if I could move among humans again. Plus, it was important for Specialty Books to shed its obscurity and enter the mainstream business community. Too many Hollow residents had no idea what or where we were. Andrea and I wanted to be the sort of establishment that welcomed all beings, dead or undead, and their money. Joining the chamber was the first step in becoming legitimate.

I was greeted at the door by a wall of high-pitched chatter. All around me, slender blond women in knock-off designer suits sipped wine spritzers and swished their hair back and forth in slow motion. A few of the braver, thinner souls were wearing suit jackets paired with capris, which to me has always seemed like the professional equivalent to wearing hot pants to the office. But on these girls, it looked fashion-forward.

They were all so . . . shiny. The last time I was around this much pink, it belonged to Missy Houston, the vampire real-estate agent who tried to frame me for murder, steal my house, and kill me. I shook through my color phobia and built up whatever psychic defenses I could muster against the waves of rampant thoughts. It was like having a really insecure mosquito buzzing around the surface of my brain. Given the "just flew in from the tanning bed" glow most of the girls were sporting, I was absolutely sure I was the only vampire in the building. And somehow, I didn't think it would be a good time to bring it up.

The floor was highly polished and very old. I felt my own sensible flats slip across the polished surface and wondered how these women negotiated it in those stilettos. I plucked at the conservative navy pantsuit I'd chosen in the hopes that it made me appear to be a serious businesswoman. Even with vampire hotness on my side, I felt a little dowdy. I checked to make sure that at the very least, I'd worn matching shoes.

I decided to give it three minutes before I bolted from the building as if my eyebrows were on fire. There was a sign-up table offering "Hello, My Name Is" tags and pastel gel pens. But none of the other ladies was wearing one, because, of course, they already knew one another. I snagged a copy of the meeting agenda from the refreshment table. It was printed on pink paper with brown polka dots, the kind you might buy from an extremely perky stationery store.

That's when I realized. There were no men. Anywhere. Not a single whiff of testosterone in the place. Had I accidentally stumbled into a man-eating coven? Was I going to be sacrificed as the ugly brunette?

I decided that my three-minute limit was up and made a dash toward the door, bumping into a willowy blonde as she poured another chardonnay. She dropped the bottle, which I quickly snagged before it hit the carpet.

"Fast hands," she said, tinkling out a laugh. "I'm lucky you caught that, or Courtney Ahern would have torn out my eyes for ruining the Persian rug. I'm Courtney Barrow. I own the Unique Boutique, the sterling-silver shop over on Dogwood."

Courtney Barrow was just as cute as a button. She was tiny, curvy, and had an intricately braided silver necklace looped around her neck. Though my proximity to a substance I was highly allergic to made me somewhat nervous, Courtney Barrow was the only genuinely friendly face I'd seen that night, so I was sticking close to her.

"Jane Jameson, Specialty Books."

Her slick, coral lips quirked. "Isn't that an adult store?"

"No, no, there used to be an adult store next door. But we bought them out and expanded into their space. We pretty much gutted the store and started all over. You couldn't have used that space for anything else, anyway. There was a lot of steam-cleaning involved. I don't know when to stop talking sometimes."

Courtney was unfazed by my babbling. "A bookstore. That's so interesting. What made you go into the book business, Jane?

"I was too tall to be a ballerina?" I offered.

Courtney giggled. "You're a hoot! Oh, you just have to meet Courtney Harris. She'd love you."

"All right, then," I said as she wound her arm through mine. "Wait, she's named Courtney, too? How many Courtneys are there here?"

"Twelve." Courtney sighed as she led me deeper into the crowd of shimmering Courtneys. I was introduced to Courtney Gordon, who had started an event-planning company for children's birthday parties, and Courtney Stephenson, who ran a specialty shop for baby bed linens. None of them seemed even remotely interested in my bookshop, and, to be honest, I couldn't figure out how I would cross-promote occult items with luxury crib sheets. I was starting to think I'd made a huge mistake joining the chamber. I wondered if Courtney Barrow would release me voluntarily or if I would have to gnaw off my arm like a coyote stuck in a trap.

"It was so confusing when we all joined at once. We didn't want to call each other 'Courtney H,' 'Courtney B,' 'Courtney G.' This isn't second grade, you know?" I smiled and nodded, because there was no derailing this chick's train of thought. "So, we tried nicknames, 'Short Courtney,' 'Blond Courtney,' 'Cankles Courtney.'

But some of the girls' feelings were hurt, so we ended up having to use Courtney H, Courtney B, Courtney G anyway. We still use Cankles Courtney, but only behind her back."

"Hmm."

"Oh, I know that sounds mean," Courtney conceded. "But trust me, you'll know her when you see her."

OK, it *was* mean, but I did recognize Cankles Courtney right away. Sadly lacking in lower-quadrant definition, she was cowering before the formidable Courtney Herndon and receiving a stern talking-to regarding the chamber newsletter's font style. Apparently, Cankles' version of Curlz wasn't curly enough.

"Courtney Herndon is the head Courtney," Courtney Barrow whispered. "She's been the chamber president for the last four years."

Did she just say "head Courtney"? There was a Courtney hierarchy?

"Courtney!" my guide exclaimed. Several women throughout the room turned to us, realized we were referring to someone else, and went back to their wine. Courtney Herndon gave me an appraising look and a thin smile.

"This is Jane. She runs a bookstore where the porn shop used to be!" Courtney Barrow squealed. "Isn't that interesting?"

"Super," Courtney Herndon said, though her voice gave the distinct impression that she couldn't give a rat's ass.

"Are you from the Hollow originally, or are you a transplant like us?" Courtney Barrow asked.

"I'm a native," I said. "What do you mean, 'transplant'?"

"Oh, well, we all married boys from the Hollow." Courtney Herndon snorted derisively, as though she did not appreciate being uprooted.

Courtney Barrow smiled fondly, ignoring Courtney Herndon, as she said, "My husband, Gary, told me he couldn't imagine living anywhere else, so I just followed him home. Same with all of the Courtneys. None of us really has to work, but we're self-starters. Except for Lisa over there." Courtney lowered her voice and nodded toward a strawberry blonde in a suit even more conservative than mine. "She runs her family's accounting firm."

"Well, that explains why I've never met most of you." I turned to Courtney Herndon. "Courtney, what do you do?"

Courtney Herndon stroked back a stray blond curl. "I do home demonstrations for women interested in cosmetic products. I do home parties, makeovers, special kits."

I nodded. "So, it's like Mary Kay?"

Courtney H's jaw twitched as she hissed out, "No, it's nothing like Mary *Kay*!" She turned on her ice-pick heels and stomped toward the wine table.

"All right, then."

"Mary Kay asked Courtney H to resign because her sales tactics were too aggressive," Courtney Barrow whispered, a conspiratorial grin tilting her lips. "She would point out a flaw and then recommend a product to fix it. Only, Courtney can be really, really . . . honest sometimes. And some customers complained. So, Courtney sent the customers letters to tell them why they were wrong . . . and then Mary Kay's corporate offices filed the restraining order."

I stifled a laugh. "Who's she working for now?"

"She says she's an independent contractor."

"So she's mixing up her own makeup in her basement? Given the restraining order, that can't be—"

Courtney Barrow lowered her voice even more. Even with vampire hearing, I'm sort of surprised I could hear her. "She's still selling the Mary Kay stuff. She had loads of it when she quit. You know, your upline always tells you that you can't sell from an empty wagon? Well, she took it seriously. She has enough lip plumper to sink a cruise ship. She just takes off all the packaging and replaces it with her own stickers she prints at home."

"That is both brilliant and deranged," I whispered back. Courtney Barrow giggled again, which was becoming less annoying.

She nodded to a tense blonde in the corner, who seemed to be scanning the room over and over, searching for some sort of infraction. "That's Courtney Ahern, the one who's crazy about the carpet. This house used to belong to one of her in-laws, but she persuaded her husband to give the tenants the boot and renovate the place for our headquarters. But now she's paranoid one of us will do something to ruin the house's potential resale value."

"What does Courtney A do?" I asked. "Sell something that's nothing like Amway?"

Courtney Barrow guffawed. "I'm going to like you!"

"Oh . . . good."

Courtney Herndon stood, cleared her throat, and silenced the room. The various Courtneys filed into the meeting room, where we were directed to cozy tea chairs instead of the usual folding monstrosities. I sat through the approval of the minutes, the agenda, and the pledge. I came up with my own identification system for the Courtneys as they debated the proper color scheme for the annual business directory. Courtney Barrow, the only one who'd bothered to be friendly, was "Nice Courtney." Courtney Herndon was "Head Courtney." Courtney Gordon, who appeared to be some sort of sycophant/enforcer, was "Toady Courtney." Courtney Ahern was "Coaster Courtney." I couldn't come up with a better-fitting nickname for Cankles Courtney and felt a little bad about it. I moved on to picking which chamber member I would eat first if we were stuck on a desert island. I settled on Courtney Jensen, or "Fitness Courtney," because it was obvious that woman hadn't even seen a carb in years, and high-protein diets give blood a rich, oaky finish. I'd almost nodded off when I heard my name being called.

"What?" I almost shouted, bolting upright in my fancy laced chair.

"It is Jane, right?" Head Courtney demanded. "You're the new member?"

"Er . . ."

Head Courtney's smile tightened as the other ladies tittered. "We were just discussing the Fall Festival charity for the animal shelter."

This was so much worse than being caught sleeping in math class. I nodded and slapped on my "pleasant face."

On my right, Nice Courtney sat frozen in her chair, a Stepford smile pasted on.

"Now, Jane, I think it would be a great idea if you gathered together the prizes for the games? Normally, we solicit donated items from businesses in the community. And since you're new, you probably have all kinds of contacts that we haven't even thought of yet!"

Well, I could ask Dick about that trunkload of pirated *Knight Rider* DVDs I gave him the year before . . .

"So, we'll just put you down to head the prize committee."

"It's just my first meeting," I said. "I don't know if I'm qualified—"

Head Courtney's eyes narrowed. "There's no better way to get to know us better than just to throw yourself into the work. Really, it's the best way to make friends here at the chamber, showing what a team player you can be. You do want us to think you're a team player, don't you?"

Why wasn't my sister in this club? Seriously?

"I'm willing to help with—"

"Great!" Head Courtney cried, interrupting my attempt at shirking the games in favor of decorations or something less "commitment-y." "Lisa will give you all of the information from last year."

From across the room, Lisa rolled her eyes and shared a commiserating look with me. This was followed by a report from the jack-o'-lantern committee and the treat committee, who lamented the lack of volunteers for making gluten-free snacks. I had never so earnestly wished that I could die of natural causes. Boredom was a natural cause, right? After the game committee and the inflatable committee, I wondered whether there was anyone in the room who was not on a committee.

"Now, the planning committee has come up with a list of acceptable costumes. I know some of you older members like to get started on your kids' costumes early."

The oldest member in the room looked to be about thirty-five. And she did not look as if she took that as a compliment.

I raised my hand. "So, wait, this is a Halloween party?"

"No, if we call it a Halloween party, some families won't come. So it's a Fall Festival."

"But we're going to have pumpkins . . . and costumes . . . and candy."

Head Courtney glared down at me. "Is there going to be a problem, Jane?"

There could be a problem. Believe it or not, vampires tend to hole up on All Hallows Eve and refuse to come out until the last trick-or-treater has been dragged home kicking and screaming. You'd stay home, too, if you were confronted with a holiday that parades around the worst cultural stereotypes pertaining to your particular species—bluish pallor, black capes, stupid accents exaggerated by clownish fangs—and presents it as "all in good fun."

"Right, sorry," I said. "It's just that . . . is the chamber really supposed to hold fund-raisers?" I asked. "I thought the Chamber of Commerce was about community building and economic development, bringing in new employers—"

"Well, this is the way *we* run the Chamber of Commerce," Head Courtney said through gritted teeth. "The Half-Moon Hollow Animal Shelter is a cause we've supported for years. Why, just last year, we collected five thousand dollars in cash donations."

"People will just give you cash for the shelter? Without a carnival?"

Head Courtney's disapproving sneer was now an all-out death glare.

"Right. Sorry," I mumbled, staring down into my lap as a sign of submission.

For the rest of the meeting, I sat still and silent, just praying to get out alive. And I was incredibly angry with myself. Why the hell was I afraid of these women? If I wanted to, I could beat them all senseless, take their fancy foufou designer wallets, and make them forget I ever did it.

Not that I would ever do that.

The best way to show that you're independent is actually to be independent. Develop outside interests, attend cultural events, anything to show your wayward vampire mate that you're not sitting at home pining away.

—*Love Bites: A Female Vampire's Guide to Less Destructive Relationships*

I slunk up my front-porch steps, exhausted and in serious need of sedatives and/or lobotomy instruments. Andrea, on the other hand, looked cool and collected, stretched out on *my* porch swing, scratching *my* dog behind the ears, and sipping a tall icy beverage that I promptly stole from her.

"Hey!" she cried. "I used your best liquor to make that! And there wasn't much to choose from."

"It's an emergency," I told her between swigs of what I think was a daiquiri. Because of my sordid history with the demon alcohol and the inevitably humiliating results, I don't usually imbibe. But tonight I was making an exception. I slumped onto the swing with Andrea and sighed. "Not that you're not welcome here at River Oaks, but has it occurred to you that making yourself frosty cocktails while I'm not home is breaking and entering?"

"Yes, it did. But I was thirsty, and you left me your key ring to close up."

"I'm way too trusting. Am I going to come home one night and find you taking a bath in my tub and wearing my clothes?" She arched her eyebrow, looking from her own stylishly cut silk blouse and slacks to my suit—which had been purchased by my mother. "Never mind."

"I'm not going to go all single white female on you. But I do love this place. I still have a hard time believing you own a home with a name."

"Well, for all of this, my sister is willing to sue me, steal from me, and have me audited. So, you might want to reconsider your whole romantic image of gentility."

Andrea sighed heavily. "Why must you destroy my illusions? How was your networking?" she asked as I tried to beckon my dog. Fitz sniffed and rested his head on his paws.

"I'm not trying to say anything about sisterhood or women in power, but what a bunch of bitches."

Andrea laughed and pulled a pitcher of daiquiris from behind the porch swing. She poured herself another drink, grinning as she said, "I thought you might feel that way. My boss at the gift shop used to complain about the meetings."

"You knew?" I cried, chucking a cushion at her. "You knew, and you let me walk into that den of iniquity unprepared?"

"Hey, hey! If you can't respect the daiquiri, at least respect the shirt," she griped, swiping at the liquor I'd made her spill on her celery-colored blouse. "I know better than to ask you to respect me."

I blew her a kiss and poured more daiquiri as Andrea began her tale in an ominous tone. "Margie said it happened slowly. One cold October night, a Courtney attended her first meeting, then another and another. It was as if the chamber was a hive being invaded by really perky Africanized bees. And pretty soon, they were proposing extra events and creating committees to run those events, and they built a power base. They elected themselves as officers, moved the headquarters, rewrote the bylaws, and made life miserable for the old-school members. One by one, the charter members all left. Margie quit after they gave her a demerit for wearing brown shoes with a black suit. To Margie, that translated to: You're over forty, get out."

"What happened to all the men?"

Andrea shrugged. "I don't know. I guess they just quit, or they got too many demerits . . ."

"I think the Courtneys ate them," I countered.

"Your guess is there's some supernatural reason for the pink chamber seal?"

I nodded. "My guess: coven of succubi."

"Well, you should fit in well, being a vampire and all." She narrowed her eyes at me. "You did tell them that you're a vampire, right?"

I sipped my drink to avoid answering.

"I thought you said you weren't going to live in the coffin anymore!" Andrea cried.

"I'm not living in the coffin. I'm just not volunteering any information that wouldn't come up in an introductory conversation. Do you walk up to people and say, 'Hi, I'm Andrea. I'm a natural redhead."

"I'm not a natural redhead."

"I knew it!"

"Don't deflect the question. So, I guess you're not going back, huh?"

"I have to," I mumbled. "I'm in charge of the prizes for the charity carnival."

Andrea hooted. "They've pulled you in!"

"They did not!"

"They made you their prize bitch! And not in the dog-show way. You might as well have given them all your milk money and then done their homework for them."

"I told you, they're scary. And blond. We've established that I don't do well with scary blond people. And you're starting to talk like me the more time we spend together. I think we can both agree that having one person in the world who talks like me is too many."

"Jane, maybe you could see this as an opportunity to grow as a person, to face your fears, to be a little less wracked by insecurity."

"I am not wracked by fear and insecurity. I have completely normal fears: failure, clowns, spiders. What's weird about that?" I groaned. "Oh, who am I kidding? It's all gone pear-shaped."

Andrea patted my head. "No more *Kitchen Nightmares* for you."

"It's Gordon Ramsay. I can't help myself. All the yelling and the cursing . . . it's so forceful. And he takes off his shirt at least once every episode to change into his chef's uniform."

She snorted. "Freak."

"Look, I'm going to stick it out. I have to. Joining the chamber is good for the shop . . . it's going to be good for the shop. Please, God, let it be good for the shop. And at least we know that they'll let you quit if it's not the place for you . . . or you exceed the maximum weight allowances."

Andrea snickered. "You know, maybe you'd be a little more confident if you jazzed up your wardrobe a bit."

I smirked. "You're just looking for an excuse to take me on another humiliating shopping excursion."

"Keep it up, and I'll put you in a stylish poncho," she said, giving me a mock evil glare.

I shuddered. "Vampires should not wear ponchos." I made kissing noises and beckoned my dog. "Come here, Fitz."

Fitz yawned and scooched even further under the porch swing, nuzzling his head into Andrea's hand.

"Traitor," I muttered.

"Oh, you got a shipment at the shop. I put it on your hall table," she said, rising and dislodging Fitz's head from her knee.

"Why didn't you just leave it at the shop?" I asked, following her through the front door, pitcher in hand.

"Well, I thought maybe you'd want these for yourself," she said, smirking, handing me the opened box. About a dozen books with blazing neon titles winked out at me.

"*Forbidden Thirst. Blood Lust. Penetrating Fangs. The Misadventures of Millie,*" I read, thumbing through the slick paperbacks. This went way beyond the cover of your average bodice-ripper. Let's just say more was being inserted than fangs. "I didn't order this! This is . . . porn! Vampire porn, but porn all the same."

"I think the publishers prefer the term 'erotica.'"

I shot Andrea my best withering glare. She shrugged, all wide, innocent eyes betrayed by her madly twitching lips. "Well, you said you were going to be lacking in sexual companionship. I thought maybe you decided to expand your horizons."

"Your perception of me is disturbing." I shuddered. "Is there a packing slip?"

"'Hope you enjoy these samples. Let me know about ordering. Talk soon, Paul,'" Andrea read aloud before showing me the innocent slip of white paper. "Who's Paul?"

"Paul Dupree, one of my suppliers in Atlanta. He specializes in vampire publishing. Normally, he sends me diet guides and self-help books."

"Technically, that could be considered a form of self-help." Andrea wriggled her eyebrows suggestively.

"Ew. I'm leather-bound editions, not this!"

"Maybe he just got stuck on leather-bound," she said, cocking her head to get a better look at Millie, who seemed more than thrilled to be tied up, hanging upside down, and leered at by a vampire with implausible pecs.

"Did Dick give you a list of dirty quips? You're enjoying this way too much."

She snorted. "I've seen some of the titles in your personal library. I don't think I would be too judgmental."

"I'm not going to enter into a censorship debate with you. I have other things on my mind right now—Stop laughing!" I cried when she collapsed onto a chair. "All I can say is thank goodness Gabriel's not here to see this. He'd probably go after Paul and rip his arms off for sending me this sort of thing, professional relationship or no . . . or he'd just say, 'This porn stash is probably for the best' and gift me with a lifetime supply of batteries."

Andrea doubled over, laughing. I was glad someone could enjoy my pain. The truth was, I didn't need any form of artificial stimulation. My body refused to believe that Gabriel and I were no longer together, unwilling to give up the orgasms he gave me, even if they had to be manufactured in my dreams. Every night, I had vivid, full-color dreams of Gabriel, his body, his lips, that thing he used to do with his index finger. My cruel subconscious dredged up memories of real encounters or provided elaborate scenarios, like the dream where Gabriel was a police officer and I had to use all my wiles—and a lap dance—to persuade him not to give me a speeding ticket. Or there were the dreams where he just stalked into the house, threw me down on the kitchen table without a word, and took me. Each night, I woke up in the middle of a screaming, head-spinning orgasm and was brought crashing down when I realized that I was alone. I was caught between being afraid to go to sleep and wanting to go to bed hours too early.

Finally recovered and rubbing at the stitch in her side, Andrea wiped her eyes. She sighed. "Still haven't heard from him?"

"Nope." She followed me into the kitchen, where I dropped the empty pitcher into the sink and pulled a Faux Type O out of the fridge. "And I'm caught in that hellish 'I want to call him, but I would rather he call me, because that proves he wants to talk to me' limbo. When did my life become a tragic episode of *Felicity*?"

"I don't know what that means."

"It means that I feel like I'm waiting for that very special boy to call, only that very special boy isn't breathing. And he told me it was probably for the best that we part ways more than three thousand miles from home, *and* he hasn't deemed it necessary to contact me in two weeks. Not even to make sure my plane didn't crash into the Atlantic. At this point, I'm not entirely sure he's not going to stay in Europe until he hears that I've moved away or become a nun or something."

She patted my head fondly. "Well, next to being married, a girl likes to be crossed in love a little now and then. It is something to think of and gives her a sort of distinction among her companions."

My face softened into a smile. "You read *Pride and Prejudice*."

Andrea rolled her eyes. "Well, I figured if I'm going to survive working at the shop, I would have to. And you only hinted that a person of any intelligence was required to read at least one Jane Austen book, like a thousand times."

I tapped a finger to my chin. "That doesn't sound anything like me . . ."

It was two days from the reopening. The cash-register drawer was stuck. We were missing a rather large shipment of what I considered our cornerstone product, *The Guide for the Newly Undead.* And I was beginning to suspect that Andrea was slipping extra espresso into her magical mystery coffee potions because "caffeinated Jane" amused her.

The only thing we had going for us was a local dairy that was willing to deliver to an account as small as ours and to a location as bad as ours at night. In fact, it was a delight to come downstairs from Mr. Wainwright's old apartment to find a tall man in an indecently tight blue Half-Moon Dairy uniform stocking our little coffee-bar fridge with half-and-half and heavy cream.

"Wow, is that our dairy guy?" I whispered. Andrea didn't bother removing her eyes from the sight of Dairy Guy's delicious blue-clad bottom swaying as he loaded the fridge.

"Yep," Andrea answered absently.

"He's going to be coming here regularly, right?"

We simultaneously tilted our heads as Dairy Guy's hips changed angles. Andrea sighed, "Yep."

"Maybe we should arrange for Dick to be elsewhere on delivery nights," I whispered. "Because you're drooling. And I don't blame you because milk does a body goooo— Oh, my God." My jaw dropped as Dairy Guy turned, and I recognized him as little Jamie Lanier, whom I used to babysit every summer.

Jamie loomed four inches over my tall frame. His warm green eyes twinkled at me from under a faded blue ball cap he'd slapped over his wavy dark blond hair. (Curse my weakness for all-American boys!) Every inch of him was toned and tan, and he smelled like Irish Spring soap. I bit back a sigh.

This was the danger of living in the small town where you grew up. Local hotties have to start off somewhere, and generally, it's as the annoying towheaded Little Leaguer who would only eat smiley-face pancakes from ages five to seven.

"Miss Jane! Hi!" He flashed those devastating dimples. "It's great to see you!"

"Jamie. How's your mom?" I asked, flinching at his use of "Miss," a sure sign that he thought of me as a senior citizen. "Still teaching?"

"Yep. But she says she's going to retire now that I'm graduating and she and dad are going to have the house to themselves."

"You're graduating from college?" I said, an insane note of desperation in my voice as I tried to do the age math in my head.

"Actually, I'm still a senior at Half-Moon Hollow High. I'm just working at night to save for tuition."

Forgive me, Lord, I'm the biggest pervert in the world.

"Say hi to your mom for me," I said as he packed up his hand truck and headed out the door. He waved at us from the delivery van as he pulled away. I stared at the ceiling, then told Andrea, "You may laugh now."

She guffawed, collapsing against the bar as she held

her side. "I'm sorry. It's just, the look on your face when he said he was graduating from *high school*!"

I rubbed my hands over my face. "My eyes, they burn."

"I can't believe I get to relive this humiliation with every delivery," Andrea said, rubbing her hands together in anticipatory glee. "This is already my favorite job ever!"

"I think you forget sometimes, I am fully capable of hurting you—" We turned to the front door as a woman in a smart peach raincoat came into the shop, clutching her purse close to her side with one arm and carrying an enormous beribboned basket with the other. Courtney Barrows, Nice Courtney, eyed her surroundings suspiciously, apparently afraid to touch anything. "Courtney?" I said.

"Jane!" She sighed, relieved to see me.

"And it isn't even my birthday!" Andrea was clearly thrilled that one of the chamber members had showed up for my brainwashing initiation so soon. She whispered, "Which one?"

I cleared my throat. "Courtney Barrows, this is my associate, Andrea Byrne. Andrea, Courtney Barrows. Courtney owns the Unique Boutique, the sterling-silver shop over on Dogwood."

"Nice to meet you," they chorused. I half expected Courtney to curtsy.

"It's not that I'm not happy to see you again, but what are you doing here?" I asked.

Courtney let out a breathy laugh. "I know! I don't normally come into this part of town, especially at night. But your store hours are just so odd, I wanted to make sure I caught you," she said, hauling the giant gift basket onto the counter. "The chamber sent you this, and I volunteered to bring it by. It's a welcome muffin basket. There's an orientation folder, a directory, the memory book, and a suggested list of places where you should go begging for game prizes."

Well, that capped it. If I'd learned anything from Missy the psycho real-estate agent, it was never to trust people bearing gift baskets.

"Memory book?" Andrea asked.

"It's a little scrapbook for our special events, fundraisers, that sort of thing."

"Like a yearbook!" Andrea exclaimed cheerily, then scowled when I pushed the basket at her with more force than was probably necessary. She stifled a giggle and took it to my office. "I'm taking these muffins, by the way! They're of no use to you!"

Courtney shot me a questioning look. I smiled. "I'm on a no-carb, no-sugar, no-gluten diet. But Andrea will love them. It was really nice of you to bring it by. You didn't have to come all the way down here."

"Well, I just liked talking to you so much at the meeting, I thought I'd come by for a visit. I just— I joined the chamber to make some friends. And the ladies at the chamber . . . I didn't know what I was getting into when I joined. They're sort of . . ."

"Scary?" I suggested.

"And blond?" Andrea shouted from the back of the shop.

I shot Courtney an apologetic smile, but she didn't

seem offended in the least that I'd been talking about the chamber members behind their backs. "Yes. But you were so nice. You know, you're the first person I've met at one of those meetings that hasn't made fun of the fact that my husband runs a construction company. As if my money is dirty or something, just because my husband's not a doctor or a lawyer."

"I was raised by a teacher and a meddlesome home-maker. I mock no one," I told her, then amended, "unless they deserve it."

"You've lived in the Hollow your whole life. You don't know what it's like to try to meet people here when you don't know anybody."

"I think you've been hanging around the wrong Half-Moon Hollow residents. See, I would imagine your husband probably outearns ninety-five percent of the people in this town. Frankly, I admire anyone who can operate heavy machinery without hurting innocent by-standers."

She giggled. "See? I told you! You're a hoot."

"That you did. Pull up a seat."

Courtney gave an exaggerated look around, her face open and pleasant as she climbed up onto the bar stool. "Your shop is, um, really interesting."

"Thanks. Coffee?" I asked. I pushed a bunch of but-tons and hoped a cappuccino would come out. Andrea came running at the rumble of the cappuccino machine, like a mama bear protecting her young. She shooed me away and finished making Courtney's drink herself.

Courtney seemed almost shy as she handed me a little

pink-wrapped box. "And I had a little gift made up for you."

"Oh, thanks," I said, opening the box. Inside was a little keychain attached to a silver disc inscribed with my initials. "That was really nice."

Vampires are allergic to silver. Touching it feels like a combination of burning and being forced to watch *Glitter* over and over again. Your eyes burn, there's an unpleasant squelching sound, and you're left with dirty gray streaks that are very hard to wash off. I knew what I was in for when I politely held the little circle in my palm.

Andrea's eyes widened as my hand began to sizzle like bacon. I mouthed, "I know!" Andrea started asking Courtney incredibly complicated questions about how she wanted her coffee. As soon as Courtney's back was turned, I put the keychain on the counter and silently yowled, shaking my hand back and forth as the dirty gray stain faded from my skin.

"You OK, Jane?" Courtney asked, smiling sweetly.

"Fine." I chuckled. Andrea rolled her eyes in my direction. "I'm just fine. I just have some allergies, a little eczema acting up . . . Wait, no, this is stupid. Courtney, you should probably know that I'm a vampire, have been for about a year now. If that's going to get me banned from the Half-Moon Hollow Chamber of Commerce, so be it. I just don't have the time or energy to try to fool you into thinking I'm normal."

"Oh, I knew that," Courtney said, patting my arm and turning over my burned hand to examine my palm. "The keychain was just a test to make sure. But it was obvious the other night what you are. You didn't touch any of the food. Your teeth are a little sharper than they should be. You're so pale and, well, sort of glowy. Your skin drove Head Courtney crazy, by the way. She kept trying to figure out what you use on it. I didn't say a word."

My forehead wrinkled. "So, what do you plan on doing with this information?"

"Nothing," she said, smiling pleasantly and sipping her coffee.

"I'm confused," I told Andrea, who shrugged.

"It's just, you're so much nicer than any of those so-called normal girls," she said, patting my hand. "I figure, if you're up front with me, you can't be all bad. And personally, I want to see how long it takes the other girls to figure it out and how many different ways they manage to put their collective foot in their mouth."

"You've got a bit of a dark streak in you," Andrea told her. "My boyfriend's going to love you. On second thought, maybe I should keep you two separate."

Courtney giggled. "Besides, I experimented a little with vampires in college. Every girl does."

I arched my brows at her. "You know I'm a completely straight vampire, right?"

Courtney threw her head back and laughed. She turned to Andrea. "Don't you just love hanging out with her? You never know what she's going to say!"

"Every day's an adventure," Andrea said dryly.

Remember to fight fair. No name-calling, no use of words like *always* and *never*, no bringing up old issues to avoid the topic at hand—and no dismembering.

—*Love Bites: A Female Vampire's Guide to Less Destructive Relationships*

"Are you sure the whole pewter-figurine thing isn't too kitschy?"

I repositioned the graceful fairy statues near our selection of amethyst geodes, which I'd moved because I wanted to make room for a display of *The Guide for the Newly Undead* next to the register. Now I was moving them around like my own personal nude pixie army. I bit my lip and bounced up and down on my heels as I considered their current formation.

"It's too kitschy."

"If you rearrange the fanciful bric-a-brac one more time, I'm going to stake you," Andrea promised. "I thought we agreed that you would get a full day's sleep before the opening."

To say I was a nervous wreck on reopening day was a massive understatement. I must have changed my outfit ten times, which is almost painful for someone who doesn't care that much about clothes. First, I put on an embroidered blue top and some jeans and decided it looked too casual. So, I changed into a red T-shirt and an Indian skirt—too hippie-dippy. The khaki slacks and polo shirt made me look as if I worked at Best Buy. Finally, I embraced the cliché: black slacks, black beaded top, tear-shaped carnelian earrings that looked like little drops of blood, and the black boots Andrea had practically forced me to buy at gunpoint. And then I got to the shop and immediately wanted to run home and change when I saw Andrea's crisp white blouse and beautifully cut gray slacks.

Mr. Wainwright had come by and given his wholehearted support, then promptly disappeared, saying that he didn't want to make me nervous on my first day. He promised to bring Aunt Jettie back at the close of business to celebrate my "entrepreneurial triumph."

It was oddly lonely to have the shop open without my former employer's spectral presence. But Dick and Andrea were there for me, running last-minute errands, cleaning up last-minute messes, holding a paper bag to my face when I did some last-minute hyperventilating— the irony of the latter compounded by the fact that I didn't technically breathe.

"I tried to sleep, and then, despite my very specific and effective internal clock, I was lying there at noon today with a racing brain. I kept thinking I really jumped into this without thinking it through," I said, putting the

Spring Blooms fairy behind the Autumn Mystery fairy
and then switching them back again. "I mean, I figured,
I've already got a location, stock, and more capital than I
needed. What else would I need for a successful business?
What if I picked the wrong types of books? What if there
were no bookstores specifically catering to vampires because most vampires are out living their unlives instead
of reading? What if the coffee bar was a stupid idea?"

"Well, it was certainly a stupid idea to give you what
amounted to three double espressos last night." Andrea
sighed, arranging pastries from Half-Moon Hollow
Sweets onto a fancy doily.

"I knew it!" I hissed at her. "I knew you were slipping
me extra caffeine."

"I thought it would be much funnier than this."

"I'm so sorry my wacky antics—which you caused—
no longer amuse you," I said flatly.

"Call it a misguided experiment," she muttered, tossing
the pink bakery box aside and wiping down the counter. An
array of muffins, cookies, and lemon bars winked out at me
from the glass case, mocking my inability to digest solids.

It may have seemed like a bad idea to give people
sticky pastries and staining liquids, then invite them to
peruse our books. But I wanted the shop to be the sort
of place where you could sit for hours at a time and feel
welcome—and therefore guilty enough to buy several
expensive books. As an added precaution, we'd put the
rarer volumes in a glassed-in special collections case, to
which I carried the only key.

"We open in ten minutes, and nobody's here yet," I

said, switching the fairies back to their original position. Andrea reached over and smacked my hand.

"Ow! No hitting!"

I shot a significant look at her boyfriend, who was conscientiously stacking midnight-blue shopping bags embossed with the new Specialty Books logo near the register. I considered it a supreme gesture of trust to allow Dick to stand that close to an unlocked cash drawer. At my indignant glare, he shrugged and slung an arm around his glaring girlfriend. "I've seen you fight. My money's on her."

"I'm not paying you, right?"

Dick shook his head.

I muttered, "Good."

"Am I your first customer?" I looked up to see my father standing in the doorway.

"Daddy!" I cried, throwing my arms around him and nearly bowling him over. "Yes, you are."

If there was anyone who could help with my "Improve relationships with family" goal, it was my father. I am an unabashed Daddy's girl. Not like Carol Anne Mussler, whose home life took on a decidedly creepy aspect after she dedicated "Every Breath You Take" to her father at the high school's annual talent show. But what more could I do than pledge my undying favoritism for the man who gave me my lifelong love of reading? The man who defended me from Mama and Grandma Ruthie's repeated attempts to make me into a Jenny clone? The father who loved me unconditionally, despite my growing catalogue of flaws? If Daddy hadn't decided to give me the unfortunate middle name of Enid, he would have been a parent without fault.

Daddy stroked my hair back from my eyes. "What's the matter, Pumpkin, afraid no one will show up?"

I mulled that over for a millisecond. "Um, yes. That would be it."

Daddy opened his wallet and handed me his Mastercard. "Well, point me to the coffee bar, and start a tab for me. And then bring me one of those books on how to be a better parent to an adult vampire."

"Well, if you gave me a valid credit card, you've got my vote for Father of the Year."

Dad took a long look at the ritual candle selection. "Does that mean you can give me a good deal on a magic wand and an owl?"

"I would respond, but we just established a storewide no-hitting policy," I said, poking him in the ribs.

He tucked a hand under my chin. "It looks great, honey. Everything. I can tell how much work you girls put into it. I'm very proud of you."

"Thanks, Daddy. Is Mama coming?"

Daddy cleared his throat. "Mama sends her support in spirit. But Jenny had some meeting tonight, and she needed Mama to babysit."

"Hmm. Convenient." I rolled my eyes.

Behind us, the bell tinkled, and the door opened. A goth teen with a pasty face, pierced nose, and lime-green-over-dirty-blond ringlets slumped into the store. She was a vampire, but she was so young. And she was obstinately avoiding eye contact. I took the direct approach, saying in my most pleasant tone, "Hi, welcome to Specialty Books. Can I help you find anything?"

She stopped and stared at me. I think she was willing me to disappear. OK, then.

"Are you looking for something in particular or just browsing?" I asked, dialing down the cheerful factor a few points.

The green-haired teen queen was now staring *through* me.

"I think she's pretending to be invisible," Andrea whispered from behind the counter.

I did not want to alienate my first non-blood-related customer, so I stepped out of her way. As she passed, I reached out to her, gently prying at the edges of her mind. Generally, I can't read vampires, but she seemed so new, I guess would be the word, that I wanted to see if I could get a few impressions.

Instead, I was flooded with the chaos of adolescent thought bubbles. She was lonely and was afraid of what would happen if her mom found out she'd driven the family car into the worst part of town. She wished I would just leave her the hell alone so she could look for the latest *Buffy* Season 8 comic and read it in peace in one of those cool purple chairs. She wished she'd brought enough cash for the comic and a mocha latte, because the coffee smelled pretty good, and she loved, *loooved* chocolate and missed it like crazy. She even missed her mom telling her that chocolate gave her zits. Her mom didn't talk to her much at all these days. Her whole stupid family seemed afraid of her, but they were even more afraid of kicking her out of the house. It was just *great* to be allowed to stay in your own room because your dad's afraid to talk to you. She didn't know why I was hassling her; it wasn't as if she was going to steal or anything. Old people always followed her around in stores because of her hair. She wished she'd never dyed it green, but then her mom made such a big deal out of it that she felt she had to keep dyeing it over and over just to try to get a little attention—

I had to fight to pull myself out of the swirling vortex of her thoughts. I shook my head, trying to throw off the feelings of gloom and isolation.

God, I was glad I wasn't a teenager anymore.

"You'll find the *Buffy* comics over in our graphic-novels section, near the back," I murmured quietly. She turned, eyeing me warily. "Andrea, could you get our first official customer a tall mocha latte with the 'special' syrup? On the house, of course."

The *Buffy* lover, whom I'd decided I was going to like, even if it killed me, had eyes the size of saucers when I winked at her. "Th-thanks," she stuttered, in a voice that was higher, shakier, than the voice in her head. "I'm Cindy."

"Really?" I asked, eyeing the nose piercing. "I did not expect that. Cindy, I'm Jane. That's Andrea. Let us know if you need anything."

"OK." She turned on her heavily booted heels and headed for the graphic novels.

"And for the record, I'm not that old," I called after her.

A remarkably more cordial Cindy parked in a chair with her comic and sipped her coffee. She proved to be quite the good-luck charm, as her arrival brought a stream of steady peals of the front entrance bell. Several vampires, whom I'd never seen before, came in and sipped warmed blood and discussed forming an undead book club. Zeb and Jolene stopped by for pastries (for Jolene) and a book titled *The Drama of the Half-Were Child* (for Zeb.) They cozied up at the bar near my dad and chatted about the impending Lavelle. They still hadn't told Zeb's mother about the pregnancy. After Mama Ginger broke into the trailer, rearranged all the furniture, "organized" their mail and bills, and cleared most of the food out of Jolene's fridge, Jolene had adjusted the disclosure date to when the baby left for college. She'd also added those biometric fingerprint locks to her plans for the new house. Seriously, you don't mess with a werewolf's food supply, even under the guise of being "helpful."

Several members of the Friends and Family of the Undead, a group dedicated to helping the loved ones of newly turned vampires, perused new releases in the self-help section and were thrilled when I offered to host the meetings at the shop on Thursday nights. A few of my currently human former library patrons braved the bad part of town and bought up Anita Blake titles they probably wouldn't have purchased in a "mainstream" bookstore. They also floated the concept of forming a book club focusing on supernatural works, starting with Alice Sebold's *The Lovely Bones*.

I missed the children and children's books. I missed old tattered copies of *Harold and the Purple Crayon* and tracking down the copy of *Behind the Attic Wall* that had been lost and nearly kept by careless girls (including my-self) a total of fourteen times. But this new enterprise was certainly rewarding. We actually sold books. To live customers. Which hadn't happened at Specialty Books in a while. Of course, by live, I mean present at the time of sale. I couldn't guarantee heart or lung function.

I was helping books find their way to people again. I would have teared up a little if I'd had time. These misty thoughts were interrupted by the appearance of a pe-tite brunette with a heart-shaped face and high, sharp cheekbones. She had on a thickly ruffled blouse paired with a long black skirt. A delicate cameo pin secured the neck. She was a vampire, and she stared at me for a while before finally approaching the counter.

"Can I help you?" I asked.

"No, I believe I'll just browse about for a while. I think you might have exactly what I'm looking for." She smiled, the tips of her fangs peeking out over her thin, whitened lips.

"O . . . K."

Directing two men who I suspected could be ghouls to the financial-planning section kept me distracted from this odd customer. There was something not quite right about this woman, and it wasn't just her taste in old clothes. Her eyes were feverish and bright, and I couldn't seem to look into them for too long. Her skin was pale even by our standards. She smelled wrong, like liniment and camphor, the combination of which was almost overpowering when she approached the register carry-ing copies of *Love Bites, How to Survive Sire Abandon-*

ment, *30 Days to a Healthier Undead You*, *I'm OK, You're Undead*, and, oddly enough, *A Walk to Remember*.

"You have a wonderful selection," she said, her dark eyes boring through me.

"Thank you. Did you find what you were looking for?"

"Not quite. But this will do for now." Her voice was flat as she handed me cash, which was quickly becoming my favorite medium of payment.

"Well, please come back. And let me know if I can help you find it."

"I'm sure you can," she said, smiling at me with an intensity that, frankly, was starting to weird me out a little.

She faded into the crowd (crowd!) of customers and out the door. An hour before closing, my feet were so sore I didn't even think of asking Andrea whether she'd noticed Creepy Cameo Chick. Instead, we totaled out the drawer, rejoiced over every large bill, and promised each other that Cindy the Goth Good-Luck Charm would be welcome to free lattes whenever she wanted them.

Mr. Wainwright and Jettie reappeared and admitted to a tiny fib. Mr. Wainwright couldn't stand the idea of missing my big night and had spent most of it watching the sales floor in invisible ghost mode. Mr. Wainwright waxed poetic over every sale and declared that the shop had probably made more in-store customers that night than in the previous year. He declared Andrea and me to be marketing geniuses. Aunt Jettie just smiled and claimed to have "known it all along." Dick popped a bottle of champagne so expensive I dared not ask where he got it, and we sat at the coffee bar toasting a good night.

All in all, Gabriel certainly picked the right moment to walk back into my life.

"Jane?" he said, tentatively walking toward me, holding a bouquet of fat, vibrant yellow sunflowers tied with raffia and ribbon.

I was surprised at how much trouble I had looking him in the eye as he crossed the room, and at how gratifying it was that he looked like ten miles of bad back-country road. Gabriel was paper pale, the hollows of his cheeks dramatic and drawn. And if I wasn't mistaken, there was a little nervous twitch to his upper lip. If he felt half as bad as he looked, well, the vindictive part of me thought that was a pretty good start. And I was touched that he knew I would know that sunflowers meant "adoration" and "warmth." But even after weeks of missing his voice, his face, I found that more than anything, I just wanted him gone. I didn't want to have this conversation now. I wanted to bask in my success for just a little while longer. I should have known better. If my history has taught me anything, it's that once I start enjoying a little good fortune, the karmic balance shifts to kick me in the face and restore the status quo.

"Hi," he breathed, as if he had spent an entire evening planning that single syllable.

"Hi," I conceded after considerable thought.

"How have you been?" he asked.

Really? We were starting off with awkward pleasantries? Because I was in an "apologize or be destroyed" sort of mood. Hmm. How have I been? Sharpening a lot of stakes. Watching *Kill Bill* over and over again . . .

Gabriel pressed the flowers into my hands as I asked, "What are you doing back?"

He shrugged and smiled. "It's your big night. I wouldn't miss it."

"Well, you did miss it. You've missed a lot of nights recently. So many nights, in fact, that I started to think maybe you weren't coming back. Thanks for putting me in that position."

"Jane, that's not fair," he said quietly as Jettie and Mr. Wainwright disappeared. Dick and Andrea had a sudden and overwhelming desire to reshelve misplaced stock.

I sat down and laid the flowers aside. "Look, Gabriel, I'm tired, and I don't have the patience for empty banter. I've had a very long night. A great night, in fact. And you weren't here for it. I did all of this without you. The funny thing is, I didn't need you. I didn't need you to protect me or take care of me or shield my delicate self in your big strong manly arms. I'm getting to the point where I kind of like not needing you. In fact, I've decided to start a no-strings-attached, purely carnal relationship with Dick to meet some of my needs, so you don't even have to show up for that."

Dick's smirking face rose over the diet and health-maintenance shelves. "Well, Stretch, if you're offerin'— ow!" he cried as Andrea's hand snaked up from behind and slapped the back of his head.

Gabriel pushed through an obvious distaste for the mental picture the words "purely carnal" invoked and said, "Jane, let me explain. I haven't called because I've been stuck in meetings every night for the last few weeks. First, a manufacturing plant I'd hoped to purchase in Leeds had labor problems. And then a real-estate deal fell through in Italy. I had to soothe some very insulted Czech tempers when my interpreter called one of them a 'horse's ass' when I was trying sell them a film-processing plant—"

"You're lying to me." At this point, I was thankful for the gut-burning anger that was preventing tears from welling up.

Gabriel started. "What?"

"You're lying, right now. To my face."

"No, I'm not."

"Yes, you are, because when you lie, you get this little wrinkly line between your eyebrows." I tapped him on the forehead. "You don't think I've noticed, but it happened every time you got one of those fancy linen envelopes and tried to explain it away as business correspondence. It's like a little exclamation point in the middle of your forehead that screams, 'I'm lying!'"

"I do not!" he cried.

"You've got one right now!" I yelled, pointing to his head, over which he slapped a protective hand.

"I've explained to you—"

"You've explained nothing to me. Nothing. And this is not an issue that will go away if we ignore it hard enough. Weirdly timed 'business' calls I'm not allowed to overhear. Secret notes at every hotel that you destroy immediately after reading. Notes that talk about what you and some other woman 'are' to each other. How I can't satisfy you the way she 'does'—"

"You read the notes?" he demanded, his voice reaching that "boyfriend in trouble" pitch that only dogs can hear.

"I didn't want to, but damn it, Gabriel, what else what I supposed to do? Just keep pretending that nothing was going on? Pardon me if the only logical conclusion I can come up with is that you're cheating on me. If there are other less crazy options, please tell me. I would love to hear them."

"I can't believe you would think, after all we've been through, that I would want to be with someone else!"

"Which is something that someone who is cheating would say."

"Stop!" he yelled. "Just stop it, Jane. I've told you, there are things going on right now that I can't tell you about. It's for your own good. I asked you to trust me, and you can't stand to be happy, can you? You're just waiting for the other shoe to drop, and when there are no problems, you invent them."

"Well, that's . . . painfully accurate. But let's explore why I might look for problems, shall we? Since I've met you, I've died. An insane blond Realtor tried to frame me for murder so she could turn my family home into a tacky condo development. My sister is suing me because she's decided that I don't deserve any part of my family's history. My grandmother has stopped speaking to me, a vampire, but she's perfectly OK with being engaged-to-be-engaged to a ghoul. My tenth high school reunion is coming up, and I'm the only Undead American in my graduating class. Oh, and my suppliers believe I'm lonely enough to need porn."

Gabriel's eyebrows drew up at this, but I continued my tirade. "And despite all of that, the only thing that's really knocked me on my ass is thinking that, yes, you've been with someone else. That you've touched someone else, told her you love her, despite all of your sire-childe, 'I'm drawn to you because of your innocence and how good you smell, I'm going to love you forever' bullshit. If there's another explanation, I would love to hear it. Because what in the world could be worse that that? What could be so bad that you don't think I could handle it?"

"Please, just trust me," he said, clutching my face between his palms like a life preserver. "Trust that everything I do is to protect you. Trust that seeing you being threatened tears at me in a way that I can't explain. Just trust me, Jane."

"Threatened in what way? What the hell are you talking about?" I pried Gabriel's hands away. "And why should I trust you? You're jealous and secretive, and you have a tendency to kill people, somehow deluding yourself that it's for my own good. I don't want to trust you. I don't care anymore, Gabriel. I just don't care what you have to say. I wish you and her—at least, I hope it's a her—my best."

"Jane—"

"Shut up! I've given you a dozen chances to explain." The more I spoke, the angrier I got, until I was shouting loudly enough to rattle the windows. "All you do is make excuses and tell me half of the truth. This is a textbook bad relationship. And you know what? I'm glad I am discovering this now, before I spent one hundred years of my life thinking that I was lucky to have you."

"I hope all your books keep you warm at night!" he yelled, stomping toward the door.

"Hey, you're room temperature at best, buddy. You never kept me that warm to begin with!" I shouted back, tossing a particularly weighty Tolkien volume at his retreating back.

Well, there went my "healthy, normal relationship" goal.

"Ow! What is wrong with you?" he roared, stalking back to me.

"You!" I yelled.

"So, hit me, but don't bother with the books," he demanded, grabbing my shoulders.

"You don't get to touch me!" I slapped his hands away.

Dick emerged from the back room, his face thunderous as he told Gabriel, "Son, you'd better back off, *now*."

Gabriel's face softened, and his hands dropped to his sides. "Just let it out, so we can get through this." He was almost begging now. He leaned his forehead against mine and pulled my hands gently into his. "This is what we do. So, let's just fight and then fight some more until we get this out of our system and we can go back to normal again."

"No," I said, my own voice shaking as I backed away

from him, toward my office. "I don't want to feel like this anymore. And we are anything but normal. Just stay away from me, Gabriel."

"But I love you."

"I know you think so." I nodded and stepped back behind the closed office door, waiting until I heard the front doorbell tell me that he'd walked out.

If a man is callous and fickle in life, being a vampire won't suddenly make him sensitive to your needs.

—Love Bites: A Female Vampire's Guide to Less Destructive Relationships

There is nothing sadder than a vampire in her bathrobe, drinking Hershey's Blood Additive Chocolate Syrup straight from the bottle and watching *Fatal Attraction* over and over again.

I hadn't gotten so much as a call from Gabriel since the ugly scene at the shop. Even though I probably would have hung up on him if he had called, he could have at least made the gesture of letting me hang up on him. But it appeared that Gabriel had learned his lesson from the first time I stopped talking to him. Complete radio silence. Every once in a while, I thought I could sense his presence outside the house, but it seemed like wishful thinking on my part. I walked outside, hoping to catch a glimpse of him. But there was nothing, not even a trace of his scent on the breeze.

Gabriel, it seemed, had moved on. And if he hadn't moved on, he was doing a damn fine impersonation of someone who had. So I decided to follow suit.

For the past four nights, I'd served coffee, helped customers select books, and kept our new mascot, Cindy, in comics and lattes. The crowd wasn't quite as big as opening night, but it was certainly respectable. And we seemed to be developing regulars, human and vampire.

But when Sunday night, our closed night, came, I found myself in my bathrobe in the kitchen, staring down the Hershey's bottle. The phone rang, and even though I really, really hoped it was Gabriel, I was still contrary enough not to answer just in case it *was* Gabriel.

Instead, Mama's voice echoed from my answering machine through my impossibly empty kitchen. "Jane, honey, it's Mama. Daddy told me all about what happened with Gabriel. I don't know why you told Daddy about it instead of me . . . but anyway, I think you just need to stop being silly and call him. It's not like there are a lot of available vampires out there. And you two are so good together. Whatever Gabriel did, I think you just need to—"

The machine cut her off. God bless technology.

Before Mama could call back, Andrea and Jolene came barreling into the house like the cavalry, armed with DVDs; dessert blood, obviously for me; ice cream, obviously not for me; and wine, obviously not for Jolene. There was also an alarming assortment of junk food, including ready-made cheesecake filling in a tub, which I didn't even know existed. And now that I was aware of it, I was extremely disgruntled that I couldn't eat any of it. At the sight of this cornucopia of girlie comfort, I promptly burst into tears.

"I love you guys." I sniffled. "I'm fine. I'm not crying 'cause of Gabriel. I just really love you guys."

Jolene wrapped her arms around me and made soft wuffling noises as I snotted up her T-shirt. I had really good friends, girlfriends, which was something I'd never had in life. Somehow they complemented each other to form some sort of perfectly balanced break-up safety net.

"Aw, honey, it's all right," Jolene soothed. "He's a bastard. Zeb was too busy mumblin' empty threats to make it clear what Gabriel did, but he's a bastard."

"Oh, have we already reached the 'calling Gabriel names' portion of the festivities?" Andrea asked, returning to the kitchen with my corkscrew. "I thought we'd at least get her drunk and watch a movie first."

"I thought we were supposed to get her drunk and put her panties in the freezer," Jolene said, her pretty face scrunched in confusion.

"I think you're mixing up your female-bonding customs," I told her. "That's 'thirteen-year-olds at a sleepover,' not 'vampire boyfriend may or may not have cheated on you, but either way, he's an emotionally unavailable asshat.'"

"Oh, how the hell am I supposed to keep up with all your weird human rituals?" She grunted, prying the lid off Ben and Jerry's Mint Chocolate Cookie and digging in. "If this was a werewolf thing, we'd just go pee on his front porch so no other females would come near him for months."

"I hadn't thought of that," I admitted.

I surveyed Andrea's outfit of artfully worn jeans and what was obviously one of Dick's T-shirts, advertising the joys of Hot Springs, Arkansas. "I thought you said you were getting rid of Dick's tacky T-shirts."

"Oh, this isn't tacky, this is vintage," she said, turning proudly to show off the way the shirt hugged her curves. "I put a seam here and there. It's a little more tailored, so instant classic."

I peered down at my own happy-face pajama pants and a baggy T-shirt advertising the annual 4-H Hog Call. "I hate you. What'd you bring?" I examined the stack of videos. "*Steel Magnolias* and *Beaches*? Are you trying to comfort me or get me to commit suicide?"

Jolene shrugged. "When I want an excuse to cry, I watch *Steel Magnolias*."

"What about this one?" I held up a copy of *9 to 5*.

"I think Jolene got confused about the theme," Andrea said. "But still, female empowerment, dosing your boss with rat poison. It could work."

"I'm your boss," I reminded her.

"That does pose a problem," Andrea agreed as my eyes narrowed.

"Zeb said we should bring over the first season of *Buffy the Vampire Slayer*, but Andrea thought you'd get all depressed," Jolene told me.

"Yeah, because what's the point of watching *Buffy* if you're not watching the second-season episodes with

Spike in them?" I asked, uncorking the bottle of wine. Andrea poured me a large glass. "Hmmm. I wonder if it would be unethical for me to turn James Marsters? And then force him to fake the Cockney accent? And then make him my love monkey?"

"Yes, the Council would probably notice that." Andrea snorted.

"Frankly, I'm surprised some crazy, recently turned fan girl hasn't already thought of it," I muttered into my wine.

Andrea pulled a DVD case with a blank cover out of her purse. "I also brought this. It's an unrated version of the BBC production of *Pride and Prejudice,* the Colin Firth version. Dick got it from one of his . . . sources. There's a rumor that during the bath scene, you get an accidental peek at Mr. Darcy's bum."

"Oh, Lord, she's crying again," Jolene groaned as I gave her neck another moist hug.

I blubbered, "I'm just so happy!"

We indulged in buttoned-up Austenian dramedy for a few hours, consuming more calories than should be allowed by law. I painted my toes a bold eggplant, which Gabriel had always disliked. He said it made my feet look hypothermic. Thanks to her accelerated pregnancy, Jolene's brief flirtation with crippling morning sickness was over. She polished off the Mint Chocolate Cookie and the Cherry Garcia but not the Chunky Monkey, which Andrea specifically chose because Jolene hated banana. I became concerned about Andrea's wine-to-ice-cream consumption ratio and what sort of color she might turn my carpet if she got sick. But then I had a few glasses myself and just didn't care. Fitz couldn't decide whom he'd rather spurn me for, Andrea or Jolene, both of whom he adored. But since he had a better chance of Andrea sharing food with him, he snuggled up with Andrea.

"Do you consider yourselves Colin Firth girls or Colin Farrell girls?" Jolene asked, munching on her thousandth or so mini-Snickers as Mr. Darcy informed Elizabeth that he most ardently admired and loved her.

"Can't I have both?" Andrea asked with a dreamy sort of leer. "One of them could run the video camera."

"That answer, by its very nature, makes you a Colin Farrell girl." I snickered.

"I'm just saying what you're both think—" Andrea let out a shriek and dropped her half-melted tub of ice cream on my floor.

At least it wasn't vomit.

"What?" I squinted at her whitened face in the flickering light of the TV.

"There's somebody out there!" she cried. "I saw them! They were looking in the window."

"Who was it?"

"I don't know!" she cried. "It was all blurry."

"I can't imagine why," I drawled, looking pointedly at the two empty wine bottles at her feet.

"Jane, I'm serious, there was someone standing there, watching us through the window!" Andrea insisted.

I shook my head. "But I haven't picked up on anything."

I looked to Jolene, who shrugged. "I usually have to be pretty focused to sense something watching me."

Jolene and I went to the window and saw nothing reflected back at us but darkened woods.

"Hit pause. I'll go check it out." I sighed.

"What if it's Gabriel? Or what if it's some townie
lookin' to mess with a vamp?" Jolene asked. "And you're
wearin' your bathrobe."

"Either way, I get to hit something, so yay. They're
probably gone by now, anyway." I shrugged. Andrea did
not look convinced. "Fine."

I shrugged out of my robe, reached into the hall
closet, and pulled out a Louisville Slugger, which had
been sharpened to a wicked point.

"Why do you have that giant phallic symbol in your
hall closet?" Andrea asked, pointing to my bat.

"I'm a woman living alone in the country. Vampire
or not, I feel the need to take some precautions. Why do
you think I keep that pair of muddy men's boots out on
the porch?"

"I thought it was a tacky decoration," Andrea said,
shrugging.

"I'm comin', too," Jolene said, rolling her shoulders in
a way I knew meant she was preparing to wolf out.

"You're not going anywhere, pregnant lady. You just
stay here and keep your belly covered. Besides, someone
has to keep Lushy here company. Lock the door behind
me. Call Dick if things get weird."

"When aren't they weird?" Andrea grumbled as I
walked out the front door. I crept around the house,
bat on shoulder, to the den window. There was a fresh
smear of scent on the air, a cold, angry presence. Some-

one had been standing outside my window, watching as we gorged ourselves and watched silly movies. Someone had intruded on what was supposed to be my sanctuary.

That just pissed me off.

The scent was emotional, unfamiliar, dark and red and desperate. I followed it to the tree line and, against my better judgment, walked into the dense grove of oaks that surrounded my house. Night is rarely quiet in Kentucky, especially in the hazy weeks of late summer. Mosquitoes buzzed near my head but apparently knew better than to try to graze on my undead skin. Bullfrogs croaked their love songs from the slow-moving creek that flowed into the long-abandoned pastures. Growth had given way to ripening and rot, a wet, sad smell that rose up to meet me with every step, covering the trail of the intruder.

I moved quickly through the trees, cringing with every acorn that crackled beneath my feet. A draft of icy, frigid air seemed to snake around my ankles, rising to twine around my body and squeeze at my chest. I froze, turning toward a bank of poplar trees on my left, the source of the strange sensation. I couldn't see anything, anyone, even with my clear, inhuman vision. I closed my eyes and tried to search for the mind of whoever was out there. It was like scratching my fingers at a slick marble wall, cold, hard, and impossible to get a grip. Even with my limited psychic practice, I could tell that the clammy blast of air clinging to my skin wasn't coming from whoever might be out there. It felt like an internal alarm, an organic warning even stronger than a sense of dread or foreboding. My body was trying to tell me that something bad was coming.

I took an instinctual step back toward the house, where I could lock several doors against this sense of impending doom. Instead, I locked my legs against the impulse to run. The time for running was over. Time to be proactive, I told myself.

Mustering up all the bravado I could, I yelled, "Hey! I know you're out here. I don't care who you are. I don't care why you're here. If you have something to say to me, you don't skulk outside my window like a peeping Tom, understand? You come to my door and approach me like a grown-up evil being."

I waited another few beats, but the only presence I felt was the frogs, their tiny hearts fluttering in the dark. "I thought so. Stay away from my house, you freaking coward!"

I turned on my heel, stepped into a mud slick, and went flying, landing on my back with a thud and whacking my head against a stump.

Through the lacy green canopy of leaves, the stars twinkled, mocking me.

"Oh, shut up," I huffed, pulling myself to my feet. I was lucky I hadn't impaled myself on my bat or some handy branch. Now fully sober and disgruntled, I trudged back to the house.

Jolene and Andrea, who had cleaned up the ice-cream mess in my absence, fired questions at me as I went upstairs to change out of my muddy clothes.

"I'm pretty sure there *was* someone out there, so I owe you an apology," I told Andrea.

"Who do you think it was?" Jolene asked, rubbing her stomach nervously. "I cracked the door open just a little to get a sniff, but I couldn't tell. Also, Andrea closed the door on my face."

"She told us to stay inside," Andrea said, as slowly and patiently as she could. "And some of us don't have superpowers."

"Do you think it was Gabriel?" Jolene asked.

"Well, it wouldn't be completely out of character, considering he pretty much kept watch outside my house for the first few months I was a vampire. But it didn't smell or feel like anybody I know. It smelled . . ."

"Angry," Jolene finished for me. "And desperate and sort of like bug spray."

"That's about it." I nodded. "So, who's ready for Elizabeth to visit Pemberley?"

"Aren't you going to call the cops?" Andrea demanded.

"And tell them what?" I laughed. "That I smelled an intruder? After several glasses of wine? And I chased after him in my pajamas with what is probably considered an illegal weapon? No. I'm going back downstairs, and I'm going to finish watching our movie. I'm going to drink that Hershey's syrup straight from the bottle. And if peeping guy wants to come back, he's getting a crotchful of my left foot."

"What if it's Gabriel?" Jolene asked.

"Especially if it's Gabriel," I muttered.

Andrea leaned over to Jolene and whispered, "Well, the good news is, she seems to have moved on to the angry stage."

The next night, Dick greeted me at the door wearing a T-shirt that I can only guess he rescued from Andrea's culling process. In blurry white letters, it read, "If you can read this, please put me back on my bar stool."

"You are all class, my friend," I told him.

"Come on, Stretch, we're going out."

"Andrea told you what happened the other night, didn't she?" I grumbled.

"My lovely lady friend keeps no secrets from me. Come on. Andrea's taking care of the shop tonight. We're going out." Dick hustled me up the stairs, where he threw open my closet door and selected a clingy red tank top that I normally wore as a camisole under other shirts. He tossed it at me, along with a black push-up bra that was hanging out of my underwear drawer. When he tried to open the drawer a bit to peek inside, I smacked his hand. I went to the closet to pick an overshirt, but Dick shook his head. "Just wear the tank top."

"It's not meant to—"

"Wearing something on top of that is a waste of your God-given gift of cleavage," he insisted. "It's practically blasphemy."

"I know I'm your first female friend, so it's taken some adjustments for you. But we're not going to have in-depth mammary discussions. Also, I'm not changing in front of you," I told him. Dick rolled his eyes and turned his back.

When I remained clothed, he sighed his martyr's sigh and slunk outside my bedroom door, calling in, "Whatever you girls did to banish the Ghost of Jackasses Past obviously didn't work, because you're all still sulky. So, you're going to take this like a man. No ice cream. No fruity drinks. No movies where whiny women 'find their power.' You're not a girl, Jane."

"I think my God-given gift of cleavage proves otherwise," I muttered as I pulled the tank top over my head.

Dick snickered. "You know what I mean. You're not like other girls. If you were, you'd be sitting in a dark room somewhere, making a scrapbook of painful memories and reading *Women Are from Mars, Men Are from Uranus* or something. You're sort of a guy at heart, Jane. And you know what guys do when we're suffering?"

I poked my head out of my room and informed him, "If this involves going to the Booby Hatch and watching my cousin Junie do her tribute to famous interns, I'll pass."

Dick ignored me. "There are three things guys do when we're suffering. We drink, and we don't talk about our feelings."

"Oddly enough, I find that extremely appealing. What's the third thing?"

Dick handed me my purse and ushered me out the door. "I'll tell you later."

"Why do I see cow tipping in my immediate future?"

When I found myself sitting in the parking lot of the Cellar, staring at the sputtering neon sign, I asked Dick if he'd lost his ever-loving mind.

"It's the Cellar, you loved the Cellar," Dick said, jiggling my shoulder. "That one time. Come on, Norm asks about you all the time."

"As in 'Whatever happened to that girl who got her ass handed to her in my parking lot and was suspected of setting Walter on fire?'" I snorted.

Dick dragged me out of the car. "No, as in 'Whatever happened to that girl who kept me from being a Norm-shaped smear across the parking lot?'"

The Cellar was packed compared with the single night I'd spent there the previous year. Norm, the ironically named cuddly bartender, was busy, his work complicated by the house band blaring painfully earnest Elton John covers. But there were humans and vampires on the dance floor, and everybody sitting at the bar seemed companionably drunk.

"Norm!" Dick crowed over the din.

Norm shook his broad, balding head and chuckled. "That never gets old."

"Place is busy tonight," Dick observed.

Norm opened his mouth to answer but started when he saw my face. "Jane! I almost didn't recognize you! Haven't seen you around here since, well, the night Walter died."

I smiled and hoped none of Walter's friends overheard this conversation. Technically, Missy did the actual killing, but that report wasn't as widely circulated in the vampire community as the one accusing me of setting Walter on fire. . . . Oh, wait, Walter didn't have any friends.

"I've been meaning to thank you," Norm said, grasping my hands in his own warm, thick paws. "Most vamps, especially newborns, probably would have wanted to stay out of that mess and let me fend for myself. You helped me, and I appreciate it. You don't pay for drinks here, ever, got it?"

If I could have blushed, I would have. Instead, I just gave him a crooked smile and said, "Thanks."

"Hey, I was there, too," Dick objected.

"You were in the can," Norm said with considerably less warmth. "And I've seen you drink. You'd run me out of business. What can I do for you?"

Dick grinned liked a winsome, irresistible toddler. "A bottle of tequila and two shot glasses, please, Norm."

"That'll be twenty-five dollars, up front," Norm told him.

"I ask you, where's the trust?" Dick grumbled as he dug bills out of his wallet.

Norm handed over his best bottle of tequila, which I could only imagine was a nod to me, a bowl of lime slices, salt, and shot glasses.

I grimaced. "I'm not so sure about this. I know this is going to shock you, but I've never actually done tequila shooters. I've always been more of a 'mixed drinks that taste like snow cones' kind of girl."

Dick poured two shots and nudged a lime slice my way. "I'll bet you're a natural, honey."

I sighed. "Set me up."

Following Dick's motions, I licked the salt, pinched my nose, and knocked back the shot, wheezing when it hit my throat. Dick forced the lime to my lips and I bit down, careful not to swallow any vomit-inducing pulp. The heady, antiseptic burn of the liquor mixed with fresh, tart citrus juice. Dick laughed and tapped his shot glass twice on the bar. "What do you think, Stretch?"

"I think my throat is melting." I coughed, though the room started to tilt pleasantly. "Give me another one."

"That's my girl!" he crowed, pouring another shot.

Three shots later, I was a much mellower vampire. Hell, I was even admiring the finer points of the band's rendition of "Rocket Man." So, when a tall, handsome vamp came my way and asked me to dance, I was just relaxed enough not to embarrass myself completely.

OK, what I said was, "I have to go to the bathroom," and then I ran to the back of the bar. Which was only a little embarrassing.

In the ladies' room, I stared at the ceiling and wondered why I didn't get any share of the Early feminine wiles, so aptly handled by Jenny, Mama, and Grandma Ruthie.

"You are a ridiculous person," I told myself. "That was a perfectly nice-looking, nonthreatening person, who, for some reason, seems not to find you repulsive. And if you were a woman who had normal emotional responses and a regulated sense of paranoia, you would actually give that man a chance to take you home tonight. Go back out there, and stop being a spaz."

I shoved the door open, fully committed to non-spazdom, and heard someone on the other side yelp. I stepped out to see that I had smacked some poor guy with the door and spilled his beer down the front of his shirt.

"Well, there goes that," I said. "I'm so sorry!"

The vampire now wearing his beer laughed and wrung out his shirt. "So, are you anti-drinking, or do you just really hate plaid?"

I laughed at the situation and the funny. "Both, actually. I had a traumatic childhood involving hard-drinking lumberjacks." His smile was wide, friendly, his fangs incongruent with the sweet chocolate eyes. "Can I buy you another beer to replace what you're wearing?"

"Nah," he said. "It was my friend's round, and he tends to buy domestic. But you can dance with me. To cover my chest, so no one will see the stain on my shirt . . . that you caused. Not to make you feel obligated or anything."

"Why would I feel obligated?" I laughed and let him lead me to the dance floor as the band struck up "Your Song." I hadn't slow-danced since Zeb and Jolene's wedding, when Gabriel twirled me around the floor to the strains of "My Heart Will Go On." Oh, thinking about Gabriel was really not going to help me right now. I pushed those images away as this delicious man, who smelled pleasantly of Polo cologne and beer, put my arms around his neck and pulled me close. Normal, healthy relationship, I repeated over and over in my head. Normal, healthy relationship.

"I'm Charlie."

"Jane."

"I noticed you earlier, you know. You're one of the only women in here whose smile looks real. Sometimes when people are turned, they lose that. It's nice to meet someone who hasn't."

"Thanks." I smiled.

"See? There it is again," he teased, his dimples winking as he smiled back.

Charlie was the type of guy I would have loved meeting when I was living. Sincere, friendly, open, and out in the world. Of course, I never went to bars when I was living, so technically I wasn't out in the world.

"So, how's a nice girl like you doing shots in a place like this?"

I smirked. "Why don't you guess?"

"You lost a bet?" Charlie asked. I giggled—yes, it's pathetic, I know—and shook my head. "You're new to Alcoholics Anonymous, and you're unclear on the rules?"

"Good guess, but no."

Charlie bit his lip and considered. "You're in the witness-protection program and that guy is your inept federal handler?"

We glanced back at Dick, who was giving Charlie the "male relative" death glare.

"That's my friend Dick. I've been having a rough time lately, and he's trying to cheer me up with good booze and bad Elton John music, forgetting that I intensely dislike both. But I do like Dick, so I'm making the best of it."

"That's nice of you." There was the smile again, drawing my attention to his mouth. It looked soft and sweet; obviously, he made Chapstick a priority.

As we swayed and turned in silence, listening to the insistently poignant music, I caught sight of Dick watching us from the bar. He looked concerned, not necessarily judging me but definitely concerned. One didn't have to be a mind reader to tell that he was wary of Charlie and the fact that Charlie's hands were making contact with actual skin. It was only the skin on my arms, but it still seemed to disturb Dick.

I turned my back on him. Charlie took this as a hint to hold me closer, so that his lips brushed my forehead. It felt good, uncomplicated. His hands stroked my back in slow circles, urging me ever closer. It would be so easy to tip up my head and let him kiss me. But something was holding me back. Actually, it was several somethings: the knowledge that Dick was watching, doubt over whether a nice girl would move on this fast after breaking up with her vampire sire, and the possibility that for all I knew, this was the guy who had lurked outside my house the other night. I really didn't like that last one.

Why couldn't I be the casual-romance girl? Why couldn't I pick up some strange guy at a bar, flirt and kiss, and have no-strings-attached sex? Why did my brain always prevent me from behaving like a normal person?

Kissing. I would start with kissing.

So I did. I parted my lips and felt the cool, wet slide of his mouth across mine. He slipped his hands under my chin, tilting my face toward his so he could take even more of my mouth. He was gentle. He was sweet. And it felt wrong.

You know when you can tell you're making a huge mistake—not just buying ugly shoes because they're on sale or choosing the wrong Christmas gift for your mother but "the world is off its axis, spinning out of control into the abyss of space" wrong? I was making a huge mistake.

Even though it was possible Gabriel was out, enjoying a "purely carnal" relationship with a woman who enjoyed high-quality stationery, at that very moment, it felt wrong for me to be kissing someone else. It felt like a betrayal.

I pulled back from him and sighed. "I'm so sorry, Charlie. You're really nice. And that was a *really* great kiss. I don't want to lead you on or send out mixed signals, which is, ironically, exactly what I'm doing right now. But I just got out of a weird relationship, and I'm not ready to do this yet."

"I can be your rebound guy," he offered affably. "It won't hurt my feelings, honest."

I stared at him for a beat, my hormones waging war against my more rational parts. Stupid rational parts! I groaned. "That's really tempting, trust me. But I'm more of a wallowing-in-self-pity/angry-outburst type than a rebounder."

"Story of my life." He sighed. He pulled out his wallet and handed me a business card for Dr. Charles McCraffrey and his ear, nose, and throat practice in nearby Willardsville. He was a doctor. A vampire doctor but a doctor all the same. It was a good thing my mother wasn't there to witness this. "If you change your mind, please give me a call. It was very nice to meet you, Jane."

"You, too, Charlie."

"What happened with Mr. Hands?" Dick asked, glaring in Charlie's direction when I slumped back to the bar stool.

"You're the one who wanted me to share my 'gift' with the world," I reminded him. "Pour me another drink."

Dick obliged, asking Norm for a bottle of water. Apparently, I was being cut off. "That was a really nice guy," I told Dick. "And a doctor. Do you know what the chances are of meeting a nice, noncrazy vampire doctor at a bar in Half-Moon Hollow? I have a better chance of being struck by lightning and winning the lottery at the same time."

"Well, maybe we should go out and buy some tickets," Dick said.

"Don't humor the cranky vampire. What is wrong with me? Why can't I just meet a nice guy and go home with him? Why do I have all these weird hang-ups about feelings and meaning and making sure I have this intuitive bell going off in my head before I can let someone into my pants? You know, even when Gabriel and I had sex for the first time—"

"I don't know if I want to hear this," Dick said, shaking his head.

"I had to be all angry and 'out of control.' I couldn't just get lost in the moment. I needed an excuse, which is ridiculous, because there's no reason *not* to want to have sex with Gabriel. I mean, he has an *amazing* body—"

"What part of 'drinking and not talking' did I not make clear?" Dick demanded.

The band kicked into "Benny and the Jets." A skinny, pimpled vampire and two of his buddies appeared behind Dick and tapped him on the shoulder. "Dick, I want to talk to you."

Dick looked thrilled for the interruption. "Todd, thank God. What can I do for you?"

"I want my money back for those Springsteen tickets," Todd demanded, his Adam's apple bobbing indignantly.

Using a patient, paternal voice, Dick said, "Now, Todd, I gave you a good deal on those tickets. I didn't even charge a handling fee. You couldn't get a price that good from Ticketmaster."

"Those tickets were to a concert two years ago!" Todd shouted, a cue for his companions to put on their mean faces and look intimidating. I rolled my eyes and took a swig of water, which did nothing for my thirst, blood- or liquor-wise.

"They were collector's items!" Dick shouted back. "It's not my fault you didn't look on the tickets to check the date. I never told you they were for a concert *this* year."

"Well, you sure the hell didn't tell me they weren't!" Todd whined. "I took a girl all the way to Memphis for that concert. There was nothing there! Marcy was convinced I was trying to trick her into something. I felt like an asshole!"

"But Todd," Dick said, giving Todd what could be construed as a sympathetic headshake, "you *are* an asshole."

A lot of things seemed to happen at once. One of Todd's friends took a swing at Dick, missing and pinning me against the bar as he fell. I reached into my purse, feeling for the little keychain canister of vampire mace Gabriel had given me for Christmas, but couldn't find it. It wasn't attached to my keys or caught loose in the lining. Crap. I thought about stepping out of the way and letting Dick handle this, but then Todd smashed a pilsner over Dick's head. I yelled, "Hey! What the hell are you doing?" and shoved Todd back. The smaller of Todd's buddies gave me an admirable upward right hook to the jaw, knocking me back on my butt.

Have I mentioned that most male vampires have no compunctions about hitting girl vampires?

I scrambled to my feet, picked the Girl Hitter up, and slammed him to the floor. Todd spun me on my heel and punched me in the eye.

Ow.

The dance-floor crowd was now circled around the ruckus, cheering Dick on as he kicked Todd in the knee-cap and hit him in the throat with a pool cue. The taller of Todd's friends smashed *another* pilsner and the tequila bottle over Dick's head, so I kicked him in the crotch and felt a vicious little thrill when he howled and toppled over.

As Todd turned and advanced on me, I grabbed a chair, sidestepped him, and broke it over his back on "B-b-b-benny" and knocked him to the floor on "the Jets."

"Outside, Dick, now!" Norm yelled, apparently hitting his limit in terms of broken bar paraphernalia. Dick grabbed a pool cue and chased the three of them out of the bar. I felt I had no choice but to follow, along with most of the patrons in the bar. The gentleman with the spanking-new crotch injury elected to get into his car rather than suffer further humiliation.

Todd was getting winded, and his other friend was whining about something in his face being broken.

"Just give me my money, and we'll call it a night," Todd wheezed.

"I'll tell you what, you get in your car and get the

hell out of here, and I'll keep my girl here from kicking you in the goods, too." Dick smirked. "She's done it before. She'll do it again."

Todd look one look at my size-nine boots. I smiled, my fangs fully extended over my lip. Todd ran for it. The crowd groaned in disappointment and dispersed.

After I handed over cash to cover the broken stools and pitchers, a more forgiving Norm allowed us back into the bar to press ice to our rapidly healing faces.

"You should know better," Norm told Dick.

"Hey, Jane threw just as many punches as I did!" Dick cried.

Norm shook his head. "She was hitting in self-defense. You started it."

"Todd hit me first. Besides, how was I supposed to know he was dumb enough to head all the way to Memphis without even looking at the stupid tickets? I thought he would have figured it out weeks ago."

Norm pointed a fatherly finger at Dick. "You know what I mean. If you didn't do your back-alley deals at my bar, I wouldn't have all that many fights. Why did you even come tonight, anyway? You knew Todd would come looking for you, and you know he loves Cover Band Night."

"I forgot all about it," Dick said, avoiding eye contact with me. Norm muttered something under his breath and turned his back to help another customer.

I stared at Dick, who busied himself pouring the remaining ice from his face pack into my water glass and stretching his freshly healed jaw. "Dick, what's the third thing?"

Dick stared at me, his face blank. "Did you get a concussion, Stretch?"

"The third thing that men do to get over a breakup. Drinking, not talking about your feelings, and then what?" I said, growing suspicious. "It's fighting, isn't it? You set this up."

"I don't know what you're talking about," Dick said, still not making eye contact.

"You set this up," I repeated, poking him in the sides.

"Yes," he mumbled in the tone of a little boy who'd burnt his Mother's Day breakfast in bed. He smirked. "I didn't arrange for him to hassle me, but I figured, you're sad, you're angry, you didn't get to hit anything the other night. Todd was going to be there anyway, so why not let you get some stuff out of your system? I always feel better after a good cathartic tussle."

"You did all this for me?" I laughed.

He shrugged. "You feel better, right?"

I thought about it for a second and realized that I did. That beating the tar out of a Bruce Springsteen fan with poor attention to detail had made me feel better than all the liquor and ice cream and Bette Midler in the world. "I sort of love you, Dick."

"While my heart and all my other parts belong to a certain adorable redhead, I love you, too, Stretch," he said, giving my shoulder a brief squeeze. "You're the sister I never really wanted."

"Nice."

When you're having relationship problems, channel your energy into productive projects. Join a charitable group, or volunteer with an animal shelter or a soup kitchen. (It's best to avoid the temptation of blood drives.)

—Love Bites: A Female Vampire's Guide to Less Destructive Relationships

Once I decided not to let moping take over my life, it was a lot easier to get up and going in the evenings.

I cleaned the house from top to bottom, something I'd neglected during the busy months before the shop opened. I did a total inventory of the valuables to make sure Jenny and Grandma Ruthie hadn't managed to sneak into the house while I was out of town. I reorganized my library, and found about fifteen paperback copies of *Pride and Prejudice*. I also found a few titles that Mr. Wainwright had sent home with me from the shop to help me "acclimate to my new culture": *Love Customs of the Were,* a few volumes on exotic were species, and *The Spectrum of Vampirism*. Mr. Wainwright loaned it to

me the year before to help me find my way through the
subtle levels of vampirism. Honestly, it's like Scientology.
I boxed them up and set them in Big Bertha's trunk, so
I'd remember to return them to the stock.

And finally, I packed up everything associated with Gabriel: the ticket stubs from our first movie date, the little
platinum unicorn necklace he'd given me for Christmas,
the travel guides I'd pored over before we left on our trip.
I put them in a cardboard box and took them down to
the root cellar. Maybe one day, I'd be strong enough to
take them out again or even throw them away, but for
the moment, I just wanted them out of sight.

In the wake of our repetitive bonding experiences,
Andrea, Dick, and I developed a new schedule at the shop.
Andrea and I would open, brew coffee, go through mail,
and prepare orders for shipping for about an hour before
customers started showing up. Andrea generally needed
a nap around midnight, so Dick would show up and give
me a hand until closing. In the interest of keeping Andrea
from being completely nocturnal, she got Wednesdays off,
and Dick helped me open. The routine was relaxed but
organized enough to suit my compulsive librarian's soul.

So, imagine our surprise when we arrived on a
Wednesday night to find a man in wrinkled khakis sleeping against the front door of the shop. Sadly, it wasn't all
that odd to find a drunk sleeping it off in our doorway,
so Dick rousted him with a few shoves to the shoulder,
while I gathered the delivery parcel Rip Van Winkle was
using as a pillow.

"You're going to have to find some other place to rest your head." Dick sighed, pulling at the man's shirt. "Come on, buddy."

Rip snorted and yawned. "Jane Jameson?"

"I told you not to put it on the door!" Dick exclaimed, pointing at the little sign that read, "Jane Jameson, Proprietor. You have enough problems without *giving* the crazies your name."

"I'm looking for Jane Jameson," the man said, yawning and scratching at two days' worth of beard growth. "I'm Emery Mueller, Gilbert Wainwright's nephew."

As advertised, Mr. Wainwright's nephew, Emery, was both milquetoast and mealy-mouthed. Emery was the son of Mr. Wainwright's only sister, Margaret, who had moved to California in the 1960s and married a radio evangelist. Mr. Wainwright had only seen Emery on rare visits to the Hollow before Emery moved to Guatemala to teach English at a mountain seminary. He'd described Emery as an odd little boy who'd grown into an odd little man. And considering the level of oddity in Mr. Wainwright, that was saying something.

The cherry on this sundae of genetic improbability was that Emery and Mr. Wainwright also happened to be Dick's descendants. Dick had watched over the Wainwright family, the illegitimate product of a prevampirism dalliance with a servant girl, for generations. He considered Mr. Wainwright to be the "pick of the litter," stepping in to pay for his college tuition and proudly watching as Mr. Wainwright became one of the first Hollow boys to volunteer for duty in World War II. Dick was afraid that his less-than-upstanding connections might put the family at risk, so he'd only confessed to the relation the previous year, after Mr. Wainwright died. Watching those two bond, a vampire who appeared to be in his thirties giving fatherly advice to a ghost in his seventies, was as mind-boggling as it was touching.

Dick was obviously not as impressed with the latest branch of the Wainwright family tree. I thought living in South America was supposed to make you all tan and scruffy-sexy, like Harrison Ford. Emery just seemed pale and clammy, like gone-over cheese. He wore horn-rimmed glasses and a permanently constipated expression. His skin was pitted with old acne scars, which might have remained unnoticed if not for his tendency to flush and blush at the slightest provocation. His hair and his eyes were the same color, which I can only describe as "dust."

Ever since Emery had responded to Mr. Wainwright's death with a telegram telling us to proceed with the funeral without him, Dick and I had a running bet about when Emery would show up. I guessed four months, Dick guessed six months, and Mr. Wainwright guessed a year. We still had no idea how we would collect a wager from a ghost.

"Four months!" I cried triumphantly to Dick, who slapped a twenty-dollar bill into my hand.

"Hi, Emery, I'm Jane," I said to a clearly confused Emery. "This is my friend Dick."

"You sent the e-mail." Emery yawned. "To let me know about Uncle Gilbert."

"Yes, several months ago," I said, smiling in that overly sweet way only Dick knew was insincere. "Why don't you come inside?"

"Oh, thank you. I drove that rental car all the way from Louisville without air conditioning. It was terrible," he said, heaving himself off the ground.

My lips quirked involuntarily at his pronunciation of Louisville. Not because he had an accent or anything. One's Kentucky street cred can be determined based on how one pronounces Louisville. Luh-vul, you're from west Kentucky. Louie-ville, east Kentucky. Louis-ville, you're from Illinois.

"I know it seems odd to show up unannounced at this time of night. And it's so nice to meet you," Emery simpered as we led him into the shop. "While I dearly love doing the Lord's work, I'm so glad to be back here. I spent many hours as a child in the store, poring over the books."

"Really?" I said, arching a brow. "It's just that they're all, you know, occult books. Mr. Wainwright said you were very devout, even as a child. He said you tried to baptize him with bottled water when you were nine."

Emery flushed pink and cleared his throat. "Yes, well, spending time here was a taste of the forbidden fruit. I was fascinated by the books because they were so different from anything in my house. It drove my mother crazy."

Mr. Wainwright appeared behind Emery and nodded. "He did spend a lot of time here. And it was his predilection for the woodcarvings of the nude rituals practiced by eastern European vampire clans that upset his mother. I had to hide all the books that bared what his mother called 'lady bumps.' It was horrifying."

Dick excused himself so he could go out to the parking lot and laugh. I was stuck chewing on my lip and praying for a straight face. I flipped on the light switch, and Gilbert gave a loud gasp at the appearance of the shop. "It's so different!"

"Yes, well, we've renovated extensively since you were here last."

"You must have spent a fortune!" he exclaimed. "It's certainly nicer than anything in the neighborhood . . . you might have outpaced yourself there."

I shot a "What the hell?" look at Dick, who had just walked back in.

"And look, everything is so orderly! You could find anything you wanted now. Uncle Gilbert never did have a head for alphabetizing." Emery smirked. "But I guess he had you for that, among other things. He wrote to me about you once. He was very fond of you, a young, pretty vampire girl who was willing to spend so much time with him. Obviously, he had to be fond of you, if he sank all his money into renovating the shop and leaving it to you. I'm glad he had someone to make his last months so pleasurable, someone who took care of him. Even if it was only an employee."

Call me oversensitive, but had Emery just implied that I exchanged sexual favors for cash and redecorating?

"I don't think I appreciate what he's implying," Mr. Wainwright said, staring at his nephew.

"Me, neither," I muttered, to which Emery gave me a confused look. I cleared my throat. "Mr. Mueller, I don't want you to get the wrong idea about my relationship with Mr. Wainwright and how his will was written. I didn't set out to take over the shop or get in good with your uncle. I was just lucky enough to be hired by one of the sweetest men on earth, and he became a close friend. I didn't know he planned on leaving me the shop, and I wasn't even sure I was going to keep it at first. In fact, I was thinking very seriously of selling—"

"Oh! I think that's for the best, the right thing to do," Emery said quickly. "I'll do anything I can to help speed things along."

I was caught off-guard by his sudden enthusiasm. Who was he to be so enthusiastic about tossing out his uncle's legacy? Especially when that legacy technically belonged to me now?

"Give him what for, Jane," Mr. Wainwright said, smirking at what he recognized was my temper building. Emery wasn't smart enough to see it himself.

"As I was saying, I thought about selling. But I decided the best way to honor your uncle's memory would be to keep this place going. So I sank my own money into renovations. It didn't cost your uncle a penny. And the business seems to be taking off, so we're not going to be closing anytime soon. Um, for now, anything you want to take, you're welcome to, especially stuff from his personal effects or private collections. He didn't spell that out in the will, but I wouldn't feel right keeping everything."

"That's very kind of you." Emery sighed, picking up his duffel. "For now, I'm going upstairs to bed. I'm sorry if I'm being rude. I'm just so tired. Jet lag, you know."

"Oh," I said, exchanging a look with Mr. Wainwright. "Actually, there's no apartment there anymore. We turned it into storage and office space. I can recommend some hotels in town, though, depending on how long you're planning on staying."

Emery's lips thinned in a way that showed that he was clearly insulted by this change. "I see. I didn't anticipate that."

"I'm very sorry," I said. "If I'd known you were coming, I would have made hotel arrangements for you."

"I don't enjoy hotels," Emery said sulkily. "You never know who's stayed in the room before you or whether the facilities have been cleaned properly."

"He is absolutely phobic about germs." Mr. Wainwright chuckled. "But only American germs, for some reason. He thinks people in other countries are cleaner than we are. Don't let him talk you into staying with you, Jane. The last time he was a guest in my house, I woke up at three A.M. to find him steam-cleaning the inside of my dishwasher."

The thought of Emery staying with me hadn't even occurred to me. Yes, I had room to put Emery at my house, but . . . no. I was not inviting a mouth-breathing stranger into my home. A vaguely rude mouth-breathing stranger at that. I wondered if Dick would invite him to stay at Andrea's place. But given the way Emery was fastidiously wiping at his hands with hand sanitizer, as if we had some sort of germ that was more powerful than what they had in Guatemala, Dick didn't seem inclined to bond with him.

"Come on, Emery," Dick said, taking Emery's duffel bag onto his shoulder and patting him on the back. "I know a good boardinghouse in town. Very clean. The owner owes me a favor. I'll get you settled in."

Dick escorted Emery to his car and came back into the shop under the guise of forgetting something. "That's the fruit of my loins?"

"I think your genes lost their mojo somewhere along the way," I teased.

Dick was indignant. "Those are not my genes. Margaret must have mated with a jellyfish or something."

Mr. Wainwright shook his head. "You're not too far off."

"Look at Gilbert. He wasn't exactly strapping when he was young, but he had guts! He had gumption! He wasn't afraid of hotel sheets!"

"Thank you, Dick," Mr. Wainwright said, smiling proudly.

"And you!" Dick cried. "What are you thinking, telling him he can have anything he wants from the stock? What if he runs off with something valuable?"

"Well, he's probably got more rights to anything here than I do," I said.

Mr. Wainwright winced. "Oh, please, don't say that in front of him, dear. He'll take everything that's not nailed down and donate the proceeds to a questionable charity."

"Are you softening up to the doughy young missionary?" Dick asked me.

"There's nothing wrong with missionaries," I said, grinning at him. "Besides, he is your great-great-grandson, your own flesh and blood. And we both know you could use a little churching up. It might be interesting for you to talk to him, to hear things from his point of view."

Dick made a sour face. "His point of view is that we're evil and should be struck through the heart with a stake wrapped in wild roses."

"Wow, that seems harsh."

Dick walked out, putting his "determined to be polite" face on. I busied myself with getting the coffee bar ready for that night's crowd.

"How have you been, Jane, dear?" Mr. Wainwright asked. "Your aunt told me about your difficulties with Gabriel. She said you took it rather hard."

"Well, after going through the female and male break-up recovery rituals, I can determine that, one, I'm going to be OK. And two, the male break-up ritual is more fun but harder to heal up from. I'm fine, really. I'm just keeping busy and trying not to think about it."

"I can haunt Gabriel's house for you, if you'd like," Mr. Wainwright offered.

"Thank you, that's very sweet, but I don't think you can really scare someone after you've spent Christmas Eve with them. Unless you're my grandma Ruthie."

Mr. Wainwright chuckled. I rummaged through the drawers behind the bar and then got on my hands and knees, searching for the tiny canister of vampire mace. It had obviously been detached from my keyring at some point, and it didn't show up in a thorough postfight search of my purse and house. And it wasn't the sort of thing I wanted lying around the shop.

"Mr. Wainwright, have you seen a little metal tube, about the size of a Chapstick?" I asked, lifting a chaise longue with one hand to search under it. Mr. Wainwright, who was always entertained by my feats of vampire strength, shook his head. "Great. Either I'm going to have to wait for Fitz to pass it or pray I don't step on it and mace myself."

The front bell rang, and Zeb walked into the shop, pale and shaking. Wordlessly, he walked to the coffee bar and climbed onto a stool.

I snapped my fingers in front of his face. "Zeb, are you OK? What's wrong? Is it Jolene? Is the baby OK? Did one of Jolene's relatives get trapped by the Department of Fish and Wildlife? Did the police find your dad's still? What?"

"Two of them," he said, his eyes oddly dilated.

"One of Jolene's relatives was trapped by the Department of Fish and Wildlife *and* the police found your dad's still? What are the odds of that?" I wondered.

He snapped out of his funk long enough to look annoyed with me. "No, two of them, on the ultrasound. There's two babies."

"Twins?" I laughed. "But that's great! And considering the number of multiple births in Jolene's family, not entirely unexpected."

"Congratulations!" Mr. Wainwright cried, and then he caught sight of Zeb's stricken expression. "I'll be going now."

Zeb scrubbed his hand over his face as Mr. Wainwright faded out of sight. "I was prepared for one baby. I don't know if I can handle two."

"It's a little late for that. There's a very strict no-return policy on babies."

"I don't know what I'm going to do, Jane."

"Well, what do you want me to do? Take one off your hands? There's not much I can do, except pay someone else to babysit. Are they boys or girls?" I asked.

"Don't know yet; it's too early to tell. To be honest, I didn't catch much after 'two heartbeats.' One of them was doing a sort of Homer Simpson shimmy. I'm guessing that's the one that takes after me."

"Look at it this way: you're lucky it's not triplets or quadruplets."

That seemed to cheer him.

"If you keep going, you can form your own basketball team," I suggested. He furrowed his brow and frowned at me. "Too soon?" He nodded. "I'll fix you some herbal tea. It's soothing," I said, patting his hand. "How's Jolene? Is she craving pickles and ice cream yet?"

Zeb groaned. "If only. It's more like Canadian bacon and ice cream. Peanut butter and turkey sandwiches. Tuna noodle pie. She actually made what she called 'bacon chip cookies' the other day—a chocolate-chip cookie recipe with bacon pieces instead of chocolate chips. She said it's her body's way of getting as much protein as possible for the babies, but I swear if I see her eat one more of those pies, I'm going to yark."

"Well, the good news, is whenever I regret not being able to eat, I'll call those images to mind. I'll never want solid food again." I shuddered, rubbing my stomach.

Zeb perked up as he said, "By the way, I got a call

from the reunion committee today. They wanted some pictures of you for the memorial wall."

"But I'm not dead!"

Zeb smirked. "Well, that's not the way the committee sees it."

"That's it. I'm not going to this thing."

"Oh, come on," he said, accepting a cup of chamomile. "You've got to go to the reunion. It'll be fun! You can scare the crap out of all our former classmates."

"It will be fun for you. You're married to a beautiful woman who adores you to the point that she'll probably maul the first doofus who tries to give you a commemorative wedgie. And she'll be pregnant, so everyone will know you've had sex with her. I, however, will most likely be going solo which will probably just cement all those lesbian rumors. Oh, wait, dead lesbian rumors."

"So, you haven't made up with Gabriel yet, huh?"

I shook my head. Cindy the Goth Good-Luck Charm walked through the door, acknowledged me with a nod, and headed for the graphic novels. "You know, I used to be alone, and I got along just fine. It's simpler this way. Less messy, less complicated. Less time wondering what the hell is going on in my own life and whether it's my fault. At least, this way, I know it's my fault."

Zeb grimaced. "Well, that's cheerful."

"I do what I can," I said, shrugging as the front doorbell rang. "I met a really nice doctor the other night. And then he saw me beat a guy senseless, so I don't think he's going to want me to call."

"You beat some guy senseless?" Zeb cried.

"Dick made an attempt to cheer me up. It was either a bar fight or cow tipping."

Zeb's nose wrinkled. "You and Dick have a complicated relationship."

I shrugged. I put a mocha latte on the counter for Cindy and left it out for her, like cookies and milk for an Emo Santa Claus. "Besides, Adam Morrow's going to be there, and I'm still feeling a little weird about him."

I'd had a huge crush on Adam since elementary school. He was the blond, dimpled football hero to my tuba-toting band geek. I never really got over that teeny-bopper obsession with him, which was why it was so difficult for me to see that his efforts to get "reacquainted" a few months before had nothing to do with me and everything to do with Adam's weirdo sexual fascination with vampires. It turned out that despite attending school with me for twelve years, he hadn't remembered the name of that "egghead who used to annoy him in class" until someone reminded him at my almost-grandpa Bob's funeral. I dropped Adam like a clove of garlic and mended damaged fences with Gabriel before it was too late.

Of course, I didn't realize at the time that it was already too late and Gabriel had moved on to Jeanine. I've really got to work on rerouting my thought process so every subject doesn't come back to Gabriel.

It seemed unfair that I felt some measure of break-up anxiety over Adam when we never technically went out. But to this day, I couldn't even hear his name without a rush of guilt and embarrassment. I would have enough to deal with at the reunion—such as my placement on the memorial wall—without delving into those issues again.

"But crushing Adam's hopes and dreams is going to make the reunion even better! You, the untouchable hottie that he can't, well, touch. It's going to be such a blow to his ego!" Zeb exclaimed. "I never told you this, because you had that thing for him in school, but I always wanted to just punch that guy in the face with his 'Oh, I'm tall and blond and dreamy, and everybody loves me because I'm such a nice guy' shtick. Maybe there were other guys in the class who were just as nice. Maybe there were some guys in the class who should have been Swing Choir president but didn't get elected because Adam was 'so dreamy.' Maybe there were some guys who wanted to take Dawn Farber to Homecoming but ended up going stag because Dawn was holding out for Adam 'just in case.'"

"Maybe *you* shouldn't go to the reunion," I said, sorting through the day's mail. "Should I start putting horse tranquilizers in your tea?"

As Zeb ranted on, I sifted through the day's mail, mostly bills and publishers' catalogues. An ivory linen paper envelope slipped out and fluttered to the counter. I stared at it for a moment, wondering if I was imagining the spidery black writing that spelled out my name and the shop address. There was no return label. The postmark was in Half-Moon Hollow.

"You OK, Janie?" Zeb asked, reaching over to jiggle my shoulder. "You're pale. Paler than usual."

I nodded and handed the heavy envelope to Zeb. My hands were shaking. "Could you open that for me?"

Zeb arched an eyebrow, concern stretching his mouth in a grim line. "Sure."

I took the letter from his hands and laid it on the bar to keep it steady enough for me to read. There was no opening greeting, just cramped paragraphs crowding the elegant slip of stationery.

> *You don't know who I am, but I have been watching you for a long time, Jane.*
>
> *Gabriel Nightengale isn't the man you think he is. He's not even the vampire you think he is. Gabriel takes advantage of those who are weaker. He doesn't care for you. He is incapable of caring for anyone but himself. Even his jealousy and possessiveness, his claims that he wants to protect you, come from his desire to own you, to keep you to himself, like a favorite toy, until he is through playing with you.*
>
> *I was once like you, young and innocent. Gabriel claimed he was drawn to me because of that innocence, my goodness. He said he could follow my scent across the world, that it was part of what bonded me to him. He said he loved me. Foolishly, I thought he was exciting and dashing—a dark prince taking me away from a life of boredom, from*

*a gilded cage of limitations and demands. He
killed me. He damned me, as he has damned
you.*

> *You are nothing special. You are not
different from any girl who has ever walked
the earth, despite what he may have told you.
And when you have served your purpose,
he will grow tired of you. He will use and
abandon you as he used and abandoned me.*

> *I know where you go. I know with
whom you spend your time. You seem to
enjoy your little life. For your sake, for the
sake of the people you care about, you should
stay away from Gabriel.*

> *A Concerned and Vigilant Friend*

I looked down and saw the corner of a photo sticking
out of the envelope. I tipped it and slid several photos
out into my hands. I gasped as I recognized the subjects.
Gabriel and I in a hotel room. The camera was obviously
outside a window, but I had no idea where we were or
when the picture had been taken. We were stretched
out on one of the wide hotel beds, a rare moment of
relaxation on the Trip from Hell. My feet were draped
across Gabriel's lap as he painted my toenails a delicate
strawberry color. There was another picture of us in
London as we walked toward the theater. I was wearing
the red dress I'd bought just to attend a performance of
As You Like It. There was a photo taken while we were

in Rome. I was sitting at a little outdoor café, alone and looking worried, because Gabriel had just gotten up to take another "business call." Another photo of me, this time alone on my front-porch swing, reading *New Moon* by Stephenie Meyer, a book I'd chosen in hopes of exorcising my own traumatic vampire break-up issues. The camera seemed focused on the teardrop trailing down my cheek, as if that was the whole point of the picture. The final photo featured Andrea, Jolene, and me sprawled out in my living room, watching TV.

Andrea *had* seen someone at my window that night. This person had taken pictures of us, laughing and eating junk food. They'd probably followed me out into the woods on my idiot's errand. I realized how foolish I'd been to leave the house. This person could have doubled back to the house and hurt Andrea, hurt Jolene and her babies. My stomach twisted into a cold, watery knot. This person had followed us for months, had been privy to intimate, happy moments I wanted to keep private, had enjoyed watching me work through pain. My fangs snuck over my lip. The razor-sharp tips caught the tender flesh and made blood well into my mouth, sending my senses into overdrive. I growled.

"Janie, what's wrong? What does it say?" While I was reading, Zeb had stepped around the bar and had an arm wrapped around me. "Bad news?"

I fought to get my temper in check, to get my emotions under control. I didn't want to worry Zeb with this. He had enough to deal with, worrying over Jolene and the babies. Through force of will and a barrage of unappetizing imagery (basically, any episode of *CSI*), I made my fangs retract.

"No." I blew out a breath and faked a smile as I refolded the letter over the photos and stuck them under the counter. "It's fine. Just really persistent junk mail."

"It doesn't look like junk mail. What's with all the pictures?"

"Don't worry about it, Zeb."

Zeb didn't seem convinced, but then customers started coming in, and I didn't have time to answer questions. I waited until Zeb's back was turned to fish the letter out and read it again. Obviously, this "concerned and vigilant friend" was the same person who sent Gabriel letters in Europe. Was it the mysterious Jeanine, the woman whose name had popped up frequently on Gabriel's cell phone in the last year? And if it was, who the hell was she? And how long ago had Gabriel "used and abandoned" her? And perhaps the most important question, what was she doing in the Hollow?

8

It's important to remember to spend time with your family. It's important to temper your absorption into the vampire culture with contact with the human world.

—*Love Bites: A Female Vampire's Guide to Less Destructive Relationships*

When a smell is powerful enough to wake a vampire up at noon, it's time to call an exorcist.

The sex dreams hadn't subsided since that horrible fight with Gabriel at the shop. In fact, they seemed to grow more intense after Gabriel's return. In this particular dream, I was strapped into complicated Victorian underwear. Gabriel was wearing an old-fashioned cut-away tux. We were in an expensive-looking hotel room, lit by gas lamps. Still clad in his white shirtsleeves, an enthusiastic Gabriel peeled my corset away, pushed me back onto the bed, and kissed his way from the curve of my linen-covered breast to the lacy little pantaloons I was wearing. He smiled up at me, the way he used to when we made love, as if I was the most beautiful creature on the planet. I felt my human flesh grow warm and pliable under his hands. He stripped the last of my underthings away, lapping away at my core with strong, sure strokes. He nibbled and kissed until I was panting. When he finally touched the very tip of his tongue to that vital little bundle of nerves, I exploded, screaming his name as I rode wave after wave of dark, shuddering ecstasy.

And then I felt the pain. My eyes flew open. Gabriel's fangs were sunk deep into the flesh of my thigh, twin trickles of blood flowing onto the sheets as he fed greedily. He snarled up at me, my blood dripping obscenely from his fangs. I screamed again, for entirely different reasons. And he launched himself at me, snapping his teeth against my throat and draining me. He rolled away, sated, and disappeared into the sheets. Horrified, I raised my bloodied hands and saw them turn slowly gray. They seemed to decompose before my very eyes. I was a corpse, rotting and decayed.

That certainly explained the smell.

I woke up with a start and immediately clamped my hand over my nose. As I shook off the last blood-smeared images of the dream, my stomach roiled. I had not smelled anything that foul since an eighteen-wheeler packed with live hogs overturned near my elementary school. My nostrils actually burned with the scents of decaying fish and ammonia. I sat up slowly, my body sluggish in the wake of the peaking sun. I felt as if I was swimming through molasses. I pressed a dirty sock against my nose, which frankly smelled a lot better than whatever was wafting through my house.

"Aunt Jettie!" I yelled. "Has there been a septic-tank explosion?"

Ignoring the weird cotton-wool sensation of daylight consciousness inside my head, I padded toward the stairs. The smell was getting stronger. I steadied myself and resisted a strong urge to gag. I crept downstairs and checked the bathroom to make sure there hadn't been some sort of sewer mishap.

"Whatcha doing, honey?" Jettie asked, appearing over my shoulder as I carefully took the lid off the toilet tank. "Do you have any idea what you're looking at?"

"Not particularly. I'm just trying to figure out where the stench of death is coming from. No offense."

"None taken. What stench?"

"You don't smell that?"

"I don't smell anything. I don't have a nose," Aunt Jettie reminded me gently.

"Trust me, you got the better end of the deal."

I wandered toward the front door, my eyes watering as the smell took on a new hideous note with every step. It was coming from the porch. Fitz was waiting by the door, thumping his tail on the floor because he thought I was about to let him out. Obviously, whatever was out there, Fitz was desperate to roll in it. Considering the Great Dead Skunk Caper of 2002, this was not a good sign.

I put on the Jackie O sunglasses, a heavy raincoat of Aunt Jettie's, and a floppy straw hat and wrapped a scarf around my face. I pulled back the blackout curtains and hissed at the slap in the face even obscured noontime sunlight dealt me. I squinted through the light. I couldn't see any dead animals or toxic waste strewn across the lawn, but it did seem to get stronger the closer I got to the window glass. I snapped the curtain shut and backed away. Fitz whined and did the "let me out to play" dance.

I gently shoved him away from the door. "Sorry, buddy, I don't think they make doggie shampoo strong enough."

There was no way I could leave the house to clean it up, so I was stuck. I went to the attic, the farthest point of the house away from the porch, and slept on an old velvet sofa. Well, I tossed and turned and kept a pillow clamped over my face.

When the sun finally set, I grabbed my car-wash supplies out of the garage and dragged the hose to the porch. There was a slimy, creamy yellow substance smeared on the front door, the banister, the porch swing, the railing, the boards of the porch itself. It smelled like burnt almonds and the orifice of a dead horse. Smashed against the front door was a weird-looking round hull the size of a volleyball. It looked like a spiky, greenish coconut.

"What in the name of all that's holy is this?" I wondered, holding the shell at arm's length.

I turned to see Zeb's car pulling to a stop in front of the house.

"Hey, Jolene sent me over with some flyers for the next FFOTU meeting." His head tilted at the curious object in my hand. "Where did you get—mother of God!" Zeb yelled. "What is that smell?"

"I don't know. I think my front porch has been slimed or possibly defiled by a sea monster." I held up my fingers to show him the buttery yuck. "I've been trapped in the house all day while this stuff baked in the hot sun. I just wish I knew what this thing was, so I would know which haz-mat team to call."

A smug grin spread across Zeb's face, and he crossed him arms and leaned back in the porch swing.

"What?" I asked. "Care to let me in on the joke?"

He examined his fingernails nonchalantly. "I'm just reveling in knowing something you don't. So, this is what it feels like . . . to be the smartest person in the room. I like it. I feel all . . . tingly."

"Zeb."

"Sorry," he said, nudging the husk with his foot. "That's a durian. I saw it on the Travel Channel. That guy who thinks turtle gall bladders are a great lunch option swears they're a delicacy. He did a whole segment on them for his Indonesia episode. You know, people are seriously injured, even killed, by these things every year? They fall out of the trees when they're ripe, and *splat*. It's like having a spiny cannonball dropped on your skull."

Zeb sniffed. "The odor is so strong that Asian governments have banned them from subways, elevators, hotel rooms, basically any enclosed space where people can't escape the smell."

"You're enjoying your position as smart guy way too much," I told him. "So, someone brought stinky fruit all the way from Indonesia to play the world's cruelest olfactory joke on me? How do I get rid of it? Burn down the house?"

Zeb rolled up his sleeves and held out his hands for a brush. "A little elbow grease, some borax, perhaps a nuclear device."

"Thank you, that's very helpful," I said, slapping the scrubbrush into his palm.

The smell did not come out. We scrubbed for hours to deslime the porch, but apparently the wood of River Oaks is very absorbent. The project did give us quality time to spend together not talking. I resisted my natural urge to jabber and just worked. Companionable silence was sort of nice. It felt mature.

Zeb finally broke when he realized that we'd nearly scrubbed the paint off my porch but hadn't made a dent in the smell.

"I think we made the smell angry," Zeb said, wrinkling his nose. "The good news is that we just happen to have intimate information of a personal nature about a certain vampire who knows how to obtain a pressure washer at eleven P.M."

"One, I hope you mean Dick," I said as he dialed his cell phone. "And two, whatever intimate personal information you have about Dick, please don't share it with me."

We went inside for some cold drinks. Zeb stripped his shirt off, wiping the durian remains from his hands. "You know what, I have to say the whole unkempt-workman thing is a good look for you. You should go home to Jolene right now all sweaty and manly."

"I can't. I smell like . . ." He shuddered. "I can't go home to Jolene like this. I'm always telling her not to come home stinky after she's rolled in something dead."

I stretched out on the porch steps, flexing my tired legs. "Wait, you do mean in wolf form, right?"

"Yeah," he said, looking at me as if *I* was the crazy one.

"Your marriage is not like other marriages," I told him. "So, how are you guys? Have you adjusted to the whole twins thing yet?"

"You were right," he said sheepishly.

I smirked. "I usually am."

"I don't have much of a choice in the matter. The babies are on their way, so the best thing to do is just hold on and enjoy the ride. And when you think about it, it's pretty cool," he said, pausing to take a drink. "Besides, Jolene's cousin Raylene is having triplets, so it could be worse."

"Well, there you go."

Zeb wiped his forehead off and considered. "This stinky-fruit drive-by is a weird thing to do to someone. Do you think Gabriel did it?"

"This isn't really Gabriel's style. This involves a certain whimsical malice that he lacks. Besides, he's not mad at me. He just can't seem to grasp why I'm mad at him, which is infuriating. And even when he was mad at me, he was much more likely to lecture me sternly or give me a spanking than leave putrid fruit paste on my porch."

"I'm going to ignore the spanking reference," he said under his breath.

"Probably for the best," I agreed.

"So, who do you think is the fruit bomber?"

I shrugged. "Could be some random person in town who doesn't like vampires. Could be a member of the Chamber of Commerce who has decided they don't want me there after all. Now, that's the place for whimsical malice. Heck, this could be Dick's idea of a hilarious practical joke to lift my spirits. It could be anybody."

"That's not comforting." Zeb said.

Or, I thought, it could be my mysterious pen pal, hoping I would be disoriented enough from lack of sleep and olfactory overdrive to stumble out of the house in full daylight to investigate the smell.

"It sucks to be this popular," I said, reaching into the front hall to pull out my purse. "Which is why I went to the scary sporting-goods store last night and bought this."

I pulled my new stun gun out of its holster and pressed the trigger, smiling as the arc of current connected between the two prongs.

"You bought a stun gun?" he cried. "Why did you buy a stun gun?"

"Do you want to smell my porch again?" I asked. "There's some stuff going on right now, Zeb. I need something for protection, and I lost the mace Gabriel gave me. And I lost Gabriel. I can't depend on anybody to protect me. I think we can agree that buying a gun would be much more likely to end in my shooting myself or innocent bystanders."

"But you're a vampire! You have superstrength. I've seen you kill someone with your bare hands. Well, there was a wooden stake in your bare hands. But still."

"I don't like carrying this thing around with me, either, Zeb. You know me, I only resort to violent impulses when I feel I have no option—"

"Or you're cranky or startled, or your blood sugar is low, or you have a hangnail—"

I cut him off with a glare. "This will keep me doing too much damage to the other person while still giving me enough time to get away. And this will keep me from getting my hands dirty or, you know, dusty."

"You know you're going to end up electrocuting yourself, right?"

"I know it's highly likely," I conceded.

As if I didn't have enough odd, emotionally hamstrung men in my life, Emery Mueller started spending a lot of time at the shop. A lot of time. Enough time that I started to consider making up with Gabriel just so he could reach into Emery's brain and wipe out any memory he had of where the shop was located. It was a skill neither Dick nor I possessed.

After seeing that I would not be closing the shop after all, Emery claimed that he wanted to keep an eye on the "family interests." So, he spent every night at the shop, annoying the hell out of Andrea with questions about her "alternative lifestyle." It appeared that he'd developed a bit of a crush on my favorite blood surrogate and frequently asked her to join him at church. When she refused, he blamed it on the influence of her "unfortunate choice of suitors" and spent most of his time giving her the moon eyes. Andrea spent most of her time trying not to be creeped out by her boyfriend's great-great-grandson's advances.

How many women could say they had *that* problem?

Dick stopped showing up on Wednesday nights, claiming he was calling in sick for "terminal disappointment." At least he offered an excuse. Mr. Wainwright just disappeared.

Emery became my own personal Mr. Collins, an irritating rash in human form. And just like the supercilious, socially inept minister from *Pride and Prejudice,* he got bolder with every visit. First, he asked to see a copy of his uncle's will, which I happily provided, along with copies of his uncle's bank statements at the time of his death. However, I started to get annoyed when Emery demanded copies of the current books for the shop, along with inventory lists, my own financial records, and a list of any books I may have taken from the shop. He commented on the number of sales per night, on the high overhead involved in the coffee bar. Then he took up residence behind the counter and casually went through drawers he had no business opening. The more time I spent with him, the less I wanted to give him. I felt the need to protect Mr. Wainwright's possessions from his sweaty, grasping hands.

"Do you happen to know a woman named Jenny McBride?" I asked after he requested the contact information for Mr. Wainwright's lawyer so he could set up an appointment with him. "About yea tall, blond, judgmental?"

Hey, considering that my sister was inadvertently in cahoots with Missy the psycho Realtor, I considered it a fair question. Emery's response was an expression both confused and constipated. For some reason, his not comprehending exactly how annoying his behavior was brought all of my repressed Gabriel-related anger to the surface. I felt the need either to slap Emery or warn him that I was about to slap him.

"I'm only looking after my uncle's legacy, Jane," he sniffed. "You've made valiant attempts to organize the stock, but, to be honest, you've only made a small dent in the problem. You have library experience, but that doesn't make you an expert on antique or rare occult books. Frankly, I don't think you know what you have here. You could let a priceless volume walk out of this store for a song and not even realize it. I think you should shut down for a few days and let me bring in an appraiser to look over the older stock."

"With all due respect, Emery, since your uncle left that legacy to me, it's mine to sell if I want to, at any price," I said. "In fact, I'm not legally bound to offer you anything beyond mementos from Mr. Wainwright's personal effects, but I'm trying to be nice. Now, when I took over the shop, I got a new insurance policy. And I have estimates for the value of the stock. I'll give you copies of that, but as far as giving you a complete inventory or letting you have some outsider go through the stock title by title, I'm afraid that's not going to be possible."

"And why not?" Emery demanded, his face flushing an unpleasant shade of purple.

"Because I said no," I said in my "talking to preschoolers" voice.

"I don't see why you listen to every bit of advice Andrea and that Dick character give you, but you just write off everything I have to say. They don't have the vested family interest in the store that I do."

"They're my family," I shot back, tapping into my reservoir of Gabriel-related anger. "And they spent more time with your uncle in the last months of his life than you did in the last ten years."

Emery blanched as if I'd slapped him. "I think I should go somewhere else before we say anything we're going to regret."

Emery made a show of slinking out the door with a kicked-puppy-dog expression.

Andrea poked her head out of the supply closet, where she'd been hiding. "You got Emery to leave after less than an hour. Can you teach me how to do that?"

Unfortunately, by "somewhere else," Emery did not mean he was leaving the shop permanently. Oh, no, he stayed and stayed and . . . stayed. He sat at the coffee bar and made moon eyes at Andrea. He hung around in the stacks, claiming to be looking for a few books that held special sentimental attachment for him. (I'd hidden the books with the naked-lady-bump engravings.) He annoyed newly turned vampires by trying to get them to take religious tracts. Hell, even Cindy the Goth Mascot would turn and walk out if she saw Emery. She'd gone four consecutive days without a latte. I was starting to worry.

For me, the breaking point was when Emery interrupted my reading yet another letter from my "concerned and vigilant friend," this one telling me how Gabriel had taken her from an innocent, sexually inexperienced girl to a strung-out love junkie by assuring her that he enjoyed her naiveté, her unpredictability.

I remember feeling Emery standing over my shoulder as I read:

> *"Gabriel told me that he liked not knowing what I would do or say. He said my innocence was a refreshing change. I don't have to ask whether he said the same to you. He says this to all the women he beds. He is as skilled at lying as he is at loving. His ability to manipulate emotions through just the right mix of sweetness and feigned overprotection is unparalleled."*

"What do you have there, Jane?" Emery asked. I ignored him.

I remember Emery clearing his throat and holding his too-soft hand out imperiously, as if I was caught reading *his* mail. My upper lip pulled back from my teeth in what I considered a warning expression. But Emery was oblivious to it and the hostile tension that seemed to be rolling off me in waves. I remember turning my shoulder slightly, so my back was to him, and continuing to read. Emery's fingers closed over the top of the page and pulled it out of my hands. I think I had some sort of rage blackout, because I do not remember snarling and flashing my fangs so viciously that Emery ran out of the store. But Andrea said there was a small urine stain on the carpet to prove it, so I had to believe her.

Andrea and I both made elaborate and sadistic threats against Dick if he didn't take his great-great-grandson out for some quality time. Andrea's threats were far more effective, as they apparently involved refusal of certain "privileges." So, Dick took Emery out for an evening of bonding and bowling, practically by force. I hoped Emery would end up with a really embarrassing tattoo.

With the shop cleared of Emery's presence, I yelled, "OK, Mr. Wainwright, you can come out now. It's safe."

He materialized, looking a little chagrined.

"So, what have you been up to?" I asked cheerfully, then glared at him.

"Jane, I'm sorry."

"Uh-huh," I said, narrowing my gaze but eventually smiling despite myself. "You said Emery was eccentric and personality-free. You didn't tell me that he was . . ."

"An enormous pain in the rear?" Mr. Wainwright suggested.

"I was going to say 'infuriating pustule on the butt-cheek of humanity,' but yeah. He's driving me crazy! He questions every decision I make. He insinuates himself into conversations and situations that are none of his business. It's like hanging out with my mom, only without the loving part."

Mr. Wainwright put his insubstantial hand on my shoulder. "He has that effect on people. I'm surprised you lasted this long."

"Hmph. I just don't think I can let him come around the shop anymore, Mr. Wainwright. I mean, he's chasing customers away. I just got the place up and running, and he's killing sales."

"By all means, toss him out on his sanctimonious keister. It will be good for him."

"Excellent," I breathed.

"By the way, I thought you had a Chamber of Commerce meeting tonight?" he asked. "You have it marked on the calendar in the office with little skulls and crossbones. Really, you executed an amazing amount of detail with a Sharpie."

"Yes," I grumbled. "I do have a meeting. But I really don't want to go."

"But I was so proud of your joining the chamber. I had no patience for that sort of thing, really. There were too many people involved."

"There still are," I muttered. "I really don't think the chamber is for me, after all, Mr. Wainwright. Those women are just—well, they're just mean! They've called every day for the last week to remind me that as the newest member, I am responsible for bringing at least three kinds of mild cheese, wheat crackers, and four bottles of California white. And I'm supposed to submit weekly progress reports on how my quest for freebies is going. When I suggested that this was excessive, I was given five demerits. I don't even know what that means! There has to be something going on. Demon possession or a man-hating cult or—ooh! Witches! They could be witches."

"Isn't that kind of obvious?" he asked.

"Don't use logic on me."

"Jane, you're not a quitter."

"Well, that's just not true."

Nice Courtney was the only chamber member who was happy to see me walking through the door with my basket of yuppie goodies.

"Jane, honey!" she cried, breaking from the pack to greet me at the door of the chamber house and relieve me of my boozy burden. "I'm so glad you're here. We just got another new member. You've got to come meet her."

A blonde in a shell-pink twin set turned when Nice Courtney tapped her on the shoulder.

Jenny gasped. "What the—"

"Hell?" I finished for her.

Jenny looked around furtively and dragged me into the foyer. "What are you doing here?" she demanded.

"I joined last month. What are you doing here?" I shot back.

"I joined tonight."

"You're not a business owner."

"Yes, I am," she shot back, handing me her business card.

"What, so I started a business, and suddenly you have to start one? How transparent are you?"

Jenny rolled her eyes. "This has nothing to do with you."

"Well, it's a hell of a coincidence."

"I've wanted to start my own business for years, and now the boys are getting older. There's a huge market out there for people who would love to create a kind of memory craft but can't so much as cut a straight line. People like you. I'm just making it a little more upscale. And technically, you didn't start one, you inherited it, just like you've inherited everything else. The house, Missy's holdings, the shop—is your long-term plan based on making friends with the elderly chamber members so they remember you in their wills?"

"There are no elderly chamber members. The Courtneys sacrificed them to their evil god," I growled, ignoring the confused look on Jenny's face as she searched the
room for a face over forty. "And I don't think I'm going
to take crap off someone who was trying to smuggle
valuables out of my house in her craft bag."

Jenny protested, "I wasn't stealing—"

"What do you call taking items that don't belong to
you from someone else's home without their permission? Aggressive borrowing?"

"I'm not going to have this conversation with you
now, Jane. You're being ridiculous. Look, no one here has
to know that we're related," Jenny said, glancing around.
"We can pretend not to know each other. You can be
some person I don't know that well and don't want to
spend time with."

"Fine, fine, it'll be just like school. You stay on your
side, and I'll stay on mine." I turned on my heel and ri-
fled through my bag. "Where the hell is the wine?"

I stuck my fingernail in the cork and used a tiny bit
of vampire strength to pop it out. I did, however, manage to resist the urge to glug straight from the bottle
and snagged a wineglass instead. Full glass in hand, I
stomped off to find Nice Courtney. She gave me a questioning look as I took her wine glass and drained it. "Do
you two know each other?"

"Apparently not," I muttered.

Head Courtney called the meeting into session. I
stewed while Jenny was introduced and officially welcomed into the group. There was clapping and squealing

and cooing. It was a noticeably warmer reception than what I received. They even gave her a little pink rose corsage.

Typical.

My sister had decided to take her love of scrapbooking to another level. The scary level. She started a company called Elegant Memories, a personalized and customized scrapbooking service using specialty handmade papers made from the hairs of Turkish virgins or something. Of course, she was accepted into the fold like a Borg returning to the Collective.

The fact that I could correctly make a reference to the Borg was probably part of the reason I was not being accepted into the Collective.

I spent most of the meeting plotting ways of getting Jenny out of the chamber. (Shaving her head came up, or telling Head Courtney that Jenny was a natural brunette. Somehow all of my solutions were hair-related.) And then I switched to trying to find ways of getting me out of the chamber, which was less productive, since I was interrupted by—

"Jane?" Head Courtney repeated sternly.

"Huh?"

"I asked how the prize collections were going."

Crap. Head Courtney had sent me a strongly worded e-mail listing the acceptable prize options for the Fall Festival: gift baskets, gift certificates of no less than $100 each, vacation packages. Very few businesses (that were not chamber members) were willing to give up such treasures for what was essentially a children's carnival.

So far, a doctor's office had given me oversized promotional pens advertising a drug for erectile dysfunction, and I'd charmed a local beauty shop out of a gift certificate for a free lip waxing.

"Not well, actually. I managed to get a few things, but with the number of participants you're talking about, it's just not going to be enough. I was thinking maybe we need to change our focus for the carnival prizes. I was thinking we might aim for smaller items, so we would have plenty of small, inexpensive prizes instead of a few big prizes. Things like stuffed animals and candy, you know, things that *kids* would like to win."

Since this was supposedly a kids' carnival and all.

Head Courtney's lips pressed together in a tight, pissed-off line. "Jane, I must not have explained your assignment thoroughly enough in the repeated e-mails I sent you."

"It's not that. I just think—"

Head Courtney snapped, "I didn't tell you to think, I told you to gather prizes for the Fall Festival."

I had a brief, colorful fantasy of latching onto her neck and drinking her dry. But I reconsidered instantly. I'd read somewhere that Botox turns the blood bitter and astringent. Instead, I smiled thinly and said, "That's kind of condescending."

Head Courtney sniffed. "Maybe you're not chamber material after all, Jane."

A way out! A way out!

I started to reach for my purse, "If you really feel that way . . ."

Toady Courtney stood up and whispered to Head Courtney, something along the lines of, "But none of us wants to do it, either."

Dang it.

Head Courtney cleared her throat. "Since you're struggling with your very simple assignment, Jenny is going to be joining your committee."

"What?" Jenny cried.

"Why?" I yelled. "Why would you do that?"

"Jenny has the organizational and people skills necessary to complete the task."

Damned if she didn't have a point there.

Jenny spluttered. "Courtney, I don't think this is a good idea."

"Now, Jenny, new chamber members are expected to make sacrifices. You want to make a good impression, don't you?"

"But-but-but," Jenny stammered.

OK, that made me giggle a little.

Nice Courtney leaned over and whispered, "What's so funny?"

"Nothing," I assured her. "Absolutely nothing."

Jenny and I were assigned a meeting schedule, a color-coded chart to record our progress, and little pamphlets with suggestions on what phrases to use to wheedle, I mean, encourage donations. If we didn't collect at least two hundred items by the next meeting, we would both be given twenty demerits.

Eventually, I was going to have to ask Nice Courtney what that meant, exactly.

It's normal to "relapse" into old patterns. The important thing is to try to avoid hurting bystanders.

—*Love Bites: A Female Vampire's Guide to Less Destructive Relationships*

I was not invited to the McClaine clan baby shower. After my participation in Zeb and Jolene's disastrous wedding events, I was considered a bit of an event jinx by Jolene's family. So, they held it at noon, outdoors, at the McClaine family farm.

I'm not sure if my absence made the party better or worse for Jolene.

Apparently, because the McClaines are such a fertile family, baby showers aren't so much gift-giving occasions but a recycling of the most recent babies' clothes, blankets, and so on, for the use of the new arrival. They do wrap the items for the new mother to open, though.

There was cake. There was a corsage of roses made from tiny baby socks. There were hostile cousins who still resented Jolene as the golden child of the pack, despite her humbling experience at her wedding rehearsal, when Zeb dumped her while under the influence of posthypnotic suggestion.

It's a long story.

As Jolene's pregnancy progressed, the McClaines had stepped up their campaign to keep Zeb and Jolene's home from being built. The pack had scared off every construction crew in three counties, showing up during the day to "supervise" the work. When the more obtuse crews didn't pick up on the subtle intimidation, the pack would use scary subliminal wolf behavior to scare them off—prolonged stares, low growls, and, in one instance, peeing on a plumber's van. The Lavelle house was basically a concrete pad and some framework that had been up for so long it was starting to buckle under the elements. Jolene and Zeb had no choice but to hire Buster Dowdy, the laziest contractor in this end of the state. He frequently spent his billable hours at the site, in the back of his truck, drinking beer and napping.

The climax of the shower was a weird diaper-related shower game in which the prize was being allowed in the delivery room when Jolene's babies were born. Jolene had not been informed of this, and she vehemently protested when her cousin Lurlene, the current president of the We Hate Jolene Club, was named the lucky winner.

"Stop laughing!" Jolene cried later, as she told me and Andrea how she tried to explain that watching her deliver twins wasn't something Jolene was willing to raffle off. We were an odd combination—the vampire, the human, and the weeping werewolf. But it felt right, somehow, for us to be sitting in the trailer's tiny guest room, sorting through baby clothes and comforting Jolene. Andrea and I were now a safety net for her.

Jolene wailed, "It's not funny! They just do not get why I don't think that was a wonderful way to end the shower. Aunt Vonnie said that they were trying to help keep me from abandoning family tradition altogether, since my human husband is insisting I go to some silly hospital instead of having a home birth, like every other woman in the family for the last thirty generations. And then Lurlene got to pretend that her feelings were hurt because I wouldn't let her 'share' in this moment and 'help' me through labor. We both know damn good and well that Lurlene doesn't give two sniffs about being there— Stop laughing!"

"I'm sorry," I cried, trying to stifle the giggles that were so clearly pissing off the hormonally imbalanced and extremely swollen werewolf. "It's indignant laughter . . . on your behalf."

Jolene sniffed as she tried to fold a tiny pink sleeper for the fourth time, finally bunching it into a ball and tossing it into a laundry basket. "And then Mama said they had a surprise for me, and I thought, 'Oh, Lord, what now?' and they covered my eyes and led me across the pasture, and surprise! There's a brand-new trailer sitting there with 'The Lavelles' already burned onto one of those little wooden porch signs? Mama said the family wanted to help me and Zeb, since they'd heard how much trouble we'd been having with building the new house. They took me inside, and it was so big." She looked around the cramped confines of the camper. "It was one of those big double-wides, with a gas fireplace and a master bathroom with separate shower. They already had it all decorated, and . . ." She sighed. "It was so pretty and new and clean. Did I mention it was new?"

Andrea smiled gently and patted Jolene's hands. "A few times. So, are you going to be moving in?"

"No," Jolene said, fully tearing up now. "Because then they showed me the nursery, and they already had it all set up. They'd already picked out all this Noah's Ark stuff, quilts and a crib set and this big mural thing on the wall. I mean, they'd done everything. And they hadn't even asked me. They never ask me. They always just assume that they're doing what's best for me. Aunt Vonnie started talking about how silly it was for me to want to move off the farm anyway, since I was going to need so much help with the babies, and how it would just be so much easier for everybody this way. And I realized it was never going to change. I'd be stuck there, and they'd just be constantly coming in without being invited and taking over everything and treatin' Zeb bad. And I lost it."

"What exactly does 'lost it' mean?" I asked, knowing full well that werewolf family arguments usually devolved into full-scale riot situations.

"I told them no. For the first time, I really, completely, no doubt about it, said no. No to the nursery, no to the trailer, no to the little wooden sign. Just no. I told them I knew that the reason we were having so much trouble finishing the house was that they were scaring off all the

contractors. I told them I wasn't going to move back
to the farm ever, no matter what they did. I told them
they'd be lucky if Zeb and I told them when we were
going to the hospital to have the babies, much less allowed them to barge into the delivery room. I told them
I would raise my babies how I saw fit and that if they
wanted to visit after the twins were born, they would
have to call before coming over, otherwise we weren't
answering the door."

Andrea's jaw was hanging freely at this point. All I
could do was mouth, "Wow."

Jolene sighed. "Yeah. And Mama burst into tears.
Aunt Lola kept asking everybody what I really meant.
Aunt Vonnie said that if I felt that way, then she guessed I
didn't want their shower gifts. I told Aunt Vonnie to take
her used Diaper Genie and shove it up her ass sideways."

"Ouch," I said, putting an arm around her shoulders.
"I know that was hard. But I'm proud of you."

Andrea nodded. "And it certainly explains why your
shower haul is so skimpy."

"I didn't take anything." Jolene sniffed, wiping at her
cheeks. "I just left."

"This whole situation sucks now, but it's going to do
you a lot of good in the long run. I'm sure Zeb will appreciate not having to live on the farm," I said, rubbing
Jolene's back.

"I've never understood why people pick Noah's Ark
for a nursery theme anyway," Andrea said breezily, folding a tiny pair of socks.

"Really." I snorted. "I mean, who wants reminders of

a natural disaster, literally of biblical portions, on their baby's walls? What are you supposed to say, 'Oh, drowning sinners, isn't that precious?'"

Jolene looked up at me through glassy eyes. "You're weird."

"I hear that a lot."

My concerned and vigilant friend's letters increased in frequency. Once a week, then twice a week. It was creepy. And they rarely varied from the theme of *Gabriel hurt me, he'll hurt you. He made promises to me. Ruined me forever. You're a big fat idiot for trusting him.*

OK, that last part was implied.

One night, I sat at the shop counter, sorting through them as Dick sipped an Americano and read a *Tales from the Darkside* comic. I tried to divide the letters into piles, based on threat level. But I kept getting the "I hate him," "I love him," and "He'll hurt you" piles mixed up with the larger "I can make your life a living hell if you don't listen to me" pile. I sighed and rubbed my eyes. There was also a disturbingly large pile of photos of yours truly taken with a telephoto lens.

Frankly, it was at times like this that I missed Gabriel's overprotective caveman tendencies. Even if it insulted my feminist sensibilities, it was sort of nice knowing someone was out there watching my back. Going through this without him made me feel incredibly alone, even though I'd told Dick and Andrea. Going home alone each night, being unsure of what was waiting for me there, was weighing on my nerves.

I muttered, "For a stalker, this chick is all over the place. She's angry and focused in one letter and eroto-manic the next. Or at least, I'm assuming she's eroto-manic for the sake of my pride."

Dick's face was blank. "Erotomanic? That sounds sexy in a way that's . . . not."

"It means someone believes they're in a relationship with someone, but that person usually isn't aware that their so-called lover exists. You have your basic I-want-to-become-famous-by-killing-someone-famous fellas. And there are the delusionals, the ones who think Ryan Seacrest is sending them secret love messages through the television. The most dangerous ones are the people who actually know you, whom you run across in your everyday routine, because the people around you really don't know whether you're lying when you say you're not involved with your stalker. Hence my confusion. Gabriel could be the victim of a stalker, or he could be a plain old cheater. But since he's acting more like a cheater than a victim . . . What?" I asked when I caught the befuddled expression on his face.

"You read up on stalking?"

"I had someone paint 'Bloodsucking Whore' on my car a year ago. It merited a Google."

"I don't like it," Dick said, grimacing.

"I think the very word *stalking* implies that you're not supposed to like it. Otherwise, it would be called 'fluffy harmless observation time,'" I said, chewing my lip. "And, considering that this woman might be danger-ous, I don't know whether to warn Gabriel, which would mean I would actually have to talk to him. Or just let whatever's going to happen happen to him, because a tiny part of me thinks he deserves it."

"Well, you know my vote, Stretch," Dick said, turning his attention back to his comic.

I think the stalking talk made Dick uneasy, because he didn't want to leave the shop that night until I was safely tucked in Big Bertha. But he had what he would only call "special plans" with Andrea, and I needed to stay late to go over some Internet orders, so he had no choice.

Around one A.M., I put the stacks of letters in my purse and headed out the rear staff entrance. As I pushed the key into the deadbolt, I saw a dark male shape reflected behind me in the glass. Even if I hadn't seen it, I would have felt him. My keenly developed sense of paranoia was a wide-open channel to the towering male presence.

I snaked my hand into my purse and ran my fingers along the leather stun-gun holster. I felt the body behind me advance, so I turned, whipping the stun gun out and proceeding to shock the ever-loving hell out of my ex-boyfriend.

"Gah!" Gabriel screamed as the current shot through his body, dropping him to the concrete like a sack of potatoes.

"What is *wrong* with you?" I yelled as the current made his torso arch off the ground. I may or may not have held it to his chest a teensy bit longer than absolutely necessary.

"S-stop sh-shocking m-m-me!" Gabriel grunted through chattering teeth.

"Sorry," I said, pulling the stun gun away to let it cool off.

"Why do you have a stun gun?" he demanded, hefting himself off the ground.

"Because people have been sneaking up behind me," I said, glaring at him. "Honestly, why would you surprise the most spastic person you know?"

"I knew you'd do something to avoid talking to me if you saw me coming," he said, dusting himself off. "And what do you mean, people keep sneaking up behind you? Are you all right? Has someone been bothering you?"

"Yes, you. When you know someone will try to evade you if you try to talk to them, that's called a hint. You need to learn to interpret social cues. And sarcasm, but that's not exactly urgent to the situation at hand. Why are you here? I haven't heard from you for weeks, and you show up now? What do you want, Gabriel?"

"I miss you," he admitted.

Despite the tiny crack that made in the hard cement shell I'd built around my heart, I kept my teeth gritted together, my tone flat and unaffected. "How sad for you."

"I miss you," he said again, backing me against the shop door. The cold of the glass and the remaining images of that horrible Victorian corpse dream were the only weapons I had to battle against the smoky comfort of his scent, the weight of his hands on my arms.

I pushed him back, without any real heat. "That's not really my problem. And you don't miss me, you're checking up on me because you don't trust me to take care of myself."

"I miss you. I miss your laugh and your voice, and I even miss your insults." He smiled, wistful, tracing the lines of my fingers with his own, up my arm to stroke the edge of my collarbone.

"Look, about opening night," I told him. "You said some really hurtful things."

"So did you," he countered.

"Well, you're way better at them."

"We can talk later. Right now, please, just admit it, you miss me," he said, pressing me to the glass again, using exactly the right parts to do the pressing. I didn't answer. Because, frankly, I was doing very well to stay upright and clothed at this point. Bastard.

As his mouth pressed ever so softly against mine, I forced my lips shut to keep from shouting that yes, I missed him. Yes, having his hands on me made me feel more set-tled than I had in weeks. Yes, his grinding me against the door was absolute heaven, and if he did it slightly to the left, it would mean the end of a disturbingly long waking-orgasm dry spell. Fortunately, Gabriel started biting my lips, which limited my speaking options even further.

Gabriel's fingers stroked up my throat, trailing the tips along my jaw and into my hair. He ground his mouth down on mine, drinking in my groans as I pulled blindly at his lapels.

This was just not fair.

"Tell me," he demanded between kisses. "Tell me you miss me."

I bit my lip. His brows drew together as I felt him slide what I called my "sensible shopkeeper" skirt over my hips. His fingers slid over my panties, drawing little circles against my skin through the damp material. His hand glided over my thighs, to peel away my panties. He tucked them in his pocket.

"Tell me," he said again, pumping one and then two fingers inside me with aching slowness.

My head slid back against the glass as my vision seemed to blur. Gah! He wasn't letting me think. If I was about anything, it was the thinking. His thumb glided over my oversensitive flesh, then plucked it like a guitar string, sending a thrumming wave along my nerve endings. I whimpered.

"You can lie to me, Jane, but your body can't. I can feel how much you've missed me, how much you want me right now." Keeping my eyes locked with his own, he brought his fingers to his lips and tasted me. He smiled. "Just as much as I want you."

My jaw dropped as I watched him lick his fingers clean. Screw thinking.

"I miss you," I whispered, hating myself as I felt his lips curve against my neck. I slid my hand between us and fumbled with Gabriel's belt buckle. Gabriel's own hand slipped along my rib cage, cupping my breast. He bent his head to press teasing little kisses over the thin fabric of my blouse before closing his mouth over my nipple.

I dropped my bag so I could slip my hands around Gabriel's neck and pull him closer. The contents spilled around his feet as he cupped his hands under my butt and hitched me higher. His kiss was the center of my universe. Without it, I would go spinning off course into the dark, seeing nothing, feeling nothing.

Through the haze in my head, I heard the faint slide of a zipper and locked my legs around his hips, crossing my ankles at the small of his back.

I grabbed the lowest rung of the fire-escape ladder for leverage as I began the long, slow slide onto him. I threw my head back, gasping, and nearly came right there. I let go of the ladder and twisted my hands in Gabriel's hair, yanking his head back, claiming his mouth with lips, fangs, and tongue. This was mine. He was mine.

I clutched at his shoulders, arching my hips in time with his. A stream of promises, profanities, and pleas poured from Gabriel's mouth against my skin. I cupped the back of his head, cradling his face against mine. I closed my eyes, inhaled his scent, and smiled, even when his fangs extended and scraped lightly across my collarbone.

If he kept doing that, keeping his mouth in sync with his movements—

I howled and put my dizzying dream orgasms to shame. I writhed and convulsed around him, pulling him tight against me with all the strength I had. I may, at some point, have said some extremely dirty things in Portuguese.

Gabriel was smiling, a big, goofy grin wreathing his face as he came, as if my muttering anatomically detailed instructions in foreign tongues was some sort of gift. And for some reason, that made me laugh, which resulted in some interesting aftershocks.

Gabriel was triumphant. "And to think you were this sweet, inexperienced librarian when I met you." He panted, pushing my hair out of my face. "Now look at you, you're a goddess. You can bring me to my knees with a word."

I blinked owlishly at him. Something about that sounded familiar and wrong. Something about Gabriel. The letters, in the letters, she'd said that Gabriel had enjoyed educating her from innocent to—

Just as I was able to cobble a coherent thought together, Gabriel glanced down at the contents of my purse and dropped me on my barely covered butt. I would say it was undeserved, but I had just Tased him.

"What is that?" he demanded, pointing to the linen envelopes as I scrambled to my feet.

"You dropped me," I pointed out.

"What the hell is that?"

"You dropped me!" I repeated. "On my ass, just then. You may not have noticed, which I'm starting to think may be part of our problem as a couple."

Gabriel dropped to his knees to look at the envelopes. "Jane, answer me. What are these?"

"Letters," I told him, plucking the papers off the concrete before he could grab them.

"She's been writing to you?"

And there it was, confirmation. My concerned friend wasn't just some crazy person with an affection for linen paper. She wasn't making up her connection to Gabriel. Gabriel knew who she was, and obviously, he didn't want me getting information from her.

I had two options here: calmly and rationally discuss my feelings of confusion and abandonment and encourage Gabriel to enter couples counseling with me . . . or pitch a tantrum, demand information, and make a giant ass of myself.

Any guesses about the route I chose?

"Excuse me," I seethed. "But you don't get to breeze back into my life, after weeks without a word, pin me to a wall with your penis, and then demand answers."

"I'm not demanding answers. I just—"

"Who is she, Gabriel? Tell me what's going on. This would be so much easier if you would just let me in."

"I can't. I can't tell you. What has she— Do you believe what she's saying?"

"I don't know what to believe, Gabriel. I mean, she's saying some things that sound pretty familiar. Her scent is what drew you to her. It's what kept you close to her. That she was special. That you loved her. That you enjoyed her being so trainable and unpredictable, particularly in the sack. Do you know where I might have heard any of this before?"

"It's not what you think," he promised, edging away from me.

"What do you mean, it's not what I think? I don't know what to think. Because you don't tell me anything! Look at me. This is the result of your grand freaking plan to protect me!" I yelled. Gabriel started to turn away. I grabbed his arm and screamed, "Look at me!"

Gabriel's face in the moonlight was a mask of misery, the shadows against his bone-white skin sharp and stark.

I didn't have to be a mind reader to see that he wanted to disappear.

"This is your handiwork, Gabriel. This neurotic mess of a vampire standing here. You made me what I am. I hope you're proud."

Looking as if he'd been kicked in the gut, Gabriel backed away from me into the shadows. Hot, bloody tears spilled down my cheeks as I shouted, "Don't come back! Don't watch my house. Don't come by. Don't call me. Just stay away!"

Gabriel's silver-gray eyes reflected back at me in the dark. I could hear his footsteps on the pavement as he walked briskly away from me without another word.

Somehow, it seemed so much worse than the first time. I sank to my knees, crying until my eyes ran dry. I cried until I was embarrassed to be crouched in an alleyway, shedding tears for someone who obviously didn't care enough to shed them for me. I pulled myself together, grabbing my purse and straightening my rumpled clothes.

"Damn it." I sniffled, looking around. "Where's my underwear?"

I didn't want to be that friend who shows up at your door with raccoon eyes and hysterics, complaining about her love life.

That's why I didn't wear mascara.

Andrea opened her door, wearing Dick's "Virginia Is for Lovers" T-shirt and no pants, drinking a Budweiser from the can. A *Wrestlemania* highlights DVD was playing in the background.

"Baby, who is it?" Dick asked, coming out of the kitchen, wearing one of those beer-drinking helmets, jeans, and no shirt.

"I take it back, you are not the same woman I met a year ago," I told Andrea.

Andrea burped noiselessly under her breath. "I'm aware."

"Everything OK, Stretch?" Dick asked, taking off the helmet. He didn't, however, bother to turn down the wrestling match. Apparently, someone was about to shave Vince McMahon's head again.

Andrea rolled her eyes at him and turned the TV off. "What's going on, Jane?" I tried to ignore the unsaid "this time" that hung in the air.

I opened my mouth, but I just couldn't find the words to express the mishmash of frustration and plain old mad I had spinning through my head. I moved my lips. I narrowed my eyes. I made angry hand gestures. But no words came out. I started to pace, gnawing my fingernails to the quick. Fortunately, they grew back almost instantly, which meant I had an endless supply.

Andrea stopped me in my tracks by grabbing my shoulders. "OK, sweetheart, I'm all for nonverbal forms of communication, but you're starting to look like an extremely pissed-off mime. Use your words."

"I Tased Gabriel!" I blurted.

"Sweet!" Dick shouted. Andrea shot him an annoyed look. "Right, sorry." Dick tried to look remorse-stricken, but the minute Andrea's back was turned, he gave me an enthusiastic double thumbs-up.

"What are you doing with a stun gun?" Andrea cried. "And how long have I been working in close proximity to you and said stun gun without my knowledge?"

I threw my hands up, exasperated. "Why is everyone so surprised that I have a stun gun?"

"Because I've seen you staple your hand to a purchase order," Andrea told me.

"Well, I can't return the damn thing now. I used it. On Gabriel. Why can't I get a reaction on that?"

"OK, why did you zap Gabriel?" Dick asked, his eyes gleaming. "Don't be afraid to go into details."

"He snuck up behind me, and I just zapped him. It was an accident. At first."

"That's my girl," Dick crowed.

"And then I had sex with him," I said, grimacing. "But just a little bit."

"I'll be in the kitchen," Dick said, beating a hasty retreat to another beer.

"And then he dropped me!" I cried, burying my face in my hands.

Andrea gasped. "He broke up with you? Again?"

"No, he literally dropped me, on my ass, on the concrete!"

Dick turned on his heel and flopped onto the couch. "I can stay a little while."

Andrea gave him a silencing glare and patted my shoulder. "So, you had a little accidental sex, big deal. It's like falling off the wagon. I'll just take away your thirty-day Gabriel-free chip, OK? Wait, you didn't stun him again afterward, did you? Is that why he dropped you?"

"No, I dropped my purse, and a bunch of the creepy letters fell out. Gabriel saw them and asked if 'she' was writing to me. Which means that this isn't just some random crazy. This is someone from his past, someone who sent him into some sort of Shirley MacLaine in *Terms of Endearment*-style panic at the idea of her communicating with me. And you know what pisses me off?"

Andrea nodded. "I've got some idea."

"He just runs off, skulks away like some thief in the night. He gets me all riled up and angry, and then he leaves me all this crap to deal with, with no help from him. It's like a relationship hit-and-run." I cleared my raw, aching throat and looked up into my friend's pitying eyes. "Andrea, I never thought to ask you directly, because I just assumed you would tell me. But just in case you're trying to protect him or something . . . could you tell me—do you know who Jeanine is? I'm pretty sure she's my 'concerned and vigilant friend.' The letters say that he made her, but maybe I'm being too literal. Or maybe she's just lying out her ass. Is it possible that she's Gabriel's sire? Because he won't share that story, either."

"Jeanine's not Gabriel's sire," Dick blurted out, clearly without thinking. And when Andrea and I turned our attention on him, he muttered, "Aw, crap."

"Dick, who's Jeanine?" Andrea asked.

Dick sighed, rubbing his hand over his face. "This is one of those 'it's better if I keep my big mouth shut' situations, honey."

"Aw, damn it, Dick," I moaned. "Not you, too."

Andrea's lips pursed. She crawled into his lap and made a pouty face. Dick groaned. We both knew he was powerless against Andrea's pouty face, or, really, any face that Andrea made. "OK, fine, if you won't tell us who she is, tell us who she isn't. How do you know Jeanine is not Gabriel's sire?"

"Because Gabriel's sire was a woman named Jessica," Dick blurted out as if he'd been dosed with truth serum. He had the sense to look chagrinned but buckled when Andrea kissed his earlobe. He cleared his throat. "Irish gal, sort of snooty. And she was, is . . . not very nice. They met at a party hosted by my parents. I don't know how she found the party or how she chose Gabriel. But she led him away from the party into a cotton crib, had her lascivious way with him, and bit him. She didn't give him the choice. We didn't have the rules we do now. Back then, no vampire would say a word if you didn't necessarily wait for written permission to turn someone. Jessica thought Gabriel would be amusing, but she got bored waiting for him to rise. She had, well, has, a really short attention span. She walked off without thinking about what might happen if he was discovered or got hit with sunlight while he was still sleeping it off."

"He was turned against his will?" I shuddered, imagining the torture such a violation would incur today. Eager to keep up a pleasant, harmless public image for vampires, the Council for the Equal Treament of the Undead enforced strict laws against forcibly turning humans. The punishment included the Trial, a combination of sunlight, silver, and sometimes a coffin full of bees, a veritable trifecta of capital punishment.

"Well, it's more like she bit him and made him an offer he couldn't refuse," Dick said. "He caught up to her during WWII, feeding on orphans lodged in the English countryside. When he saw her again, when he saw what a monster she was—as much as he resented her abandonment, being left to figure out this vampire thing all by himself, he knew he probably would have grown cruel and bloodthirsty with Jessica. He was grateful that he was left alone. But he knows that his turning out so ass-numbingly dull was all a matter of chance. That's part of the reason he felt he had such a responsibility to you. He wants you to have the right sort of influence, to become all that you can be, and all that.

"Stretch, I've known Gabriel my whole life. For him to get this worked up over something, to put you through all this, he's got to have your best interests at heart. Just hold on for a while, let him work it out for himself."

"Whose side are you on?" I grumbled.

"Mine," he said. "If you two patch things up, I won't have to hear the pair of you whining all the damn time."

"The pair of us?" I asked suspiciously. "You've been talking to him, too? Damn it, Dick!"

"We agreed you wouldn't speak to the enemy camp!" Andrea yelled.

"All I did was go over to his house and threaten to kick his ass on your behalf," Dick said defensively. "It was after the store opening, and when I saw how hurt you were, I couldn't stand it. I went over there and told him he was getting the beat-down he'd deserved since 1878. And then he cried!"

"He cried?" I asked.

Dick's teeth ground together, his expression disgusted. "Yes! He took all the fun out of it. How am I supposed to kick a man's ass when he's bawling like a baby? It was horrifying. I found myself comforting the jackass."

"What did you tell him?" I asked.

"I told him that whatever he was going through, you were worth— No! No, I am not going to do this," Dick said, standing and waving the pair of us off. "I don't want to get caught in the middle of all this. And Gabriel swore me to secrecy . . . which puts me right in the middle of this. Dang it, he's better than I thought." He pulled his beer hat back into place and yelled, "I am Switzerland, do you hear me? Completely neutral. Work this stuff out yourselves. Now, could everybody please be quiet, so I can watch Macho Man Randy Savage beat the crap out of somebody?"

"But, Dick—" Andrea cried.

"Shh!" Dick shot back, turning back to the wrestling match with a determined air.

Andrea and I watched Dick with bemused expressions. "That's my boyfriend," Andrea said, sort of meekly.

"At least yours didn't drop you on your ass," I pointed out.

10

The best way to get over a messy break-up is to spend time with a supportive group of friends. The best way to chase off a supportive group of friends is to talk constantly about your messy break-up.

—*Love Bites: A Female Vampire's Guide to Less Destructive Relationships*

To say I had some pent-up anger would be like saying Britney Spears had minor impulse-control issues. *Love Bites* encouraged me to channel those emotions in a positive direction, so I decided to pay Zeb's contractor a visit.

The minute there was enough twilight shadow for me to move unscathed to the future site of Casa Lavelle, I ran through the trees at full speed. Zeb said that Buster, who was known for high-quality carpentry work before his interest in a perpetual buzz outstripped his desire for a growing clientele, took off at exactly five P.M. every day, leaving a pile of empty beer cans in his wake.

The battered green Dowdy Construction truck was parked in the shade of a huge elm tree, where Jolene had talked about hanging a tire swing for the kids. Buster was dozing with his mouth open, his old faded Cardinals cap perched over his eyes. Long and lanky, he looked like a young Don Knotts, complete with droopy eyes and a twitchy lip.

Somehow the construction site looked even more depressing than the last time I'd been there. The place was haunted by the ghost of "supposed to be." Chalk outlines showing where the interior framework was supposed to be situated had long since faded into pale scribbles. Sitting in what was supposed to be the living room, a roll of insulation looked as if it was molding from exposure to the rain. Frayed plastic sheeting that was supposed to be protecting the framework flapped shroudlike in the breeze.

It looked as if Buster unpacked his tools every day and did just enough to make it look as if he was working, without making any actual progress. I stared at the sleeping Buster, my lip curled back. I let my fangs fully extend. This man had kept my friends dangling for months. He'd made Jolene cry. This was not going to be a happy meeting for him.

With one lithe, soundless spring, I hopped into the back of the truck and sat on the lip of the bed. I cleared my throat and hollered, "Buster!" startling him into consciousness.

"Wha!" he shouted, sitting up. "Whassat?"

"Wake up, Buster, we need to talk."

"Debbie?" He yawned, scratching his head and blinking in the low purpling light of the setting sun. "Honey, I told you, I'm sorry I said that about your sister—"

Buster's eyes slowly came into focus, and he realized that I was not his angry live-in girlfriend.

"Oh, hey, Jane," he said, yawning again. "Whassup?"

"We need to talk about your timeline for completing the house, Buster. I mean, walls painted, hardware on cabinets, light switches screwed in place, everything. What's your ETA?"

Buster cleared his throat and tried to use his "professional" voice. "Well, it's hard to say. So much of that depends on when I can get materials and extra guys out here to do some of the work. I'm just one person, you know."

"Cut the crap, Buster. What month are you aiming for?"

"It's OK, the McClaines explained it all to me," Buster said in a conspiratorial whisper. "They want Zeb and Jolene to give up on the house by the holidays. Jim McClaine even promised me a bonus if I could get them to move back in with Jolene's parents before her due date."

I exhaled loudly through my nostrils. One day, when Jolene's hormone levels were normal, we were going to have a long talk about her dad.

"The McClaines aren't bankrolling this project," I told him. "I am."

"That's not what Jim—gak!" Buster yelped as I yanked him up by the collar and pulled him out of the truck and into the barely framed house. Still holding his shirt, I hoisted him against the strongest of the wooden ribs and pinned him by the throat. Normally, I would be nervous around this much exposed, fractured wood, but Buster was too frightened to think about staking me. "Listen to me, Buster, look at me. Really look at me."

He spluttered and coughed, taking in the too-bright eyes, the pale skin, the fading light glistening off long, sharp fangs. "Yeah, I'm a vampire. I'm a vampire going through a really rough emotional transition. And Zeb and Jolene are among the few people in my life who don't piss me off right now, so I'd like to keep them happy. If that means checking up on you every day, beating the tar out of you to make sure you're sober and doing the work you promised, I'm going to do it."

I dropped him to his feet, and he promptly sank to the ground like a sack of potatoes. "But the McClaines—"

"The McClaines have told you it's in your best interest not to finish the house. Don't worry about that. Right now, I think you need to decide which of us scares you more."

"I don't do the work that I used to do," he mumbled, rubbing at his reddened throat.

"Because of the drinking? Well, consider me your own personal recovery program. The steps are, you build my friends' house—on time and in good condition—and then you get to keep all of your limbs. Sound fair?"

Buster nodded, mute with fear. He sobered considerably as we went room to room in the shell of the house, discussing what would have to be redone, how long each phase should take. By the time I was ready to leave, Buster seemed almost excited about coming back the next day. Or, at least, excited to keep all of his limbs.

"Bright and early tomorrow, Buster," I told him. "And if Zeb or Jolene asks, we didn't have this conversation."

Buster's smile was stiff, as if he couldn't remember

how to be a "people pleaser" and was working to recall the skill. "What conversation?"

Eventually, Mama found the shop. The bad news was that Mama found the shop in time for the first meeting of the reconstituted chapter of the Friends and Family of the Undead.

The good news was that seeing that many vampires gathered in one place freaked Emery out so badly that he found an excuse for leaving just a few minutes after he walked in. Maybe we could hold the monthly FFOTU meetings every week . . .

The FFOTU used to meet at the Traveler's Bowl, a restaurant featuring healthy "global" cuisine that spiraled into bankruptcy, not just because the owners tried to sell soy cheese to Hollow residents but because the police seized all of the "glass sculptures" they sold at the restaurant gift shop. It took Police Chief Don Parker several visits to recognize that they were bongs and not very complicated ashtrays. Unfortunately, it only took his son, DJ, one visit. Once you sell a bong to the offspring of a small-town police chief, it's a pretty safe bet that anyone who so much as pauses in your parking lot will be ticketed. With their handful of customers scared off, the owners had no choice but to close.

The support group consisted of twenty or so people of all races, ages, and socioeconomic classes, all of whom were bonded through the shock of knowing that (1) a loved one had died, and (2) that loved one still walked around and sometimes had violent episodes. Plus, there's the embarrassment and stigma that can come with being associated with the undead in a small rural town like the Hollow, where vampires still occasionally suffered household "accidents" involving pointy wooden objects. It helped new vampires and their families to be able to meet in a safe location just to talk or vent or learn that your newly turned son is not avoiding Sunday dinners because he doesn't love you anymore but because you serve said dinners with the good silver and he can no longer digest solid food.

The group operated under guidelines that were a mishmash of Alcoholics Anonymous and PFLAG. We did not reveal our last names. Personal information revealed during the meetings was confidential. We were not required to disclose whether we were vampire or human. But after a few meetings, you figured out who was eating the snacks and who wasn't. The common ground was that each member hurt. Each offered understanding and sympathy to the other members. Each tried to keep a sense of humor.

Zeb and Jolene actually met at an FFOTU meeting. Jolene was still recovering from the dusting of her recently turned childhood friend, and Zeb was still weirded out by my new dietary habits. Zeb brought me into the group a few months later.

The meeting started out well enough. I'd set up complimentary drinks and snacks around the "lounging area" as a sort of welcome gesture. I'd even invited Cindy in the hopes of giving her some resources to deal with her awkward family situation. I gave her the usual latte, and she sat in the back, not attempting to socialize with anyone.

All of the regulars I'd come to know were there, including DeeDee, the de facto leader of the group. DeeDee's banker husband was voluntarily turned in the midst of a midlife crisis. Instead of buying a sports car or having an affair, he decided he wanted to stop the aging process altogether. She'd felt pressured to be turned herself, aging a little every day while her husband remained forever forty-seven. In the end, she had elected to remain human, and her husband left her. She was now dating a very nice accountant who fainted at the sight of blood. But she stuck around to help other people through the transition and welcomed new members to the group. And the newest addition to the group was my mother.

Stupid grocery-store community board.

I turned my back for two seconds, and there was Mama, carrying a plate of brownies and wearing a black T-shirt with the vampire rights logo on it. And a name tag that she'd brought from home that said, "Hello, my name is: Jane's Mama!"

Was it too late to change *my* name?

I turned on my heel, hoping to escape the room, possibly get as far as Borneo, before I heard, "Janie! Baby! It's Mama!"

Cringing, I turned back to where Mama had DeeDee in an arm-lock and was dragging her over to me.

"Now, DeeDee, this is my daughter, Jane. She was turned last year! This is her shop, isn't it wonderful? I'm just so proud!" Mama cooed. "Jane, this is DeeDee."

"I know, Mama, I've known her for a while," I whispered. "Miss DeeDee, would you please excuse us for a second?"

DeeDee winked at me and made her way to the bar to get a free latte.

"I love your little shop, honey!" Mama cooed, walking me around the lounge area like a show dog and mouthing a breathless hello to every person we bumped into. "I just love what you've done with it. The colors and the chairs and all the pretty little knickknacks. Did Andrea pick all this out?"

"Nope, that would be me. I did this," I informed her.

"Well, it's lovely, but I probably would have gone a little lighter on the wall color. You know, Jenny says if you paint a room too dark, it's like losing ten percent of your square footage. You might have called her and asked her advice."

"Well, since my lawyer has advised me against speaking to her without a transcriptionist present, that might have been difficult," I said, smiling sweetly.

"Oh, now you're just being silly." She sighed and then saw Jolene and Zeb come through the front door. Zeb saw Mama and turned on his heel, trying to usher Jolene out for a quick escape. But there was no escape. This was the Thunderdome of parental intrusion. "Zeb! Oh, honey, come see what Jane's done with the shop!"

"Mama, he's seen it," I told her. "He's been here before. In fact, he helped me paint. I appreciate that you're being so supportive, but could you be a little less, I don't know, forceful about it?"

"I don't know what you mean." Mama sniffed and then launched herself at an unsuspecting Jolene for nonconsensual belly rubbing.

Andrea smirked at me. I glared at her. "Am I naked?

Normally, when I have this dream, I look down and I'm naked."

"I know, it's terrible. I'm sorry," Andrea said, barely able to control the twitching corners of her mouth.

"You don't look sorry."

"I'm terribly, terribly sorry," Andrea promised, a snicker escaping when she turned her back to fetch a bottle of hazelnut syrup.

"You're just humoring me because I sign the checks, aren't you? I would say I don't need your pity, but obviously, that's not true."

Zeb joined me at the bar, having abandoned his wife to Mama's pregnancy interrogation, the coward. Zeb gave me a sympathetic shoulder squeeze. "I meant to tell you. DeeDee put ads on bulletin boards in the supermarkets, Walmart, the events calendar in the newspaper . . ."

I groaned. "I knew this community-involvement thing was going to come back and bite me on the ass. You know what we could do instead? An awareness crusade for vampires who use sunless tanner. Nothing's as obvious as an orange vampire."

"It's good for business," Andrea told me. She shot a fierce look at Zeb as she hefted a king-size tray of fruit, veggies, and cheese cubes. "I'm going to go rescue your wife with a plate of nutritious, baby-building snacks, you weenie. Jane's mama doesn't scare me." She cleared her throat. "Much."

Zeb chuckled, watching as Andrea managed to insinuate herself between Mama and a grateful Jolene.

"So, how's the house coming along?" I asked.

Zeb's face flushed with an incredulous smile. "Great. Buster actually started putting up interior framing this week. He's got a crew coming out to do the roof soon, and he said we might be ready for Sheetrock before next month. And when Jolene's dad came out yesterday to give Buster the stink-eye, Buster just kept his head down and worked his butt off. Even Lonnie had to admit that Buster was doing good, solid work. We might actually be moved in by Christmas. Can you believe it?"

"Wow," I intoned, trying to sound appropriately impressed. I kept my eyes wide and innocent. "You must have really put your foot down with Buster."

Zeb puffed his chest out a bit and tried to sound nonchalant. "If I've learned anything from my scary in-laws, it's all about tone of voice."

As everybody circled to start the meeting, I scrambled to sit next to Mama, so I could control . . . um, introduce her. Mama had apparently taken the time to memorize the Pledge, a collection of five truths the group repeated before every meeting, and was louder than the rest of us combined as we promised: "I will remember that a newly turned vampire is the same person with new needs.

"I will remember that a loved one's being turned into a vampire does not reflect on me.

"I will remember to offer my vampire loved ones acceptance and love, while maintaining healthy boundaries.

"I will remember that vampirism is not contagious unless blood is exchanged.

"I will remember that I am not alone."

Before DeeDee could stand up to introduce herself, Mama bounced to her feet. "Well, hello, everybody! I'm Jane's mama, Sherry. I'm just so happy to be here!"

"Hi, Sherry," the group chorused, despite my attempts to pull Mama back into her seat by her sleeve.

"I'll admit that I went through a bit of bad patch after Jane came out, but I've come to accept that I cannot change what Jane is," Mama said, her voice quavering. "And I need to do whatever I can to make her feel accepted and loved by her family. Even if she tries to avoid spending time with us. And isn't speaking to some of us."

"That's my Mama," I conceded.

"Well, Sherry, it's refreshing to see a parent so vocally supportive of her child after they come out," said DeeDee.

I rolled my eyes. Can we talk about the fact that her "bad patch" involved force-feeding me pot pie and trying to give me a tan? I sulked through DeeDee's discussion of the pain and confusion of new vampires adjusting to a human world and through her preplanned talk on subconscious conversational slips that can be highly insulting toward vampires. I couldn't help but think this last topic was directed toward Mama, and I was all for it. But she was so caught up taking notes and beaming beatifically at DeeDee that I'm pretty sure the clue sailed right over her head.

The group broke up to socialize, which was usually my favorite part of the meetings, but this time, I was dodging my mother with a sudden, extremely urgent search for coffee filters in the stockroom.

"Jane?"

"Gah!" I cried, jumping and whacking my head on a shelving unit.

"Are you all right, hon?" Mama asked, cooing over my new contusion.

"No, no, I'm not," I grumbled, rubbing my forehead.

"I'm sorry. I just wanted to catch you in private," she whispered. "I just wanted to see how you're doing, you know, since Gabriel broke up with you. Your daddy and Jolene said you took it awfully hard."

"Wha— G-gabriel did not break up with me. I broke up with him. And what is Jolene doing talking to you about that? If she thinks she can deflect belly questions by baiting you with information about me, well, that's just evil and brilliant, actually. I don't think I give her enough credit . . ."

"Oh, you're so silly. Now, I'd like to talk to you about your grandma's birthday," Mama said breezily. "Your grandma Ruthie wants to make sure you apologize to Wilbur so we can all enjoy dinner without any unpleasantness."

"Hmm. Unpleasantness like bringing up the fact that Wilbur tried to stake me with his cane the last time I saw him?" I asked. Mama made a "disappointed" face.

Sometimes newly turned vampires are only given enough blood to enable them to wake from the death sleep. They have none of the vampiric strength or speed . . . or charm. They're called ghouls. I only know this because my grandma Ruthie almost married one of them earlier this year. Despite the fact that Wilbur looked like Skeletor and may have bumped off several of his wives to sustain his endless after-death retirement, he and Grandma Ruthie decided to keep dating. *After* he tried to dust me with his cane.

It turned out that Wilbur and Ruthie were a perfect match. After all, Grandma Ruthie's four husbands and previous fiancé all died under equally suspicious circumstances, involving a speeding milk truck, a brown recluse bite on the inside of the throat, a previously unknown allergy to Grandma Ruthie's famous strawberry-rhubarb pie, a golf-related lightning strike, and a miscalculation of Viagra dosage. Wilbur and Grandma Ruthie seemed very happy together, though I guess when you never know when your lover might facilitate your release from your mortal coil, it's important to keep up the appearance of happiness. Frankly, I was glad they were still so lovey-dovey. For me to win the "dead pool" with Zeb and Dick, either Wilbur or Grandma would have to meet a grisly end in a botulism outbreak next spring.

"No. Absolutely not. You all can just celebrate without me," I told Mama. "I do not apologize to people who try to kill me. It sets a bad precedent."

"Oh, but your grandma Ruthie will be so hurt if you don't show up!" Mama protested.

"No, she won't," I told Mama. "You know she won't. She'll be much happier, and things will be a lot less tense without me there. In fact, that will be my gift to her this year, not showing up."

Mama looked resigned but unhappy, which was generally how we both felt when negotiating the logistics of family gatherings. "Sometimes I just don't understand the things that come out of your mouth, baby," Mama said, pushing my hair back from my face.

"I hear that a lot," I told her.

Mama chuckled, rolling her eyes. "Now that we have that out of the way, how are you doing, really?"

"Other than spending an unhealthy amount of time faking answers to magazine quizzes so I get better scores, I'm fine," I told her. "The shop is doing well. I have sweet, patient friends with a high tolerance for whining. Zeb and Jolene keep me involved in their never-ending baby-name debate. Dick is the older brother I never really asked for. Andrea wants to start a belly-dancing class next month. My life is very full."

"Do you want to talk about it?" Mama asked.

"No, I do not."

"Honey." She sighed, tipping my chin toward her. "I know it hurts right now, but whatever Gabriel did, I'm sure he's sorry. And if he's not, maybe Adam Morrow is still interested . . ."

"No. Mama, I love you. I love that you're being supportive and that you want to put me back up in the saddle. But trust me, trust me, you don't want me dating Gabriel . . . or Adam. I'm better off alone right now." I kissed her cheek. "But I love you."

"I love you, too," she said, squeezing my cheeks. She let out a cleansing breath and returned to her normal cheerful tone. "Maybe it would help if I invited Adam's mama to the meetings. You know, maybe if she learned to be a little more open-minded like me, it would make it easier on the two of you if you just happen to start dating."

I thought about making a smart comment, but for the sake of this newfound bridge of mother-daughter understanding, instead I said, "Maybe we shouldn't make *more* connections with the guy who has a fuzzy perception of personal boundaries?"

"Oh, you're so strange sometimes," Mama said in that tone of voice that always left me unsure of whether she was going to pay attention to what I said.

The gears in my brain whirred, searching for any activity that would keep Mama occupied and safely away from Adam Morrow's mama. When all the machinery clicked into place, a wide smile spread over my face.

"Mama," I said, putting my arm around her. "How would you like to throw Jolene a baby shower?"

I received a "reminder" e-mail from Head Courtney that I had yet to submit a progress report on my collections for the prize committee. She was giving me three demerits and told me to meet with Jenny to "better implement a synergistically creative approach" to my begging freebies before a progress meeting with the Courtneys. I was going to find the person who sold Head Courtney her copy of *Who Moved My Cheese?* and smack them.

With an obvious expression of disdain, Jenny strolled through the shop's front door with her hand sanitizer at the ready. She seemed surprised by what she saw. She even smiled, just a tiny bit, at the fanciful little pottery dragon grinning at her from a table by the front window.

"How can I help you?" I asked, smiling pleasantly to the point that it was hurting my face. "We just got a shipment of self-help books. Can I interest you in a copy of *How to Stop Being a Raging Bitch in 30 Days?*"

Jenny's lip curled back, and I could practically see the acid response forming, but she bit her lip and exhaled loudly through her nose. "This is a nice place," she conceded. "Good light, nicely arranged. Probably not a color scheme I would have chosen."

"I'm sure." My teeth were grinding as I led her to the counter. I didn't offer her coffee or a scone, despite the fact that they were arranged temptingly under a nearby glass dome. This was not a social visit. This was business. OK, fine, fine, Jenny had been making me feel unwelcome for years, and now I was having a tiny bit of revenge.

She smiled sweetly, or what passed for sweetly when you've had enough Botox to paralyze an elephant. "Mr. Wainwright must have been fond of you to have left you all this."

"Here we go," I muttered.

Jenny shrugged, her eyes wide and not-quite-convincingly guileless. "I'm just saying, it must be awfully nice—"

"You think I like the fact that Mr. Wainwright died?" I asked coldly. "Do you think I wouldn't rather he was here right now?"

Technically, he was there at the moment, hovering over his favorite copy of *From Fangs to Fairy Folk: Unusual Creatures of Midwestern North America*. But I wasn't about to tell Jenny that.

"I think I'll pop out to see how your aunt Jettie's doing," Mr. Wainwright whispered.

"Coward," I muttered. I turned back to my sister. "Why did you come here, Jenny?"

Jenny tried, and failed, to look surprised by my line of questioning. "Courtney told you. We have to go over our collection plan before the meeting. I wanted to talk to you about getting some of the car dealerships in town to offer some detailing packages. I think I might have an in with the owner of Nelson Ford."

I searched Jenny's face. I even thought about peeking into her thoughts, but past experience with Grandma Ruthie had shown me that only prolonged the argument, it didn't help me win it. Fortunately, I'd known my sister long enough to discern the acquisitive, gleeful look in her eye when she was bordering on social triumph. And if she was really going to forge some sort of tenuous connection with the largest auto dealership in town, she would have been dancing some uptight little jig.

My eyes narrowed. "No you didn't. We could have handled this whole thing by e-mail. That's how we've done it so far, why change now?"

"Fine. I want to talk to you about the house," Jenny said, sighing.

"No!" I threw up my hands. "My lawyer said I'm not supposed to talk to you about the house or its contents without him being present. That's why we've been handling this frustrating yet not at all rewarding task over e-mail!"

"Jane, I think we can settle this without the lawyers."

"How do you figure?"

Jenny actually had the good grace to look slightly timid, twisting her wedding band around her finger as she said, "Well, your situation has changed. You need to stay close to town now that you're running the shop. And besides, you don't need that big old place, all by yourself—"

"If you finish that sentence, I'm going to punch you in the head."

"Don't you threaten me," she said, shoving my shoulder.

"Don't you tell me what I need," I said, shoving her back, sending her chair scooting across the floor.

"Jane, you have so much stuff! I don't understand why you need *everything* the family's handed down! You're all alone. No one even sees all those beautiful things. They won't be appreciated in your house like they would be in mine."

"I'm not having this discussion with you again," I told her, pushing back from the table. "Let's just get through this carnival from hell, I'll find a way to fake my death and escape from the chamber, and you can fight Head Courtney to the death for her position as queen of the evil hive. And then we never have to see each other again. You can pretend I died or something."

"You did die," Jenny said, rolling her eyes.

"So it should be easy for you."

"Why can't you just discuss this with me like a rational adult?" she demanded.

"Why? Are you going to behave like a rational adult?" I shot back.

She grunted and tossed her folder of chamber materials across the bar at me. "I can't talk to you when you're like this, which is *all the time*. I'm going." She huffed and puffed while she slung her purse over her shoulder. "But this isn't over, Jane. You're going to have to deal with this sooner or later."

Jenny blew back out of the shop like a bitchy hurricane, leaving a trail of scattered prize committee papers in her wake. And when she'd tossed her folder at me, she'd knocked a huge stack of mail off the counter.

Perfect.

I ran around the shop, picking up sheets of paper detailing Jenny's campaign to wheedle free floral arrangements and colonics out of the Hollow's business community. I also cursed a rather impressive blue streak that eventually began to rhyme and was soon coming out in iambic pentameter.

Andrea had enrolled us in a poetry seminar.

And when I finally managed to assemble the papers on the bar, I was confronted with the envelope. I'd been avoiding the mail for the past couple of days. Frankly, between the creepy Jeanine letters and my Visa bill, the U.S. Postal Service wasn't exactly bearing me good news lately. But I couldn't ignore today's note, the creamy linen envelope stuck between humdrum bills and catalogues.

I seriously considered tearing it up without reading it. Insight into my sire and his crazy possible ex's relationship didn't exactly make me happy. But the more I read, the more I wanted to know. Whoever this woman was,

Jeanine knew exactly how much information to reveal, how much to play close to the vest, to keep me confused, wound up, and coming back for more. She should have been a mystery author or maybe run for Congress.

I took a deep yoga breath and prepared myself for whatever obsessive looniness the letter had in store for me. And as I scanned the page, one word jumped out at me: "whore."

I really hated it when people called me that.

"*I saw you. I saw you with him, rutting in an alley like some common whore. I warned you, but you wouldn't listen. What do I have to do to make you understand that you have to stay away from Gabriel? Do I have to do something drastic to get my point across? You have no one to blame but yourself now.*"

"Oh." My hands trembled, and the letter fluttered to the counter. My stomach pitched, pushing the salty-sweet remnants of synthetic blood into my throat.

The fact that someone had watched me engage in intimate acts in an alleyway seemed far more pressing than the fact that she was threatening to "do something drastic." Personally, I thought the drive-by fruiting of my front porch was pretty drastic. But she'd *seen* us? Someone had watched Gabriel and me having sex behind the shop? She'd seen my sex faces? Heard the noises I made? Watched when Gabriel dropped me on my ass? I felt as if I'd been doused in ice water. What if she'd taken more pictures? What if she sent them to people I knew? Posted them on the Internet? What if that's what she meant by having no one else to blame?

I tried to imagine explaining nude online pictures to my mother. If she thought me becoming a vampire was embarrassing, how would she react to "accidental amateur porn star"? I leaned my forehead against the counter. "Oh, not good."

What do you do in a situation like this? I certainly wasn't going to the police, who weren't exactly helpful in cases where vampires were concerned. I'd probably pressed Andrea's and Dick's nerves to the limit with my "erotomania" talk and the relationship hysterics. Zeb didn't need to be dragged into this, what with his procreative worries. That left one person, one man who would understand the situation, my feelings of paranoia and guilt and revulsion.

And I wasn't talking to my sire at the moment.

My computerized calendar alarm sounded from the register. Andrea had set it so I wouldn't conveniently forget my scheduled progress meeting. It was being held at Puerto Vallarta, the only restaurant in the Hollow that served Mexican food without a drive-through window. The theory was that the planning committee would build better connections and work more creatively in a social setting. Basically, it was an excuse for the Courtneys to get knee-walking drunk off half-priced margaritas on a weeknight. And because Nice Courtney wasn't a committee head, I wouldn't even have her as a social shield.

"Forced bonding time with inebriated Courtneys in a restaurant, where I'm going to have to hide the fact that I don't eat," I groaned, flopping my head onto the counter. "Peachy freakin' keen."

11

If you're new to a relationship and your plans for the evening involve alcohol, consider this formula to determine your consumption: however many alcohol units it takes to get you to start complaining about your last boyfriend minus 100 percent.

—*Love Bites: A Female Vampire's Guide to Less Destructive Relationships*

I was, of course, the first person to show up at the restaurant, because, silly me, I assumed that when a meeting starts at seven, that's when you're supposed to show up. The rest of the Courtneys, and Jenny, showed up at 7:20, just as a table for ten became available in the crowded dining room. Apparently, I was the designated table saver.

This was going to be a fun night.

Puerto Vallarta was run by the Gonzalez family, first-generation Mexican-Americans whose parents had come to Kentucky in the 1970s to find seasonal work on the tobacco farms. The three siblings served affordable, delicious Mexican cuisine with just the right amount

of "authentic" mariachi-ized ambience and a smile—
even when the locals butchered Spanish while ordering
"case-o-dillias."

Hector, the oldest Gonzalez, led us to the back room,
which was set up for large parties. When Head Courtney
saw the unassuming spot under crisscrossed guitars and
a neon sign for Dos Equis, she shook her head and said,
"We would *like* a *different* table," with loud, deliberate
pronunciation. Then she repeated the phrase with big,
swooping hand gestures.

Apparently, Head Courtney didn't think that Hector
spoke English. But she did believe that when you speak
really slowly and loudly, English automatically becomes
whatever language is understood by the person you're
yelling at.

"We want *that* table," Head Courtney said, pointing
to another long table underneath huge hanging bunches
of dried garlic and chili peppers. Then she added more
hand gestures.

Hector, who had been the go-to grammarian for my
honors English class at Half-Moon Hollow High, looked
to me with a puzzled expression. I rolled my eyes and
shrugged.

Several of the Courtneys seemed to be watching me
as we approached the table. As we were seated, I mentally
reviewed the benefits of belonging to the Chamber of
Commerce. Legitimacy, contacts, free advertising. I said
it over and over in my head, like a mantra to keep me
from strangling one of the Courtneys with their imita-
tion Coach purse straps.

"Thank you," Head Courtney said loudly. Hector nodded.

"Good to see ya, Jane. I'll have a server with y'all in just a few minutes," he said in his perfect, heavily-Southern-accented English. Hector, who insisted on being called Heck in school, had always looked a little like Lou Diamond Phillips and sounded a lot like Larry the Cable Guy. I winked at him.

Head Courtney looked momentarily confused but quickly forgot her ethnic profiling as she watched me settle in with a menu, ignoring the cluster of dried garlic hanging over my head. Contrary to what movies would have you believe, vampires aren't allergic to garlic. It does, however, smell to high heaven, and we have supersensitive noses. But it had been a long time since the specimens overhead had remotely resembled usable food. The smell was strong but not unpleasantly so. It reminded me of coming to Puerto when I was living. Zeb and I would come on Tuesday nights to split a carne asada platter and chat with Hector over cheap beer.

"Are you OK here, Jane?" Cankles Courtney asked, peeking carefully over her menu. She nodded up to the garlic. "Jenny said you have . . . allergies."

I'll bet she did. I glared Jenny's way, but she seemed completely absorbed by her menu. I smiled sweetly at Cankles Courtney. "Thanks for asking, but I'm fine."

Cankles Courtney gave Toady Courtney a triumphant look, as if to say, "See, I told you! She's not a vampire."

I sighed, making a show of studying the menu. I missed carne asada. And chocolate. And ice cream. And lasagna. And cheeseburgers. Basically, I missed all food, except brussels sprouts. It still irked me that my last meal had consisted of potato skins and liquor. People who get the chair receive a better culinary sendoff.

I wasn't going to order the carne asada, because that would just be depressing, even if I used Jolene's disgusting food-craving imagery. I decided on tamales. They were mushy and messy, and it would be difficult to tell how much, if anything, I was eating. Plus, I'd never liked them much, so staring at them for an hour or so without being able to eat them would be bearable.

Our server suffered through our ordering pronunciations with a brave face. When he came to me, I ordered the tamales, and whatever remaining interest the Courtneys had in my eating habits seemed to melt away. The server stared at me for a long moment and then asked, "And to drink?"

I thought about sweet, fortifying tequila, since all of the Courtneys were planning on bellying up to the margarita trough. But I wanted to keep my wits about me so I wouldn't get wrangled into cleaning up after the petting zoo or any of the other undesirable jobs Courtney had lined up.

"Water's fine, thanks." The server seemed to sense a weakening in my resolve and continued staring at me. I took the bar menu from the little plastic console in the middle of the table. "Actually, I'll have a beer."

The Courtney on my left gasped in horror. Jenny sneered as I looked over the beer selections.

"El Torrente Sanguíneo?" he asked.

For a moment, I and my three years of poor Spanish instruction thought he was asking if I wanted a raincoat with that. I squinted at him. He pointed to a selection near the bottom of the menu. The little dark brown bottle on the illustration looked like any beer. I knew that Sanguíneo probably had something to do with *sangre*, which translated to "blood." And *torrente* probably meant "river" or "stream." So it probably translated to something like "blood stream" or "vein." Was he offering me synthetic blood?

I looked up at the server, who smiled back at me, looking a little dazzled. Now that they'd been thoroughly horrified by my choice to drink beer in public, the Courtneys weren't paying attention to what I was ordering. I guess they figured vampires wouldn't drink beer and order tamales.

"Please!" I said emphatically, smiling back.

The waiter practically scrambled over the adjoining booth in his rush to get our drinks back to us. He set the brown bottle in front of me with a flourish, a slice of lime carefully balanced in the lip. I thanked him as he served the margaritas and took a long pull from the bottle.

Ahh. Sweet, slightly spicy, a thick coating of synthetic blood rolled down my throat and soothed my nervous stomach. I was going to have to remember this brand. The waiter watched me expectantly. I wanted to smile, but I was pretty sure my teeth would be blood-stained for the next few minutes. Also, my fangs were trying to creep out of my mouth. I pressed my lips together but nodded enthusiastically. I was going to have to tip this guy in a serious way. The waiter backed away from our table but promised to be back soon.

"If Jane's done eye-flirting with the server," Head Courtney said, clearing her throat and pursing her thin, cranberry-glossed lips, "we should start the meeting."

Crap, I'd totally forgotten why I was there.

It was a good thing I'd elected not to drink. Courtney tried to stick me with petting-zoo clean-up, sitting in the dunk tank, *and* putting down the deposit on the inflatables (out of my own pocket, apparently, with the hope that the Courtneys would remember to reimburse me).

Each of the committee chairs was given a progress evaluation. Head Courtney wasn't pleased with our work. Cankles Courtney, who was in charge of food, had neglected to think of vegetarian options for the festival attendees. (Because nothing says old-fashioned family fun like a tofu dog.) Short Courtney, who was in charge of publicity, had yet to secure an interview with the local morning radio show, so that Head Courtney could educate the masses on the importance of the chamber's philanthropic efforts. Also, Short Courtney had ordered the promotional posters in an autumnal burnt orange instead of the chamber's signature pink, so five demerits for her. I was failing miserably, and I was lucky that Jenny was there to save my butt. Head Courtney placed her right hand on Jenny's shoulder while she pronounced this. Jenny tried to preen subtly but failed. I was reminded of the scene in *The Omen* when Damien realizes the extent of his evil power.

Seriously, could I buy my way out of this gig? What if I just *gave* Head Courtney $5,000 for the animal shelter? And then moved and changed my name?

By the end of the "meeting," Head Courtney had four empty margarita glasses next to her plate and was starting to tell the other Courtneys what she really thought of them. Short Courtney needed to get her roots done. Cankles Courtney had, well, cankles. Toady Courtney had almost reined her in when Head Courtney's gaze fell on me. At this point, I'd been pushing tamales around on my plate for two hours while watching my sister get fawned over. As far as I was concerned, Head Courtney could bring it on.

Head Courtney was swaying in her chair, her cornsilk-blond hair clinging to the light sheen of drunk sweat on her cheeks. "You think you're so much smarter than the rest of us. That we don't know what you really are."

"Courtney, I don't think you're feeling very well," Toady Courtney said loudly, her brown eyes wide with alarm. "Those enchiladas must have been rancid!"

"Oh, don't interrupt her, Courtney," I said, smiling and tilting my head. "I think she was on a roll."

The jig, apparently, was up. And I felt a little foolish for picking at those damn tamales. Oh, well, I might as well have some fun with it.

"Jenny told us all about it. You think we would have let you in if we had known?" Head Courtney hissed. "We would never—and now, we can't kick you out because you people sue for discrimination at the drop of a hat. We don't want you to pull a Frink on us."

Did she just call me "you people"?

The whole table was suddenly quiet, as if Courtney had dropped a glass dome over us. Suddenly, it all made sense. The stupid tasks, the poor performance reviews, the general bitchiness. It wasn't *just* that they didn't like me. They wanted me to quit. They'd managed to weed out everyone who didn't live up to their standards through intimidation and misery, but they couldn't get rid of me because I scared them. I was making *them* miserable by my mere presence. I smiled, letting my fangs peek out just the tiniest bit.

"Jenny, I'm surprised at you," I said in my blandest tone. "I thought you'd be too ashamed to tell anybody about your sister's shameful vampire condition. I mean, really, where's the benefit in outing me? Aren't you afraid of tarnishing your reputation?"

"Shister?" Head Courtney slurred. "What do you mean, 'sister'?"

The silence was broken, and a rush of whispers rounded the table of Courtneys. Now it was my turn for my jaw to drop. I stared at Jenny. "You told them I'm a vampire, but you didn't tell them I'm your sister?"

Jenny's jaw clenched. Her face turned a pasty shade of oyster gray. "There was no reason to. My sister died last year."

I waited for the twist in my chest, the pain of being rejected by Jenny once again so she could spend time with people who were better, more important than me. But it didn't come. I was used to it. She'd made her feelings clear a long time ago. There was a freedom in just not giving a damn anymore. And Jenny had granted me this gift. I was free. I could walk away. Part of me wanted to, to give Jenny and the Courtneys what they wanted. I could quit and walk out the door so they'd have to pay for my synthetic-blood tab. But the more perverse part of my personality was intrigued by the possibilities. So, I did something that shocked the Courtneys.

I laughed.

Everyone at the table winced as I threw my head back and laughed like a big old donkey. I giggled until my sides ached. I laughed for every fat girl, bookworm, and wallflower who'd ever felt powerless in the wake of the Courtneys of the world. I laughed because I knew that when I got up, Jenny was going to have to explain to the Courtneys why she had lied to them. She was going to be left holding the conversational bag for once. I laughed because this was such a silly high school drama to find oneself enmeshed in at the ripe old age of twenty-eight.

Once I'd recovered, I wiped at my eyes, hoping that there weren't streaks of blood tears running from my lashes. Other diners had lifted their heads from their tacos and were starting to stare. I stood up, prompting another communal flinch, and tossed some bills on the table, enough to make up a 40-percent tip for my buddy the waiter.

"That is my big sister," I said loudly. "Always looking out for number one. You girls are hilarious! Courtney, what a sense of humor you have! I had a great time tonight. Thanks for asking me. I'll see you at the next meeting!"

I took two steps, then turned around, prompting the entire table to press back away from me, knocking Short Courtney off her chair. "By the way, the waiter figured it out faster than y'all did. And he had a hell of a lot more class about it."

I giggled all the way from the table to the front door, to the point that Hector stopped me at the door and asked if I was OK to drive.

"I'm fine," I assured him. "Sober as a judge."

"You haven't seen Judge Frye in here after about three beers." Hector snickered. "He wears a sombrero and everything. Hey, Jane, are you going to the reunion? It's coming up pretty soon."

"I don't know . . . I haven't really thought it through."

"What's to think through?" he asked. "You see some old friends, laugh at everybody who got fat and bald, get drunk off spiked punch, and go home. Come on, I'll need someone to listen to my bad jokes. I miss seeing you and Zeb around here. You used to come in all the time, you know, before . . ."

I winced but realized that Hector was standing as close to me as he always had. The friendly warmth in his eyes was genuine. "Yeah . . . before."

"Look, I don't care. I haven't been attacked by a vampire yet. I don't figure you're going to be the one to do it. I am a little hurt that you don't come in here anymore. But I figure you have your reasons."

"I can't eat."

Hector chuckled. "Well, that's a reason. But we put that bottled-blood stuff on the menu for a reason, Jane.

We don't turn away anybody's money here, dead or un-dead. You're always welcome. But try for Wednesdays, because I want you to see Judge Frye do what he thinks is the Mexican Hat Dance."

"Thanks, Heck."

"Anytime," he said, giving me a brotherly punch on the arm. "And the reunion, think about it, OK?"

"I will." I laughed and bopped his bicep lightly.

"Ow," he said, rubbing his arm dramatically. "You didn't hit so hard in high school."

"People change," I told him, giggling as I walked out the front entrance.

Andrea and I were backed up on several days' worth of deliveries that we hadn't had a chance to open. So, we sat at the coffee bar, pretending it was Christmas.

"I think that's the cookbooks I ordered," I said, taking a load of packing peanuts to the trash as Andrea picked up an Amazon.com box. "Apparently, some chef in New York was turned and is doing amazing things with drinkable sauces that are tasty and won't make vampires vomit. So I got a dozen of them."

Andrea bounced the package gently. "It seems kind of light for a dozen books. I think it's probably that un-natural number of Jason Statham DVDs you ordered."

"He has to have filmed a nude scene at some point in his career. I don't care how many shoot-'em-up action movies I have to watch, I will find it," I said solemnly. "Oh, yes, I will find it."

Andrea rolled her eyes as she pressed the brass athame

Mr. Wainwright used as a letter opener to the packing tape. "I know money isn't really that much of a concern for you anymore, but have you ever stopped to examine some of your odder spending habits?"

"I'm comfortable with the balance I— Do you smell something?" The back of my throat itched as Andrea sliced through the tape. She squealed when the box hissed and then spattered her face with a sheer silvery mist. I tried to call out to her, but my throat wasn't working right.

I screamed noiselessly as smoke rose from my arms. My skin crackled and burned. I think I made a very undignified, strangled screeching noise as I smacked the box off the counter to the floor.

Dick emerged from the back room, coughing.

I heard Andrea screaming, "What is it? What is it?" while I dropped to my knees and gave hoarse, choking, rattling coughs. My throat was closing up. I didn't have to breathe, but the inability to draw in air was even more painful than the slow flames of pain licking at my face. I was going to die. For real this time, I could feel it. My strength was ebbing out of my limbs, and I could feel my body shutting down.

Gabriel. I would never fix things with Gabriel. Until that moment, I hadn't realized I had expected that I would. As the edges of my vision began to darken and blur, I struggled to tell Andrea to find Gabriel, to tell him how sorry I was.

"Get it out of here!" Dick yelled as he swooped behind the counter. "Keep the door open."

Andrea, still wiping frantically at her cheeks, tossed the box out through the front door. Dick propped me up against his chest and dragged a fingernail across his wrist. "Come on, sweetheart. Come on, Jane, please, calm down and drink." Dick coughed slightly as he pressed his wrist to my mouth. He hissed in pain as my mouth touched his skin. The flesh against my lips sizzled and turned black as his skin reacted to the silver on my face. He murmured soothing words as I struggled to swallow. "Good, good. You need this. It will help. There's a girl. Long, slow sips."

Despite the fact that our organs are no longer functioning, vampire cells actually reproduce at a rapid rate. When we're injured, tendrils of tissue and muscle reach out to each other to replicate the previous alignment, which is why we don't gain weight or age. Drinking the blood of another vampire, particularly an older one, speeds the process along. The blood pouring down my throat was a balm. The comfort was almost instantaneous. My skin stopped smoking; the burning subsided. My throat relaxed, allowing Dick's blood to soothe and heal.

And laced through it all, like a gold ribbon streaking through the pain, I felt love. Dick really did love me, in a sweet, brotherly manner that sent his thoughts scattered in a million directions. Images whizzed by without rhyme or reason. Our meeting in the parking lot at the Cellar. Dick coming to River Oaks and realizing that Gabriel was my sire. Me introducing him to Andrea. Dick bickering with Gabriel while I refereed. His trailer exploding. Dick spending time with Zeb. Andrea and

Dick dancing at Zeb's wedding. Sitting with Andrea at her kitchen table. All of these little scenes were tenuously connected to his knowing me. He saw his life as being better after he met me. He didn't want to lose that.

Aww.

I broke away from him and let him wrap his arms around me, hugging me close. "Don't *ever* do that to me again, do you understand?" Dick demanded, his voice rough. I nodded, squeezing his shoulders, before he released me and checked the damage to my face. I didn't mention the visions, even though we both knew what I'd seen. Dick wasn't much for big emotional displays.

Gently, he leaned me against the cabinet. I pressed tentative fingers against the raw, ravaged skin of my cheeks as Dick rummaged for a wet rag. "What. The. Hell. Was. That?" I wheezed.

Rubbing his wrist as the flesh reformed and healed, Dick said, "You were having the vampire version of a bad allergic reaction. Can you explain to me how you managed to release aerosol silver directly into your own face? What's next for you, stake juggling?"

And with that, Dick had recovered from his fit of fraternal devotion.

"Why are we assuming that I did this to myself?" I growled, my voice still hoarse. Dick gave me a flat stare. "It was worth a shot," I said, swiping the rag across my cheeks. "Andrea! Andrea opened the box. Is she OK?"

"I'm fine," she said, peering over the counter, rubbing her own face with a dust rag. "It doesn't even hurt. I'm sorry I screamed. It just freaked me out."

"Eh, just promise you'll let me have the panic attack next time we're accosted by the mail."

Dick seized Andrea's shoulders and hugged her long and hard. "Dick . . . can't . . . breathe," she wheezed.

"Sorry, delayed reaction to you using your panicked voice. I love you like crazy, woman. It does strange things to me," he said before kissing her. He winced as the silver sizzled against his lips. He pulled away, carefully sniffing her face.

"That was so sweet," Andrea said. "Until you sniffed me."

"Colloidal silver," he announced. "A pretty strong dose of it."

"The health-supplement stuff?" I said, raising an eyebrow.

"Why am I not surprised that you know what it is?" Andrea grumbled, rinsing her face under the coffee-bar tap. "OK, geek girl, would you mind filling in the people who don't memorize everything they read?"

"It's basically microscopic clusters of silver particles in liquid. New-age types use it for everything from burns to eye infections, because it supposedly keeps germs from being able to metabolize. Hundreds of health-supplement Web sites sell it. It's perfectly safe for humans, with the exception of people who take too much over a long period of time. They have a tendency to turn blue. But obviously, it seriously screws with vampires." Andrea stared at me, her expression amazed and amused. I shrugged. "I saw it on *Oprah*."

"But how did it get sprayed at us from what was supposed to be a box of books?" Andrea griped. "What supervillain did you piss off this time, Jane?"

Dick examined the box carefully. "It looks like a pretty simple device. Once the tape was ruptured and the box top split, a lever compressed on this spray can and sent the silver into the air. In fact, if that had happened in a room full of humans, it wouldn't have been a problem. But obviously, someone thought there would be a good chance you would be opening the box."

"You seem to have to figured that out awfully fast," I commented dryly.

"It's a common trick if you've pissed off a vampire," Dick said. I narrowed my eyes at him. He gave me his best impression of an innocent person's indignant protest. "Not that I've ever done it."

"So, basically, we're looking for the Unabomber or MacGyver," I muttered. "Why is someone always trying to kill me? This never happened to me when I was alive."

Don't be afraid to be vulnerable. Sometimes we have to bare our souls to our vampire mates and say, "Yes, I'm invincible and immortal, but you can still hurt me."

—*Love Bites: A Female Vampire's Guide to Less Destructive Relationships*

We'd underestimated how far the silver had sprayed. I could see faint misting spatters of the grayish liquid along the far wall of the shop. Suddenly very weary, I wondered how long it would take to clean up the mess. Not that I was much help in that department, anyway. Andrea and Dick forced me to sit across the room, farthest from "ground zero," with an ice bag on my cheeks, while Andrea wet-vacuumed the carpet. Dick was wearing a surgical mask and elbow-length rubber gloves to wipe down the bar with disinfectant.

I sat there, feeling sort of useless, as Gabriel came roaring through the front door, his eyes wild. From the panicked, crazed look on his face, I thought he'd finally snapped and was going to go to all bunny-boiler on me. But when his eyes connected with mine, there was such powerful relief there that I couldn't be afraid. He bounded across the room and tenderly cradled my blistered face between his palms, poring over the damaged skin. Even though I was still mad at him, even though I still had enough of my pride to sting at the thought of him seeing me in full Freddy Krueger mode, I threw my arms around him and buried my face in his neck.

"It's OK. It's OK." I sniffled. "I'm fine."

I relaxed into Gabriel's arms and let him rock me gently back and forth. I knew things weren't settled yet. We were going to have to have a lot of long, long talks about trust, fidelity, communication, and not dropping one's sexual partner's naked ass onto concrete. But for the moment, I was willing to skip it all. I just wanted someone to care whether my face disintegrated or not. I don't think that's a violation of feminist principles.

"What is *he* doing here?" Andrea demanded, giving Gabriel the Glare of One Thousand Suns.

"I called him," Dick muttered.

"You what?" Andrea cried.

Gabriel lifted his head from my shoulder and growled at Dick, "How could you let this happen?"

Dick looked sheepish. "I can't watch her every minute, son. How was I supposed to know she'd be attacked by ground shipping?"

The two of them shared a look over my head. Gabriel made several threatening faces. Dick responded with rude gestures. Eventually, they looked like two inebriated mimes having a dance-off.

"Would someone clue the scabby girl in on the conversation?" I demanded.

"Dick was supposed to be watching you," Gabriel admitted. "He's been watching you for me for a while now."

"Well, that explains why you've spent so much time at the shop!" I took a swipe at Dick, who lithely stepped out of the way toward Andrea. She smacked him in my stead. "I do not need the Dick and Gabriel Secret Service Detail!"

"I'm sorry. I'm sorry," Gabriel whispered. "It's not that I didn't trust you to take care of yourself. Between the letters and the pranks, I was scared. I just wanted to protect you."

"Which is probably what put me in danger. Jackass," I said, halfheartedly slapping at his arm.

"I love you. Love you so much," he whispered into my neck. "I don't know what I would have done if you'd been . . . I am a huge jackass."

"That's the sweetest thing you've ever said to me," I told him, ignoring Andrea when she said, "That's just sad."

"She's fine," Dick said. "Really, Gabe. She's going to be OK. She's a tough little nut."

"Dick saved me," I told Gabriel. "Without him, I would be a little pile of Jane ashes waiting to be vacuumed up."

"Thank you," Gabriel told Dick. Dick seemed to be waiting for a punchline, so Gabriel repeated it. "I mean it. Thank you."

Dick would have blushed if he was capable. Instead, he made a study of the floor.

"Can I see the device?" Gabriel asked.

Dick retrieved the box, which we had wrapped in a clear plastic bag.

"The label was intact, undamaged," Dick said, showing Gabriel the address flap. "You couldn't even tell the box had already been taped once until you took off the second layer."

"So, whoever it was would have had to monitor our Dumpster closely enough to wait for a barely damaged Amazon.com box with an intact label to be thrown away?" I made a face and then winced at the pressure on my burnt cheeks. "You know, I think I'm more upset by that than I am the silver thing."

"The silver is very pure," Gabriel observed. "I can smell it, even from here. Colloidal silver tends to be higher in concentration than the mix used in defense sprays, and this seems to be a particularly potent batch. If this had sprayed you directly in the face, instead of Andrea, you might not have survived. It would be like someone who is allergic to bee stings stepping on a hive. Your healing ability would have been overwhelmed, and you would have been stripped down to the bone. Young vampires rarely come back from injuries like that."

"Didn't you say your new friend Courtney runs a sterling-silver shop?" Dick asked.

"Who's Courtney?" Gabriel asked.

"I met her at the Chamber of Commerce."

"You belong to the Chamber of Commerce?"

"Hey, I haven't been sitting around moping after you. I am a very busy and important woman." Andrea gave me a smirking yet disapproving look. I amended, "I moped a little bit."

Dick rolled his eyes. "Someone who runs a jewelry business would be pretty well versed in the different forms of silver, especially high-concentration stuff."

"Oh, come on, guys, don't do this," I whined. "I really like Courtney. Well, that one, at least. I just want one normal human friend without a frightening agenda. Please don't take that from me."

"I think that hurts my feelings," Andrea muttered.

"Besides, I think we all know who—" I was interrupted as Emery sauntered from the rear of the shop. He stopped and sniffed delicately at the harsh disinfectants, shuddering.

"What's that smell? It smells like burnt popcorn in here," he said, gagging.

"Emery, how long have you been here?" Andrea asked.

"I just arrived, Andrea, dear," he said, offering her an overly gooey smile. "I came in the staff entrance."

"It was locked," Dick noted, his jaw set as he pulled Andrea just a little bit closer.

"I borrowed a key," Emery said in the dismissive tone he always used when talking to Dick.

"You're going to give that back now," I told him, not bothering to disguise the irritation in my voice.

Emery ignored me, his eyes sweeping over the disheveled room. "What happened?"

"Someone sent Jane a can of aerosol silver, which sprayed all over the shop," Dick said, watching Emery carefully for a reaction.

"Did it get on any of the more important books?" Emery demanded with a shriek. "Does liquid silver stain? Have you contacted your insurance agent?"

Sadly, that was exactly the reaction I'd expected. I sincerely looked forward to the day when Dick revealed their blood connection to Emery . . . and then Dick took his great-great-grandson out to the woodshed for an old-fashioned ass-whoopin'.

"And I'm fine, thank you," I muttered. I felt a low growl rumble deep in Gabriel's chest. I placed a restraining hand across his shoulders. As much as I appreciated Gabriel's indignant response, Emery couldn't help that he was raised to be a socially clueless tool. Plus, spilling Emery's blood would probably damage more books.

"Well, of course, I'm concerned for you, Jane, but obviously, you're fine," Emery said, giving another delicate shudder at the sight of my ravaged face. "But who knows what kind of damage this little prank has done? Who knows how many books have been ruined?"

"We're not really worried about that right now, Emery," Andrea said. "We're just grateful that Jane's all right."

"Of course, you are. You're such a good friend, Andrea." Emery pressed Andrea's hands between his. Dick's eyes narrowed into dangerous little slits.

"We'll start checking the books just as soon as we have all this cleaned up," Dick told him. "Why don't you head on home to the boardinghouse or the malt shop or wherever you wholesome types spend your evenings?"

"But I can help," Emery protested. "You probably want to clean the silver off the books as soon as possible if you're going to salvage them. Besides, it wouldn't do for poor Jane to stumble across a book soaked in silver months from now, would it? We can't have those sorts of hazards just lurking around the shop for her or our vampire customers. I'm willing to examine every single book if it means making the shop safe for Jane . . . and her friends."

"Andrea and I can handle it," Dick told him.

"Wouldn't it be better to have an extra pair of hands helping you?" Emery countered. He gave Andrea a long simpering look. "Besides, it's obvious that Andrea is shaken by the incident. I'd like to pitch in and help her however I can."

"Emery, look." I stood on wobbly legs. My head swam, and the floor tilted toward me. "I don't feel so well."

"You're going home," Gabriel told me as he caught my elbows and kept me from smacking my head on the floor. "Dick, would you mind closing up?"

I was too dazed to object or hear Dick's response. Dick and Andrea could figure out what to do with Emery. I let Gabriel lead me to his car and tuck me into the passenger side.

I stared out the window, unsure of what to say, as he drove me to River Oaks. When we got there, he let Fitz out to run and took me to the upstairs bathroom, where he carefully stripped me out of the silver-laced clothes. While Gabriel ran bathwater, I caught a glimpse of my face in the mirror and was relieved to see that it no longer looked like raw hamburger. I had a few shiny, pale pink patches across my cheeks and nose, like a human recovering from a bad sunburn.

Gabriel let me slip in under the bubbles, and I closed

my eyes to avoid looking at him while he ran a sponge down my still-healing arms and legs. He poured some of my "fancy" antifrizz shampoo into his palm and massaged it through my hair. Apparently, he didn't expect me to talk about my feelings or how awkward it was for me to let him see me naked again, especially with my fabulous shiny pink healing burns. It was just as well. I wasn't sure how I felt about him seeing me naked again, with or without shiny pink healing burns.

When he tilted my head back to rinse my hair, I caught him staring at my face. You'd expect someone in his situation to be sneaking looks about eight inches south, but he was wholly concentrated on my face. The burns must have been worse than I thought.

"I know, it's bad," I told him. "But I'm feeling a lot better."

"No, you're almost completely healed. I just— I'm trying to take in as much as I can before you're strong enough to drop-kick me out the door."

"Why are you being so sweet?" I asked.

"Because you're letting me," he said, a sad little lopsided smile tilting his mouth. "I'm so sorry."

"I missed you, too. But I didn't do anything wrong, ergo no apology."

"I can live with that." He nodded, gently pouring warm water over my head. "I would like you to consider moving to my house for a while, Jane."

"I couldn't do that. It would feel weird. And I don't think living together would be right for us at the moment. There's too much going on."

"Well, then move into Andrea's place, at least until the threats stop."

My eyebrows arched, the new skin around them stretching tight. "Andrea's place, where Dick lives? You must be scared."

"I don't want anything to happen to you."

"I'll be fine. And I'll be much more careful when I open the mail, I promise." He gave me a withering fatherly look. "I'll let Andrea open the mail from now on?" When that didn't satisfy him, I huffed. "I'll take it to the airport and have it X-rayed?"

"I will be spending a lot more time at the shop with you," he said. "You don't even have to acknowledge my presence. I will just sit in the back and watch you, to make sure you're safe. Wherever you go, I go."

"Like a stalker."

He nodded. "Yes. Jane, I don't care what capacity you let me have in your life. I just want to be there. And if that means I have to keep my distance, I'll do that."

I sighed. If ever there was a time for me to lay all my cards on the table, this was it. Naked, wounded, and vulnerable. "So, here's my basic problem with us, the reason I can't seem to relax into a relationship with you, the reason I find problems where none exist and I push you away. I—I can't figure out why you're with me!" I exclaimed, clapping my hand over my mouth. I hadn't meant for that part to come out. I had meant to say, "You lie and hide things from me."

Gabriel pried my fingers away from my lips. My hands trembled as stuff I'd been feeling for months tumbled from my tongue. "I know that makes me neurotic and sad, but I can't figure out why you want to be with me. Every other woman in your life is exotic and beautiful and has all this history. And I'm just some drunk girl you followed home from a bar, some pathetic human you felt your usual need to protect, and you got stuck with a lifetime tie to her because she was dumb enough to get shot. I can't stand the idea that you feel obligated to me. I know I'm insecure and pushy and spastic, desperately inappropriate at times and just plain odd at others. And I can't help but wonder why you would want that when there are obviously so many other options. I can't help but feel that I'm keeping you from someone better."

I let out a loud, long breath. It felt as if some tremendous weight on my chest had wiggled loose and then dropped away. No more running. No more floating along and waiting. My cards were on the table. If Gabriel and I couldn't have a future after this, it wasn't because I held back from him. Now I could only hope it didn't blow up in my face in some horrible way.

I wasn't sure my face could handle much more.

Gabriel sighed and cupped my chin, forcing me to look him in the eye. "I didn't follow you that night because I wanted to protect you. I followed you that night because you were one of the most interesting people I'd met in decades. You had this light about you, this sweetness, this biting humor. After I'd only known you for an hour, you made me laugh harder than I had since before I was turned. You made me feel normal, at peace, for the first time in years. And I didn't want to lose that yet. Even if it was just watching over you from a mile away, I didn't want to leave your presence. I followed you because I didn't want to let you go. Even then, I saw you were one of the most extraordinary, fascinating, maddening people I would ever know. Even then, I think I knew that I would love you. If you don't love me, that's one thing. But if you do, just stop arguing with me about it. It's annoying. "

"Fair enough," I conceded. "Why the hell couldn't you have told me this a year ago?"

"I've wanted to. You weren't ready to hear it."

The water cooled. Gabriel helped me out of the tub and wrapped my robe around me. I snuggled up under the covers and pulled him under with me. He held me close for a long, silent moment before I finally said, "Tell me about Jeanine. Tell me everything. I won't get mad, no matter how bad it is."

Gabriel turned me to face him, stroking my hair. "I met Jeanine on one of my first visits to Paris. Her family had old money, very old. Her parents died when she was young, leaving her to be raised by a criminally indulgent grandmother. Jeanine's mother had been prone to 'spells' during which her grandmother attended to her every need. So Jeanine learned early on that being weak and sickly was the fastest way to get attention. Batteries of doctors, nurses, and maids catered to her every whim around the clock. And yet they could never find exactly what was ailing her. Her symptoms shifted like the sands, leaving her grandmother frantic that she would lose another beloved girl. Jeanine was never forced to study subjects she found boring, never forced to meet family or social obligations she found unappealing, never made to do anything that didn't suit her down to her stamping little foot. The end result was a girl with a woefully limited education, little empathy, and no apparent conscience.

"She spent so much time pretending to be ill that she convinced herself she was. The whole of Paris society spoke in quiet admiration of this 'pale rose' who only braved the trials of public appearances every so often for the opera or an important party. She was beautiful. Mahogany hair, always curled into the latest fashions. Bottomless eyes the color of bluebells. Her skin was so—"

"I get it. She made tuberculosis hot," I said crossly. "On with the story."

In a slightly less admiring voice, Gabriel assured me, "I found her to be manipulative, spoiled, and not nearly as wan or silly as she wanted us to believe. She was what you would have quite freely called a pain in the ass. But she was also very clever. Most of her 'incapacitation' was spent reading."

"I thought you said she didn't study."

"Oh, she read what suited her. Romance novels, Gothic horror. Unfortunately, some of her library included Gothic romance tales, *Varney the Vampire* and *Carmilla*."

"Those are pretty hard-core books for the time," I commented. "Surely, well-bred and invalid young ladies did not read lurid lesbian vampire fantasies." Gabriel arched an eyebrow at me. "Not that I've read them . . . Moving on."

"As I said, her grandmother was indulgent. She would go to any lengths to lift poor Jeanine's spirits, including discreetly procuring naughty books. Jeanine recognized what I was right away. She approached me, throwing herself in my path wherever I went, the ballet, parties, even a late-night card game at a friend's home. It was becoming a joke among my friends. Her grandmother encouraged the infatuation, because she seemed to think that whatever got Jeanine out of bed and into the world was a good thing. One night, Jeanine cornered me at a ball and told me she knew my secret, but not to worry, she wouldn't tell a soul. All I had to do in return was to make her what I was."

"She wanted to be turned?"

Gabriel muttered, "For someone who spent so much time on her deathbed, she was terrified of death. The idea of becoming old and not having the choice of being confined and ill was horrible to her. She thought by becoming a vampire, she would finally be free from illness, stronger, able to get out from under the control of her grandmother, whom she began resenting long before. I refused, told her she was mistaken. I even used my burgeoning powers to wipe all thoughts or memories she had pertaining to my being a vampire. But her obsession ran deeper than my reach. Within a few weeks, she was back again and more determined. She was everywhere. I switched hotels endlessly to dodge her. She excelled at knowing my schedule before I did. Everywhere I went, there was a note from her, cajoling, wheedling, promising me her undying devotion, endless love, and companionship."

"That sounds vaguely familiar," I said dryly.

He sighed. "Finally, she found the hotel where I was staying. I came home one morning to find her on my bed."

"Slut."

"Fully clothed with both wrists slashed," he added.

"Ew."

"She was on the brink of death. She had just enough breath to whisper, 'Help me, please.' I knew it was wrong—"

"But, being unable to pass up a damsel in distress—which is a bit of a pattern with you, by the way—you intervened," I said, cupping his chin in my hands.

"Yes. I felt it was my fault she had done this. I hadn't been forceful enough in dissuading her. I could have done more. There was no blood left to take from her, but I gave her my own. Afterward, I felt used, angry, helpless. I'd panicked and turned someone who was going to be an undead terror. I was ashamed of what I'd done. I knew what sort of evil she would be capable of, and yet I still couldn't bring myself to destroy her, to keep her from rising and walking the earth.

"I slept—on the floor of the hotel room—and when I rose that night, I took her to the home of a friend, a fellow vampire. A woman, Violette, who was three hundred forty years old at the time and less likely to be manipulated by Jeanine. I hoped that when she arose, Violette would prove to be a mentor, a stabilizing influence. By that time, I'd booked passage to China."

"Dramatic," I noted.

"Necessary," Gabriel countered. "Jeanine is a prime example of a vampire who changed not at all after she was turned. She's just as neurotic and self-absorbed now as she was then. She's the only hypochondriac vampire I've ever met. She travels with a humidifier, for God's sake. She's so convinced that every place she goes will be her 'final resting place' that she carries all of her possessions with her in a moving van."

I snickered, but he continued, "And when vampirism didn't change the way she looked at herself, the way she felt, she blamed me. She believes she's a lesser vampire. She said that I didn't turn her properly. She believes she's still weak and sickly, so, obviously, she didn't get enough of my blood. She wants me to try to turn her *again*."

"Is that even possible?" I asked.

"Once your transformation is complete, that's the way you'll remain for the rest of your existence. The point is that I did turn Jeanine completely. I gave her more than enough of my blood. She refuses to believe me. I've tried to talk some sense into her, to teach her restraint, but when she doesn't get what she wants, her tantrums turn out to be massacres. She became convinced that the only 'cure' for her condition was the blood of those who had lived in high altitudes, so she drained every nun in a convent in Tibet. She's butchered hospitals' worth of doctors because they can't find any way to help her."

"She's spent almost one hundred years trying to track me down, doing what she can to isolate me, ruin my friendships, my relationships with women. She'll become dormant for a few years, while she 'recuperates' at a mineral spring or a monastery or some other supposedly curative location. And then she'll get restless and start up again. When it became clear that she was beyond my help, my focus became keeping her away from the people, the places I cared about. That's the reason I've spent so much time bouncing between the Hollow and, well, the rest of the world for the last century. She says I owe her, that I made her, and now I'm responsible for what she's become. And she's right. She's my creation. The blood of every person she's ever killed is on my hands."

Gabriel pressed his face against my shoulder, cringing as if he expected me to start screaming and hitting him. I waited a beat before saying, "So, really, I'm *not* the craziest girl you've ever dated. That's a relief."

"Your grasp of the weight of this situation is amazing," he retorted.

I shrugged. "I'm just saying."

"So . . . you're not angry?" he asked.

"Of course, I'm angry!" I exclaimed. "I'm freaking furious with you right now. If I was up to full strength, I would kick your ass from here to Sunday. I can't believe that this is what you kept from me all these months. I thought you cheated on me! You let me suffer and mope and go *months* without seeing you because of some issue with a bratty childe? You and your stupid overactive conscience! From now on, you are going to gauge the severity of your actions by answering the question, 'Would Dick think this was a good idea?' and if the answer is no, *that's* when you know you've done something really, really wrong. Either way, just tell me about it so we avoid these dramatics. If you had told me about this months ago, I would have helped you track her down and lock her in some vampire nut ward."

"That's exactly why I didn't tell you. I didn't want you to know what I'd let happen, that I wasn't even trying to stop her anymore, just outrun her. I shouldn't have lied to you. And it kills me that I hurt you in a misguided attempt to protect you, especially when it seems that isn't doing any good. All I can say is that I panicked. I was ashamed. I was trying so hard to cover my tracks that I lost sight of what was important—you."

"Why were you ashamed?" I asked.

He lifted my chin, meeting my eyes. "I was a coward. If this had happened to you, you would have stopped her. You would have gone after her with both barrels and talked her into submission. And when you left me in that hotel room, I was torn between wanting to drop to my knees, tell you everything, and beg your forgiveness and wanting you to leave, to get away so you would be far from Jeanine and her madness. I thought I'd feel better once you were home, but I was decimated. I sat in that hotel room for a week, unsure of what to do, where to go, how to feel, all the while hoping you would come back but knowing that you shouldn't."

"Technically, decimated means 'the reduction of a military force by one-tenth,'" I pointed out.

"Mmm, I love it when you do that." He sighed, pressing his face into my hair. "I haven't had anyone to correct me or fill my head with useless trivia for months."

"You poor soul," I muttered, smiling despite myself. "Besides, I wouldn't say you're a coward. You pushed a tree on top of a guy for me." I laced my arms around his waist and pulled him against me. "So, you were wrong."

"I was absolutely, unequivocally, undeniably, one-hundred-percent wrong," he agreed, accenting each word with a soft kiss on my throat.

"Which would mean . . ."

"That you were absolutely, unequivocally, undeniably, one-hundred-percent right," he said, again with the kissing.

"You know, a woman waits her whole life to hear those words." I sighed. I straightened, lifting my head. I looked up into his face and caught a flicker of uncertainty. "What? What's with the face?"

"Well, I can believe Jeanine sent you letters," he said. "And maybe even rubbing your house with exotic, unpleasant fruit. But the silver, that seems rather aggressive for her. She's absolutely phobic of any sort of silver, claims she's more sensitive to it than most vampires because of her delicate constitution. For her to send it to you, she must be getting desperate."

"Either that, or I have another stalker," I wisecracked. "Oh, crap. You said you've turned three people including me. Who was the third?" I poked him when he didn't respond. "Total honesty."

"It's a much shorter story. I met Brandley in the 1950s in London. He was a young medical student, brilliant. He spent most of his time in a lab, studying vaccines. From the moment I met him, I could tell that he was very ill. There was a taint to his scent, an undercurrent of decay. Leukemia. But when I thought of what he could accomplish, how he could benefit mankind when he had unlimited time to conduct his research, I gave him a choice: impending natural death or everlasting life.

He took it. I was so careful turning him, staying with him until he rose, coaching him through those first few days. And at first, it was wonderful to have a companion, someone to hunt with, to talk to. Like yours, Brandley's learning curve was quite steep. He adjusted beautifully to his new life. But unlike you, Brandley had an enormous aptitude for cruelty. He had no interest in study or science when he could spend his nights drowning in the blood of his victims. I tried to teach him patience, pity for his food, but for him, the meal seemed incomplete if they survived."

I chewed my lip. "Should we worry about Brandley coming after us, because I don't want to go through this whole bratty demon stepchilde thing again."

"Brandley's dead. He was killed by an angry Welsh mob who objected to his tendency of feeding off their very young daughters."

"Are you sure he's dead?" I asked.

"Well, they cut his head off, so, yes."

I was quiet for a long moment. "You have really, really bad luck when it comes to vampire children, don't you? I mean, how could you have worked up the nerve to turn me? Because it could have gone just horribly, horribly wrong."

"Who's to say it hasn't?" Gabriel muttered. "And stop using adverbs twice, it's insulting."

"Seriously, why would you put yourself through that when you'd had such terrible experiences as a sire?"

He kissed me, pressing his lips ever so softly against mine. "Because you were different. When I told you that your goodness and your innocence set you apart,

I meant it. I'd had reservations when I turned Jeanine and some reluctance about turning Brandley. But when I saw you, bleeding and dying, I knew without a doubt that you deserved a second chance, that you would make the most of your vampire life, without cruelty, without being petty or selfish. You're the best part of me, Jane, the gift I could give the world to make up for past wrongs."

"That's either incredibly beautiful or a *lot* of pressure to put on me."

Gabriel snorted. "I love you."

"I love you, too. Idiot."

"Agreed." He sighed. "I've never had a lover I've met as a human and known as a vampire. I've never made love to someone I sired. I didn't count on my feelings of love and concern and responsibility twisting into such a confusing mess."

"So, I'm your first?"

He seemed startled by the question. "Yes! The last thing on my mind was sex with Jeanine, and, well, Brandley was a man."

"So, you've never . . ."

"No!"

I threw up my hands. "Hey, vampires are hypersexual creatures. Our boundaries are not like those of humans. And then, of course, there's all that tension between you and Dick. You can't really blame me for thinking—"

"Jane!"

I shrugged. "OK. You're totally heterosexual."

"You're enjoying my discomfort right now, aren't you?" he growled.

"Immensely," I told him, snickering as I bit down on his bottom lip. "This is my proposal, simple and to the point: we track this Jeanine twit down and kick her ass."

Gabriel sighed again, burying his face in my hair. "That's my girl."

I would have gotten into a long-term relationship years ago if someone had told me about the almighty power of makeup sex.

We talked long into the night about our months apart. We seemed to see it as a competition, who missed whom more. I described my bathrobe-encased moping. He countered with the fact that he let Zeb take him to karaoke night at the Cellar to sing sad break-up songs, including "There's a Tear in My Beer." I told him about my evening of drinking with Dick, carefully omitting the bar fight, for Dick's sake. Gabriel confessed to keeping one of my T-shirts in bed with him so he could smell me while he slept.

"You are now officially a sixteen-year-old girl." I giggled, stroking his back. "Wait a minute, what did you do with the panties you stole in the alley?"

"It's best we don't discuss that," he said, nuzzling my collarbone. "We've already established that I missed you more than you missed me. Let's leave it at that. I am the truly pathetic winner."

"I wouldn't call it winning, per se," I said, shaking my head. "But I think I have you beat."

"What can be more pathetic than sexually objectifying your New Kids on the Block T-shirt?" he asked, arching a brow.

I rolled, letting his weight pin me pleasantly against the mattress as I held his face over mine. "My body craved you so much that I couldn't sleep for all the sex dreams I was having. Full-color, surround-sound, waking up in the middle of multiple-orgasm extravaganzas that tortured me every single night. I didn't know whether to be angry at my subconscious for not being able to let you go or grateful that I was able to hold on to you even in that empty, barely satisfying way."

Gabriel's mouth went slack, and I think I heard his brain shatter like glass. He wheezed, "Tell me."

I launched into detailed descriptions of my dreams, because I figured, why suffer alone? I told him about what was basically a reimagining of my losing my virginity in college, only it was Gabriel hiking me up against the stacks of the Russian folklore section of the university library. And we ended up christening the special-collections room as well as the reference section. He groaned when I told him about the one where he was my boss and I had to be "disciplined" against his desk for improperly filing a report. I recounted the scenario involving him and a pint of Chocolate Overload ice cream just to be mean. When I got to the Victorian dream, I left out the bloodier, upsetting aspects to focus on the setting and the fancy clothes. I stumbled over the, um, oral exam, because I was new to the dirty talk and couldn't seem to find the balance between sexy-dirty and gross-dirty. Seriously, Naughty Jane can only keep up the façade for so long.

"Don't stop now," Gabriel said, his eyes dark and slightly unfocused. "I'd like to know how this one ends."

"It's a little embarrassing," I confessed, suddenly wanting the bed to open up and swallow me. I'd gone from wet and ready temptress to stuttering novice in three seconds flat. If I could have blushed, my face would have lit up like a flame. "I will say that you kissed me somewhere that you've never kissed me before."

"Like in the backseat of a car?" he asked, his tone teasing.

"Yes, you kissed my Honda." I snickered, slapping at his shoulder as he spread kisses in the valley between my breasts, the little dip in my belly button. When he nudged the tip of his nose to the lace waistband of my panties, my hips bucked up from the bed. "What are you doing?"

"I told you, I want to know how this one ends," he said, peeling my underwear away. I let out a slow, jittery breath as the cool air hit my damp, trickling flesh. I made a noise between a yelp and a sigh when Gabriel's tongue made that first long, achingly slow slide against me. Gabriel murmured, "How will we know if the dream was accurate unless we let it play out?"

My hips bucked up, pressing me against his mouth as his lips danced across my center. His hands slipped under my butt and lifted me closer, my legs slipping over his back. He nipped and kissed and teased while my body pitched. Hot spikes of pleasure coiled in my belly, stretching each nerve until every stroke of his mouth was almost painful. And just like my dream, the moment the tip of his tongue flicked at that little elusive pearl of nerves, I came, howling.

Pushing my thighs apart and settling between them, Gabriel slid up the length of my body, kissing and nipping until he reached my mouth. As his tongue, still tasting of my own arousal, swept into my mouth, he filled me to the hilt. Whatever breath we had left was released in one long sigh.

He spread my knees wide, tucking my ankles around the small of his back as he withdrew. I whimpered just as he snapped his hips and drove deeper. He brought me to my peak over and over and then pulled back, drawing out our release. I lost track of time, of rhythm, of anything but the delicious friction. Gabriel brushed his lips over my closed eyelids. My eyes fluttered open as his fangs peeked over his lips. He smiled, bending his head to my throat and delicately scraping his sharp teeth against my skin. I arched my neck. He sank his fangs into my skin, drawing blood to the wound with insistent, gentle pressure. I turned my head toward the palm cupping my face, biting down on the skin just below his wrist as his movements became more frantic.

He gasped as I swallowed the first mouthful of blood. The connection, the flow of blood seemed to open up some little window between us. I'd never caught so much as a hint of what Gabriel was thinking before. And now I could feel everything he felt—the love he had for me, his relief at being able to touch me again, the pleasure I was giving him. It was all laid open for me. And when I thought, "I love you, too," he gasped again, as if he heard me. The thought sent him toppling over the edge and dragged me with him.

In my head, the lesser, dream version of Gabriel was sent packing with his stupid tuxedo jacket thrown after him.

13

There comes a time to accept that some relationship patterns will never change. The problem with being a vampire is that it can take hundreds of years for that time to come.

—Love Bites: A Female Vampire's Guide to Less Destructive Relationships

Mama had outdone herself.

With little effort or prompting on my part, my mother had pulled together a baby shower that would have made Martha Stewart turn chartreuse with envy.

"Oh . . . . my." Jolene sighed as I helped her waddle through the front door of my parents' house.

Since the ultrasounds had been unclear as far as the twins' gender, Mom had kept things charmingly gender-neutral. A hand-sewn banner shouting "Congratulations!" in appliquéd pink and blue letters hung over the foyer table. On the table, guests could "sign in" by autographing a little baby album for Jolene and offering her an invaluable piece of parenting wisdom. To our left, the parlor's chairs were arranged in a circle around a small pile of beautifully wrapped presents. A clothesline was strung on one side of the room, artfully hung with little gender-neutral baby outfits, matching socks, and hats I knew Mama wouldn't have been able to resist buying for the twins. To our right, Mama had dressed the dining table with little votives of wildflowers between plates of rattle-shaped cookies and candy-colored petit-fours.

"It's all so beautiful." Jolene sighed again. "And no one's naked."

"Well, if that's not a baby shower prerequisite, it should be," I said, shuddering as Mama came into the dining room with a huge bowl of her special strawberry "shower punch." I groaned. Every Southern woman prides herself on her own special shower-punch recipe, whether it's combining lime sherbet and ginger ale or creating a frozen ring of pulverized pineapple in a bundt pan and letting it slowly melt in a punchbowl full of orange juice. Mama had never revealed her secret punch formula to me. Personally, I'd never understood the appeal of combining bizarre ingredients in unnecessarily complicated ways when popping the top of a Coke can was so much easier.

That's probably why I wasn't in charge of the shower.

"Oh, Mrs. Jameson, it's so . . . thank you." Jolene sniffled, throwing her arms around Mama's neck. Mama, who was not familiar with werewolf strength, winced in Jolene's grip but patted her on the back.

"Oh, honey, I'm happy to do it. Zeb means a lot to John and me. That means you do, too," she said, gently peeling Jolene's arms away so she could breathe. "Now, Jane said you'd had a pretty hearty appetite lately. So I made you a little snack to pick at before everybody gets here. Why don't you go make yourself at home in the kitchen?"

I arched an eyebrow as Jolene followed her nose into the kitchen. Through the door, I heard her squeal, "She baked me a ham!"

"Zeb told me Jolene could go through a lot of food," Mama said, carefully placing the punchbowl on the table. "You sure do have an interesting group of friends, sweetheart."

"Thank you, Mama," I said, kissing her cheek. "Really, it's beautiful. Hey, what did you mean by 'everybody'? It's just going to be me, Gabriel, Dick, Andrea, you guys, Aunt Jettie, and Mr. Wainwright. You've put together a gorgeous spread for a bunch of people who don't eat."

Both Jolene's and Zeb's relatives were conspicuously absent from the guest list. I think we can all agree that was for the best.

"I may have invited a few more people," Mama said. "There are a lot of parents who know Zeb from school, people my age who knew him when he was little, who want to help him celebrate the babies. Plus . . . I may have sent invitations to all your aunts and cousins, making it sound like Jolene was somehow related to them."

"Mama!"

"Well, I had to go to all their showers and their daughters' showers," she huffed, looking slightly embarrassed. "And you're not going to need one, so I'm calling in all your chips for Jolene. No one can remember half of the names in this family anyway. They'll show up, give her a present, and walk away thinking they've done their duty for a distant relation."

"That's . . ." I laughed. "Actually kind of brilliant. I underestimate you."

"Constantly," Mama told me. "Now, I don't want you to worry about the boys. Your daddy's got a card table set up out back with enough beer and poker chips to keep them entertained for hours. He's actually pretty excited about spending some time with Dick and Gabriel. He has this list with all kinds of questions about the Civil War. And I'm so glad you and Gabriel have come to your senses, honey. You're perfect for each other. All you have to do now is get him to put that ring on your finger . . ."

"Mama, I'm not legally allowed to get married," I told her. "There wouldn't be much point in our getting engaged."

"Honey, I know this is a sore subject. I would just feel better if I knew you were settled."

"Mama, I'm going to live forever, and so is my boyfriend. I think that's about as settled as you could expect, considering the circumstances."

Mama considered that for a moment and seemed satisfied.

"Besides, I think we have a more immediate problem. As much as I appreciate you planning this expanded shindig for Jolene, what are we going to do about the extra guests? What if people don't want me around because of the undead issue? This would be the first time I've seen a lot of the aunts and cousins since ... Oh, wait, is Grandma Ruthie coming?"

"I decided it was best not to invite your grandma," Mama said, carefully adjusting the folds of a chair cover. "And honey, if anybody has a problem with you being here, they can get the hell out of my house."

I blinked back the mysterious moisture gathering at the corners of my eyes. "Thanks, Mama."

"Who's ready for some Texas Hold 'Em?" Daddy boomed as he came downstairs in his silly translucent green dealer's visor. It went well with his lucky rainbow suspenders.

Dick was going to eat my father alive.

"You guys aren't playing for money, right?" I asked.

I will admit to sweating a little when the doorbell rang.

The first guest to arrive was Iris Bodeen, a distant relative of one of my step-grandpas and an avid "band mom" when Zeb and I were in the Marching Howler Band. She handed Jolene a case of diapers and told her what a catch she'd snagged.

"Zeb was always good to my Jessica, even when she was going through her awkward phase," Mrs. Bodeen said of her daughter, who had developed debilitating acne our sophomore year. "He was kind, even when it would have been easier not to be. He's going to be a wonderful father."

Jolene beamed at her.

Nina Tipton, whose rambunctious twins had made

Zeb's life hell his first year of teaching, almost cried when she talked about Zeb's patience with them. "A lot of teachers would have just washed their hands of my boys . . . especially after the clown incident. But your husband worked and worked until they were able to sit still for a whole day without punching or kicking or trying out new wrestling moves. They would have been expelled from elementary school if it wasn't for Zeb Lavelle."

And on and on it went. It was a shame that Zeb couldn't hear these testimonials, as he was sequestered on the back porch. An avid fan of the *Gambler* movies, Daddy was doing his best riverboat-dealer shtick for Dick, Gabriel, Zeb, and Mr. Wainwright. I frequently snuck to the back window to check on the "menfolk." Mr. Wainwright seemed to be floating silently behind Gabriel giving Dick clues about Gabriel's hand. I sent Aunt Jettie outside to even the playing field.

So far, I'd managed to stay under the radar, helping Andrea keep the plates filled while Mama handled hosting duties. The guests I did come across didn't seem surprised or alarmed to see me. Well, my cousin Junie was making it a point not to speak to me. But that had far more to do with my discussing her stripping career near a microphone at a family funeral the year before than any vampire issues.

"Janie, honey, how have you been?" asked Loralee Warner, who worked with Mama at A Stitch in Time. Loralee's usual mode at any party was to camp next to the buffet and watch the proceedings from there. She was a fan of tiny food she didn't have to cook herself.

I lifted an eyebrow and searched for potential double meanings in Loralee's words. I couldn't find any.

"I'm fine, Miss Loralee. How are you?"

"Oh, my hair's grayer, and my butt's bigger, but what else is new?" She snorted. "You know, your mama told me about your, um, big changes that you've been going through."

I could only imagine what Mama and Loralee talked about while trapped in the quilt shop for hours. On Mama's frustrated days, I doubted I came across in a flattering light. "I'm sure she did."

"You know, my sister's boy, Jason, he was turned last year." She sighed. "But it turned out to be the best thing for him. He actually had to think about what he did before he did it. Was it safe for him to leave the house? Did he have enough blood to get him through the week? Was he talking smart to a vampire who was older and stronger than he was? He had to do a lot of growing up. He's almost tolerable to be around now."

"Well, there's something to strive for," I muttered.

"Your friend Jolene," Loralee said quietly. "She's not quite human, either, is she?"

"Please don't tell anybody," I whispered, looking to see if the other guests overheard her. They were far too engrossed in Jolene's opening what appeared to be a vibrating musical baby swing with five speeds.

"Oh, honey, I don't care," Loralee said. "The way I see it, you vampires and whatever Jolene is, you're just making things more interesting for the rest of us. Are there any more sausage balls?"

And with that dizzying change of subject, the conversation was over. No one in this crowd, it seemed, cared that I was a vampire. These were people who had known me since the day I was born. Their children had attended my birthday parties. They'd attended all of my step-grandpas' funerals. Being with them now was no different from when I was a human. As long as I kept the frothy punch flowing, I was welcome. Now, that wasn't to say that I would be welcome in any crowd. There was a good chance that for the next fifty years, I would walk into any conversation with a human who knew me before I was turned expecting some sort of insult or rejection—which was a result of my own neurotic nature, really. Humans were neither all good nor all bad. And just as in my interactions with vampires, I would have to approach each of them on a case-by-case basis.

The fact that it had taken me this long to come to this "stunning" conclusion made me a little sad.

I wiped my hands on a tea towel and made my way over to Jolene, who was cooing over the double bassinet Andrea and Dick had given her.

"Dick wanted to buy you a breast pump." Andrea snorted. "I learned never to take him into a baby store. Ever. He snickered every time he heard the word 'nipple.'"

"Well, that's what you get for dating a giant twelve-year-old," I told her, sitting on Jolene's left.

"Oh, honey, they're all that way," my mother's best friend, Carol Ann Reilly, told me in a world-weary tone.

"Look who's all smug and secure now that she's made up with her boyfriend," Jolene said.

"My boyfriend is more of a giant fourteen-year-old," I muttered. "Just as emotionally immature but somehow more dangerous."

"Oh, honey, they're all that way, too," Carol Ann assured me again.

It was far from the small family shower I had planned, but Jolene was positively glowing with every exchange. We cooed and awed appropriately over every little outfit, crib sheet, and stuffed animal. Hell, I got a little emotional over Jolene's shiny new wipes warmer.

By the end of the evening, my relatives were convinced that they remembered Jolene from family reunions when she a little girl. She was invited to join several Mommy and Me groups and a sewing circle. Mama considered her baby-shower-related social debts settled.

The boys were allowed back into the house after the ladies left, trailing cigar smoke and chip crumbs in their wake. Considering what Gabriel and I had been up to, I fully expected to burst into embarrassed flames at being in the same room with both him and my father. Let's just say that we'd spent several evenings experimenting, and we'd figured out that I could read Gabriel's mind if I was drinking his blood during exactly the "right moment" during sex. Unfortunately, his thoughts tended toward the possessive grunty male part of his personality. We were still working on deeper, more meaningful communication, hence the spontaneous combustion of parental shame.

I focused on helping Mama with the dirty-dish patrol. The heavily pregnant Jolene, despite having eaten her weight in sausage balls during the shower, tucked into a heaping bowl of ice cream and Canadian bacon. Daddy, Andrea, and Zeb made a furtive grab at whatever food Jolene hadn't claimed.

When Daddy finally took a break from grilling Dick and Gabriel about their nineteenth-century childhoods, Gabriel took Dick into the parlor and handed him a little leather portfolio containing the deed to the Cheney family manse. Considering that they'd spent the evening gambling, I took this as a bad sign. But it seemed to be something that Gabriel had been thinking about for a long time.

"I want you to have it back," he told Dick. "There's no way I can ever really repay you for being the kind of friend Jane needed, but I can give you this."

"I can't," Dick protested. "You know what that bet cost us. To take it back now would just make it all pointless."

"Not to be rude, but it was all pointless," I noted from across the room. Four eyes narrowed at me. "What? I said not to be rude. That's like saying 'God bless them' right after you say bad things about someone. It means it doesn't count!"

"What are they talking about?" Daddy whispered, clearly fascinated.

"Did Dick win at cards tonight?" I asked Daddy. Daddy nodded. "Well, he tended to play drunk when he and Gabriel were human, so he usually lost. Dick lost his family's house to Gabriel. The pair of them are so stubborn that it's taken them this long to get over it."

"Wow!" Daddy couldn't have been happier than a desperate housewife watching her favorite "stories."

Gabriel cleared his throat. I had the good sense to seem sheepish and mouth, "Love you."

"After all you've done for Jane, it's the least I can do," Gabriel said, pressing the portfolio into Dick's hand.

"I don't know what to say, son. I'm sorry we let it get this far. I've missed having you around the last hundred or so years," Dick said, looking the most human he had since I'd met him. He looked younger somehow, more vulnerable. He took the portfolio but then looked up, his eyes pleading. "Can I still irritate the hell out of you?"

"I don't know what I would do if you didn't," Gabriel said honestly. "I think you would sicken and die."

They shook hands and gave each other manly punches on the arm. Dick announced to Andrea that they were moving up in the world, to a deluxe antebellum home that she could redecorate to her heart's content. Then he lovingly fed her a deviled egg. Andrea blushed, especially when Dick tried to kiss her afterward. Deviled eggs are not a sexy food.

"Does this mean that we're going to be double-dating now?" I asked. Andrea rolled her eyes.

Gabriel's grin was wicked. "Yes, because I think it's only fair that since Dick got my girlfriend into a bar fight, I should be able to take his girlfriend out on the town and put her in danger while he watches. Maybe we can go to a biker convention."

Dick growled. "Hey, Jane fared better in that fight than I did."

"I thought you weren't involved in the fight with Walter," Gabriel said, his brow furrowed.

"Not that one, the other one, with Todd. The one . . . you don't know about." Dick grimaced. "Crap."

"You got her into another bar fight?" Gabriel exclaimed. "You were supposed to be looking out for her, not *putting* her in harm's way! That's it. Dick, Jane, from now on, all of your play dates are supervised. Andrea, sweetheart, I'm taking you sky-diving. It's only fair."

Daddy laughed and headed into the kitchen for another round of beers. Andrea climbed into Dick's lap and suggested alternative activities, such as bull riding, swimming the Ohio River during peak barge traffic, motocross racing without helmets, and letting me cook for her. Dick's scowl grew deeper with each suggestion. Having finished the world's most disgusting sundae, Jolene was propped up against Zeb's side, both of their hands gravitating to her enormous belly. Jettie was distracted from inventorying Jolene's loot with a fond pat on the cheek from Mr. Wainwright.

I had a family. A family that loved me, without judgment, without reserve. And my parents had somehow fallen right into this motley crew and were enjoying themselves. Sure, there were blood relatives out there who couldn't stand the sight of me, but I could fall back on these people. They would fight for me, kiss my booboos, take me out for tequila shooters when life got me down. I didn't need more than that. All was right with my world.

So, it made sense that my grandma Ruthie chose this moment to come storming through the door.

"Jane Enid Jameson!" she thundered, slamming the door behind her. Grandma was in a fine froth, her snowy white hair frazzled and her cheeks flushed. She was dressed in a pink and orange plaid pantsuit, the kind of thing that would send Aunt Jettie into a giggle fit when she was living. Apparently, it worked its wonders after death, too, because my ghostly aunt was laughing her invisible ass off. And she wasn't alone.

"Enid?" Dick snickered.

I ignored Dick's low laughter as Grandma screeched, "How could you embarrass your sister that way? She told me what you did at the Chamber of Commerce meeting. How could you? You know how important her public image is with this new business she's starting. How dare you attempt to sabotage her by telling prominent members of our community that she's—"

"Related to me?" I tried to keep my voice calm as I said, "Grandma Ruthie, as you can see, I have guests. Maybe we can have this discussion at another time."

"Don't you tell me when and where I can talk to you, young lady!" she yelled. "This is your mother's house. I'll come and go as I please."

"Mama, what is all this fuss about?" my mother asked as she came out of the kitchen. "Just calm down."

"Don't tell me to calm down, Sherry," Grandma Ruthie snapped. "It's bad enough that you've continued to let Jane into your home, but now you're letting her drag her undesirables into your living room? Hosting parties for them? This foolishness has gone on long enough."

"Don't talk like that in front of my friends," I told my grandmother.

"Oh, don't mind us," Jolene said, transfixed by the

family feud unfolding in front of her. I'm sure it was a novelty for her, considering that most McClaine family disputes ended in both parties phasing and proving their werewolf fighting skills. Usually naked.

"*These* are your friends?" Grandma Ruthie sneered, observing my motley group, my chosen family. "*These* are the type of people you spend time with under your great-great-grandfather's roof?"

"Watch it, Grandma," I warned her, seeing the expression of insult on Andrea's face. Dick, on the other hand, was used to that sort of comment and remained unperturbed.

"Now, let's all just calm down," Mama said in a different tone from the one she normally used during these confrontations. She wasn't trying to placate Grandma. She was just trying to keep us from coming to blows in her parlor. That was weird.

Grandma drew herself up to her full height and used her matriarch voice. "I will speak my mind, Jane."

"Well, then, you'll speak it in the kitchen." I put my hand under Grandma's elbow and not-quite-gently led her through the kitchen's swinging door.

Mama warned, "Now, Jane, be careful."

"Mama, I'm not going to hurt her." I sighed.

"No, no, I know that," Mama assured me. "It's just that all of my nice dishes are sitting out on the counter. Try not to break anything."

I barked out a laugh. "Mama!"

"Oh, she's had it coming for years," Daddy told me. "Your mama's just not ready to do it herself yet."

"I'm working on it," Mama promised. "She can't keep talking to you that way. I've let it go on for far too long. Maybe if I'd stood up to her years ago, we'd have a better relationship. You and I might have had a better relationship. I'm trying to set some boundaries with her, honey, but she's so old. And I'm so—"

"Scared of her?" I suggested.

Mama nodded. "Give her hell, baby."

That said, I squared my shoulders and marched into the kitchen to face off with my tiny septuagenarian foe.

"Be as rude to me as you'd like," I told her. "But don't ever insult the people in that room in my presence, do you understand me?"

"Don't you talk to me that way," Grandma snapped. "You were raised to have respect for your elders, Jane."

"I was raised to have respect for people who show respect to me. That's something you have never done. Now, why don't you go home to your half-dead fiancé and let me and Jenny figure out our issues for ourselves?"

Grandma stamped her size-six orthopedic shoe. "You will apologize to your sister, Jane. And you will end this foolishness with the lawsuit and give Jenny her share of the Early legacy. I command it."

I goggled at the raging geriatric before me and then burst out laughing so loudly that Gabriel stuck his head through the doorway to check on me. I waved him away as I leaned against the counter for support and let the bloody tears roll down my cheeks. "I'm sorry," I said, giggling. "Did you just *command* me to do something?

Have we met? Has that ever worked for you? Jenny got her share of the 'Early legacy.' She took it, out of the house one piece at a time, without asking. And so did you. You've been smuggling valuables out of that house since Aunt Jettie's funeral. Don't pretend otherwise."

"Let me tell you something about your precious aunt Jettie," Grandma spat.

In the corner of my eye, I could see Aunt Jettie squinting at the dry-erase marker Mama kept on her refrigerator. She grasped it and began to scrawl on the front of the fridge. Ruthie's face froze in horror as an invisible hand eked out, "Ruthie . . . This is Jettie . . . I need . . . to tell you . . . you've gotten fat."

"Jane, I don't know how you're doing that, but stop it. It's morbid," Grandma scolded, her face paling.

"I'm not doing it," I said. "I'm telepathic, not telekinetic. Aunt Jettie, maybe you shouldn't . . ."

Aunt Jettie winked at me. "Honey, she's had this coming for years."

"Jane, stop that right now!" Grandma yelled as Jettie called her a "natural brunette," underlining "natural" three times.

"It's not me, it's Jettie," I said. "She's been haunting the house ever since she died. I wasn't able to see her until I was turned."

"Of all the sick jokes," Grandma Ruthie spat. "How dare you use my sister's memory this way!"

"Oh, come on, you can believe in vampires but not in ghosts?"

Grandma Ruthie sneered at me.

I sighed. "What if I told you something that only Jettie would know?" I asked as Jettie leaned in to whisper in my ear.

Grandma's mouth flapped open like a beached guppy's. "I'm not going to—"

"Aunt Jettie says that if you don't cut me some slack, she's going to visit your mother and tell her all about what you were doing in Edgar Oliver's backseat when you were supposed to be at Bible study."

Ruthie blanched. "How could you—my mother's dead."

"Yes, but Jettie can go over to the Half-Moon Hollow Women's Clubhouse anytime she wants and visit Grandma Bebe. That's the way ghosts work. They can haunt wherever they choose, move from place to place. They even visit each other."

OK, that last part was a total bluff. Grandma Bebe was a sweet old lady who had no unfinished needlework, much less unfinished business, when she died. She moved into the light a long time ago. But Ruthie didn't know that. And I told her that so I could tell her this: "Jettie's even visited Grandpa Fred a few times. He's haunting the golf course."

Jettie cackled with glee as Ruthie's cheeks drained of color. "You tell her to stay away from my Fred."

"Tell her yourself, Grandma. She can hear you. Much better, in fact, than she could in life. Besides, you're engaged. Why should you care? And I don't think he's your Fred anymore. Remember till death do us part? He's dead. You've parted. Grandpa Fred's on the market again."

Ruthie turned a sickly white under her artfully applied Elizabeth Arden powder. "You lifeless Jezebel! You stay away from my Fred!"

At this point, it seemed a moot point to note that Aunt Jettie had actually broken up with Grandpa Fred earlier this year to take up with Mr. Wainwright. Aunt Jettie, obviously enjoying Grandma's discomfort, seemed to think so, too.

"They can't . . . all be yours. Though you . . . certainly had more . . . than your share," Jettie scribbled out in surprisingly legible script.

"Dried-up old maid!" Ruthie yelled.

"Black widow!" the refrigerator spat back.

"Unclean spirit!" Ruthie gasped.

"Varicose-veined ho!" Jettie scrawled, prompting an indignant gasp from Grandma.

"I will not stand here in my daughter's home and be insulted!" Ruthie shrieked. "Jane, you tell your great-aunt that I will not set foot in River Oaks until she can keep a civil tongue in her skull—which, by the way, never had the bone structure I have. And she was always jealous!"

"She can—"

The door slammed in dramatic fashion.

"Hear you." I finished.

Jettie slumped to the floor, clearly exhausted by her telekinetic efforts.

"That was awesome," I marveled. "Telling Grandma everything you've ever thought about her doesn't mean you have closure and you're moving on, does it? I was just getting used to having you around."

Aunt Jettie reached up to stroke her transparent hand along my cheek. "No, I could have insulted Ruthie while I was living. I'm sticking with you, kiddo."

"Lucky me." I chuckled. "My relationship with Grandma isn't ever going to change, is it?"

Aunt Jettie led me over to the swinging door, where my friends were crowded, listening. "No, baby, it's not. You and Ruthie have exactly the kind of relationship you want with each other. It was the same with us. Ruthie and I chose not to like each other. I'm not saying that's right, but it's the way things are. There's no law that says families have to be best friends. You can choose your own family, which you have. Of course, you can also choose to want a better relationship with people you were born to. It's up to you. Until then, sit at the fountain of my experience and learn Ruthie's weak points."

"'Vericose-veined ho' was one I hadn't heard before," I admitted as we pushed through the door, gently popping an eavesdropping Dick in the side of the head.

Dick cursed. Aunt Jettie shrugged. "You leave the TV on during the day. I've watched a lot of *Maury Povich.*"

14

When you've taken all you can, walk away. Be the bigger person. Or at least find a bigger person, and use your vampire strength on them. It's the sporting thing to do.

—*Love Bites: A Female Vampire's Guide to Less Destructive Relationships*

Given my history with my sister, it was inevitable, really, that we would end up wrestling in the mud, beating each other senseless with pieces of foam rubber.

The Half-Moon Hollow High parking lot was carefully organized into a carnival grid: flaccid, half-inflated bouncy houses in the south quadrant, food booths in the east, and no fun to be had in either.

At a normal Hollow charity carnival, the signs were hand-painted posterboard affairs. The games consisted of tossing pool rings over two-liter bottles or softballs into bushel baskets. You paid too much for a corn dog and a stuffed bear, you felt as if you contributed to your community, you went home.

This Halloween hell hole involved professionally

screen-printed signs and catered low-carb treats. I'd suggested a cotton-candy machine, and Head Courtney gave me a look that would have vaporized lesser women. And forget any preconceived notions of streamers or balloons. This was strictly a Martha affair, pumpkins as far as the eye could see, artfully arranged with corn and various raffia accoutrements.

God help us all.

The spookiest thing about this extravaganza was all of the women in matching pink sweatshirts manically scrambling to make the parking lot into a Halloween casbah, each terrified that Head Courtney would find her efforts wanting and put her on cleanup duty. Given Head Courtney's less-than-enthusiastic response to the prize boxes I was unloading from Big Bertha and the fact that the rest of the Courtneys had shunned me following my "outing," I already knew who was going to be manning that stupid push broom all night.

Gabriel had wanted to accompany me to the carnival, but I asked him not to come, just in case I ended up stuck in the dunking booth. I didn't want him to witness my humiliation. Fortunately, this carnival didn't have dunking booths. Or clowns, which, for me, was another bright side.

Andrea was covering the shop for me while I served my carnival sentence. She and Dick would have the place to themselves for the evening. Emery had announced his intentions to attend a Christian-themed haunted house called "Hell House" weeks before. Emery had been spending less and less time at the shop lately. Andrea hoped that meant he'd found a girl to go to prayer meetings with.

We didn't have time to overanalyze that possibility—or to consider warning the girl—because we were expecting a big Halloween-night crowd. Adults seeking a safely scary atmosphere. Teenagers looking for supplies to summon the Blair Witch. Having Emery standing in the aisles, trying to hand the customers religious tracts, would probably spoil the ambience.

Andrea was dressed up like Glinda the Good Witch, covered in pink sparkles from head to toe. The voluminous tulle skirt of her rented costume barely fit behind the coffee bar. Somehow she'd managed to talk Dick into wearing a Scarecrow costume. He looked like an extremely embarrassed Raggedy Andy doll and planned to stay in the stockroom for most of the night.

"Quit trying to put off going to the carnival," Andrea had told me, filling a bowl with those rock-hard peanut taffy candies wrapped in orange wax paper. "We'll be fine here."

"I'm going, I'm going," I muttered, sliding into my Pepto Bismol pink Chamber of Commerce sweatshirt.

"And I hope that you realize that as a witch, I am claiming double overtime for you making me work on a religious holiday," she said, gesturing to her girlie ensemble.

"Watch it, or I'll drop a house on you." I sneered as I walked out the door.

Since Jenny had yet to show up, Nice Courtney was helping me unload and distribute the prizes to the various game booths. Zeb was pitching in, too, but I think he was just there to get first crack at the funnel cakes. Imagine how sad he was when he found out that this wasn't *that kind* of carnival. The closest thing he could get to junk food was a sugar-free caramel apple. Nonetheless, he'd promised to come running, yelling that Jolene was in labor and we had to leave right away, if things got bad with the Courtneys.

"Well, it's still pretty much a high school parking lot," I said, hefting a box of free tote bags out of the trunk. "But I'm sure after everything is inflated, it will be a magical autumn wonderland."

"Just keep telling yourself that." Nice Courtney snickered. "Where do you want the popcorn balls?"

"Wherever Head Courtney won't see them," I muttered, throwing a blanket over the individually wrapped offerings from the A&P. "Don't you know this is a no-carb charity carnival?"

Nice Courtney giggled. "I'll smuggle them to the kids under the guise of giving them their complimentary hand sanitizer."

"I've had a bad influence on you," I said, gasping in mock surprise. When I made my escape from the chamber, I hoped that Nice Courtney and I could keep in touch. If nothing else, she'd proven to me that just because people are shiny and preppy, that didn't make them automatically evil. It was entirely a matter of choice. She'd single-handedly undone a lot of damage that had been inflicted in high school.

"Jane!" Judging from the look on Jenny's face as

she barreled across the parking lot, I guess she'd heard about my visit with Grandma Ruthie. And being Grandma's favorite and confidante, it was up to her to set me straight.

Speaking of shiny and evil personal choices.

"Oh, what now?" I muttered.

"Who do you think you are? Are you out of your mind, scaring Grandma like that?" she yelled, her face only inches from mine. "How could you do that to your own grandmother?"

"Let me get this straight. You're yelling at me for my behavior during a conversation with Grandma Ruthie, in which Grandma Ruthie yelled at me for how I behaved during a conversation with you?" I sighed. "Do you two organize a 'be a pain in Jane's ass' schedule?"

"She could have had a heart attack!" Jenny insisted.

"Oh, please, Ruthie's an unstoppable force of nature, like the Black Plague or Richard Simmons."

"That's it," Jenny growled through her clenched teeth. "Stay away from my family. Mama, Daddy, Grandma, the kids, everybody. You obviously don't care about us or what we think. So, just stay away from us."

"I know you've been lobbying for this since the day I was brought home from the hospital, but you can't kick me out of our family, Jen," I told her.

"It's not 'our family,'" she spat. "It's mine."

"Who the hell do you think you are?" I cried.

"Oh, don't pretend you care about being a part of this family." She sneered, snagging a foam-rubber "combat hammer" from the jousting game Head Courtney had banned from the midway. She jabbed it into my chest, backing me into the inflatable bouncy house. The giant clown head that hovered over the entrance leered down at me, and my latent coulrophobia forced me to change directions toward a muddy patch behind the staging area. But not before I was able to grab a foam weapon of my own.

Jenny poked me again with the hammer. "You've been waiting to get away from us for years. We're not smart enough for you, not sophisticated enough. Do you think we don't notice when you make your little jokes under your breath? You've wanted to get out of the Hollow for years. Why don't you just go? We certainly don't want to keep you."

"How would you know that I want to leave?" I demanded, smacking her arm with the foam. "How the hell do you think you come close to knowing how I feel about anything?" Jab to her chest. "From our long heart-to-hearts? All those nights you came over to watch *Sex and the City*?" Smack to her other arm. "Do you realize that the last time you and I had a conversation that ranged beyond the weather and whatever misinformation Mama's fed you was at Aunt Jettie's funeral luncheon? And I think you'd had too many toddies to remember."

"Oh, you're just all about the open, sisterly communication, aren't you?" She landed a respectable blow to my face, knocking me on my butt into the mud.

Considering my vampire strength and speed, that was just embarrassing.

"When have you ever made an effort to spend time

with me? To get to know me?" She hit my head to punctuate each point. "Oh, no, you're just so freaking above it all, you couldn't bring yourself to stop sniping for five minutes and just be my sister. Boring old Jenny with her husband and kids. Lame Jenny who likes to play Pictionary with her friends on Friday nights. Silly little Jenny and her silly little hobbies."

"You're mad because I won't scrapbook with you?" I asked, dumbfounded, though I'm sure it was more from the ringing blow to my skull after she managed to rip the foam off the plastic bar that supported it. I shook it off and jumped to my feet.

"Even when we were kids, you thought you were so much better than me!" Jenny yelled, panting as we circled the mud pit. A crowd had gathered, cheering us on. "I never had to worry about you copying me like a normal little sister. No, you wouldn't lower yourself to my level. I didn't like the right books. I didn't like the right music. I wasn't sarcastic enough for you. Not good enough for Jane. And then you get turned into a freaking vampire! I have to hear from Mama about your fabulous undead makeover, about your undead rights group and your hundred-and-fifty-year-old boyfriend. How can I compete with that?" Each sentence was punctuated with an impressive smack upside my head.

"You're mad because I'm cooler than you?" I guessed again, but Jenny was too worked up to notice I'd said anything. With a cry that would have made Xena proud, she swept my leg. My feet went flying out from under me, and I landed with a wet *thwap* on my back.

She growled. "You're always saying that I'm the favorite, that you get treated like a child. You're always bitching about Mama bringing food over to your house and folding your laundry. Do you know how many times she's brought dinner over to my house? Twice. After each of the boys was born. I had to go through twenty-three hours of labor without drugs just to get a damn pot pie! You think Daddy ever just drops by my house for a chat and some pizza? You think Mama calls me before I leave for work or checks on me at night when I'm home alone? No, because 'Jenny can take care of herself. She never needs any help,'" she cried, throwing her head back and screaming at the sky. I used her distraction to knock her back on her butt and pummel her repeatedly. Jenny, on the other hand, had resorted to flinging mud at me. Literally.

"Because you're perfect!" I yelled, throwing a glob of muck into her face. "Do you think it was easy growing up with *the* Jenny Early as your older sister?"

Jenny spluttered as she spit the mud out and landed an impressive clump in my hair, considering that she couldn't see. "Do you think I ever walked into a classroom where the teacher didn't say, 'Oh, you're Jenny Early's sister, we know what to expect from you?' I have to live up to the example of a woman who color-codes her underwear drawer. 'Jenny's so responsible. Jenny's house is always immaculate. Jenny cooked an entire Thanksgiving dinner and still had time to make place cards out of acorns and rice paper!' Don't blame me because you've had to live up to your own hype."

I pushed up onto my feet, scraping several layers of mud from my face. "And frankly, I'm tired of hearing 'Oh, that's just the way Jenny is' and 'She didn't do it to hurt your feelings, she just likes things a certain way.'"

"When have I ever hurt your feelings?" She gasped, trying and failing to stand. She slumped to the ground and looked up at me, squinting through the blood and sweat dripping in her eye.

"Let's see, holidays, birthdays, graduations, family dinners, baby showers, church functions, school plays. You put me at another family's table at your wedding reception, Jenny."

"Because I didn't want Grandma Ruthie to drive you crazy with questions about when you were going to get married," Jenny protested.

"And because I embarrass you," I said, wiping a clod of dirt from my cheeks.

"You don't embarrass me! You annoy me. You irritate me. You drive me up the damn wall. But OK, wait, the vampire thing, that did embarrass me a little bit. But still, I don't hate you."

Awkward silence. I looked into the future and saw the two of us, fighting and sniping at each other like Grandma Ruthie and Aunt Jettie. Though, obviously, I was immortal, ageless, and way hotter than septuagenarian Jenny. I didn't want that. I chose not to have that kind of relationship with her. But I didn't know how to fix it.

Fortunately, Jenny did.

"So, I hurt your feelings?" she asked, the corners of her mouth lifting slightly.

"Well, you don't have to look so dang pleased about it," I muttered.

"I'm not, I just, I didn't know I could have that effect on you," she admitted. "You seem . . . unflappable sometimes."

"It's all a clever ruse," I said, blowing my bangs out of my face. "I'm extremely flapped most of the time."

Jenny wiped at her eyes, but I think that had more to do with her impromptu facial than emotion. "You're going to outlive my boys, Jane. And their children, and their children. Don't you think I've thought of that? When my grandchildren are lying in the nursing home, you're going to be the one packing up everything they own and deciding who gets what. You're the sole survivor, no matter what any of us does. You're going to outlast us all. I think that's why I went so crazy about all those family heirlooms. I figured, it's going to come to you in the end anyway, so why don't you let us just borrow it for a little while? And when you said no, I don't know what came over me . . ."

"To be honest, the stuff doesn't matter that much to me, Jenny. I just like to screw with you, and this seems like the only way to get you. I'm sorry I've been a little petty about the heirlooms. I just wish you would have told me things like this before, you know, I died," I offered.

More awkward silence.

"What do we do now?" I asked, hesitantly sitting next to her.

"I don't know," she said, sinking back into the mud, clearly exhausted by her emotional unburdening.

"You could stop being such a hag at every single family gathering," I suggested.

She lifted her head to glare at me.

"Too soon?" I asked. She nodded.

"Well, we could stop sniping at each other and focus our anger where it belongs," I said.

"Mama?" Jenny asked. I nodded.

"It won't be like this forever," Jenny promised, placing a tentative hand on my shoulder.

"Yeah." I sniffled. "Someday Grandma Ruthie will be locked safely away in a home for the elderly/criminally insane."

"Jane!"

I brightened. "Can I pick the home?"

"Jane!"

"That wasn't a no."

"This has been good," Jenny said, laughing. "I feel . . . lighter somehow."

"It's amazing what a little foam battering can do," I said, nodding.

"Well, it's a good thing we stopped where we did, 'cause I was this close to kicking your ass."

I nodded to the mutilated grass behind us. "We can always jump back into the mud pit and settle things once and for all."

"This is one of those things where I'm just going to assume you're joking."

I sniffed, wincing at the sting in my lip as it healed. "Probably for the best."

Jenny watched as my skin closed and the bruising faded away. "That is really cool."

"Just one of the perks," I said, grinning as I pulled her to her feet.

Head Courtney came running over to the foam and mud wreckage. "What do you think you're doing?"

"Just settling some family issues." Jenny chuckled, wiping a spot of blood from her nose.

"I cannot believe you two! This is a *children's* carnival! You're ruining everything. Do you realize what you're going to have to do to work off this many demerits? Never in the history of the Chamber of Commerce—"

Zeb came running up, frantic. "Jane! Jane! We've got to go! Jolene's mom just called. She's in labor!"

Head Courtney seemed supremely annoyed at the interruption, but her laser-beam gaze did not falter from its target. My head.

"Zeb, it's not a big deal. You don't really have to fake Jolene being in labor."

"I'm not faking!" he screamed, his voice reaching an alarming soprano octave.

Turning my back on Courtney, I forced Zeb to bend over and take some deep breaths. "Zeb, calm down. Do you have the bag?"

"Yes, it's in the car. Jolene packed in June. She wouldn't let me help."

I reached to pat his shoulder, but when I saw how muddy my hands were, I pulled away. "I think we can all agree that was a wise choice. How about I drive to the hospital?"

"No, no, I can handle it," he said, showing me what he thought was a set of keys.

"Zeb, that's a pair of pliers."

"Maybe you should drive," he conceded.

"Jane, where do you think you're going?" Head Courtney thundered. "I'm not done with you yet."

"My friend is in labor. I'm going to the hospital."

"I did not excuse you!" Head Courtney shrieked. "You still have duties here at the carnival. There are balloons to be blown up. Garlands to be hung. Lights to be strung."

"My. Friend. Is. In. Labor," I repeated very slowly. "I'm going to be with her."

Courtney put a restraining hand on my shoulder. "You're not leaving. Abandoning an assignment at a special event will result in an automatic suspension, Jane."

"And then what? Detention? Expulsion? Firing squad? I don't have time for this. I'm leaving," I told her.

Head Courtney turned an apoplectic purple. "If you walk out now, I'll assign you to scoop horse poop after every Founders' Day parade for the next twenty years!"

"You know what, Courtney? I don't think I'm chamber material after all. So, you can take your precious Fall Festival and shove it up your—"

"Jane, we've got to go!" Zeb yelled from the car.

"Dang it, I was really looking forward to that one. Courtney, I quit."

"This is what I get for letting some filthy bloodsucker into the Chamber of Commerce!" Courtney howled. "We're going to destroy your bony, pasty ass, do you understand me, you undead bitch? When we get done with you, you won't be able to sell so much as a—"

I had stepped forward, ready to belt Head Courtney in the manner she deserved. But I was cut off by Jenny, who had cocked her fist back and knocked Courtney onto her ass, into a crate full of stuffed Spongebobs.

"Jenny!" I laughed, staring at her in surprise.

"Nobody talks to my sister that way," Jenny said, rubbing her knuckles gingerly.

"You talk to me that way," I pointed out.

"But that's different. I'm your sister. I'm allowed, but no one else is."

Tears sprang into my eyes, and I threw my arms around her. "Thanks, sis."

Jenny stiffened, then relaxed and squeezed me back. "Oh, well, anytime."

Zeb cleared his throat. "I hate to interrupt this beautiful family moment, but *my wife is having babies.* Jane, get in the car!"

We arrived at the hospital to find Mama Ginger attempting to wrestle her way past a formidable-looking nurse into the maternity ward. Unfortunately for Mama Ginger, the nurse was obviously a John Cena fan and maneuvered Mama Ginger into some sort of pretzel arm-lock position in which she was powerless.

At the sight of his mother, Zeb stopped in his tracks and muttered several of the seven words you're not supposed to say in polite company.

"How did she know Jolene was here?" I demanded. "I

thought you said you weren't going to call her until a few days after the babies are home from the hospital."

"I don't know," Zeb said, at this point on the cusp of tears. "She must have staked out our house! I thought I saw her car driving up and down our road yesterday, but I told myself even Mama wasn't that crazy."

"Obviously, you haven't paid attention for the last thirty or so years."

"I've got to get to Jolene," Zeb said, his eyes scanning the hall wildly. "If Mama sees me, I'll never get past her in time."

"Calm down. This is why Jolene appointed me waiting-room bouncer," I told him. "Because I'm willing to do things like this."

"Like what?"

"Like this." I shoved Zeb behind the admissions desk, out of Mama Ginger's sightline.

"Mama Ginger, what are you doing?" I called, waving excitedly.

Mama Ginger whirled at the sound of my voice, no longer struggling with the hospital's linebacker. With Mama Ginger distracted, Zeb slunk around the admissions desk, behind her back, and into the maternity ward. She didn't look pleased to see me, but I did provide the excuse to complain about her treatment in a really loud voice.

"This silly woman says they don't have a patient named Jolene Lavelle listed here, but I know she's here! I saw her mother's car out in the parking lot!" she cried, her voice reaching hysterical levels. Several nurses poked their heads into the hallway, but seeing who it was, they ducked back into the patients' rooms.

"Jolene must be listed as a private patient, Mama Ginger," I said, keeping my voice soothing. She shied away when I tried to loop my arm through hers, so I took her elbow and led her into the waiting room. "That means the nurse can't tell you if she's here. It's against the law."

When we walked into the waiting room, Jolene's entire pack was waiting there. It was fortunate that very few women in town seemed destined to have Halloween babies, because there would have been nowhere for their expectant families to sit. Jolene's aunts, uncles, and cousins were lounging on every available surface. Jolene's male relatives had that healthy, hearty, but blank look about them. Yes, they were nice to look at, but all hotness aside, I'd like to spend my time with someone who doesn't live his life according to tenets set forth on *Walker, Texas Ranger*. The aunts were convened in a corner, eyes darting from one side of the room to the other, absorbing it all. They all seemed to be enjoying the novelty of the experience, with the exception of Aunt Vonnie, whose mouth was puckered and unhappy.

Mimi and Lonnie McClaine, the only McClaines who liked me, were pacing the room, their stances defensive and agitated. Lonnie McClaine was picking a giant bouquet of carnations to shreds. But fortunately, there were backups. It looked as if the babies were about to be coronated. The room was absolutely packed with flowers and stuffed animals. Half of the flowers were pink, the other half were blue. They had teddy bears wearing tutus and bears wearing baseball uniforms. And a ham, which I guessed was gender-neutral.

Nothing like covering all of your bases.

Now that Jolene's presence in the labor room was confirmed, Mama Ginger started screeching, "I have a right to see my grandchildren born!"

The entire pack flinched at once. I threw myself on top of Mama Ginger, both to keep her from launching herself toward Jolene's delivery room and to serve as a shield—just in case Jolene's relatives still held grudges about Mama Ginger's wedding-related sabotage. From the floor, I looked up to find a circle of emotionally high-strung werewolves glaring down at us.

"Mimi?" I called. "Could you keep your family from, you know, committing public homicide?"

"Come on, y'all, calm down," Mimi chided, rolling her eyes. "My baby's having babies, I can't take time to bail your asses out of jail."

The pack let out a collective huff and backed down. Because Mimi was the alpha female and they pretty much had to.

"They're my grandbabies," Mama Ginger whined. "I belong in that delivery room! I've been waiting Zeb's whole life for this. I have the right to be in there with him!"

Mama Ginger tried to push up off the floor, and I forced her back down. Please, Lord, don't let someone I know see me wallowing all over the hospital floor on top of Mama Ginger. Or the cops, who would probably assume I was trying forcibly to drain her. "No, you don't,

Mama Ginger. Whosoever's hoo-ha is on display, that's the person who decides who gets to be in the room. And Jolene didn't even ask her own mother to be in the room, so that should tell you something. Zeb will come and get us when they're good and ready to see us. Now, just sit down and read a damn magazine."

Mama Ginger flopped onto a couch and petulantly flipped through a year-old copy of *Redbook*. In the choice between sitting with Jolene's extended family, most of whom didn't like me much better than Mama Ginger, or with Mama Ginger herself, I chose to lean against the wall. This proved to be a good call, as I had to launch myself after Mama Ginger from time to time whenever she made a break for the delivery rooms.

I could only fly-tackle a fifty-year-old woman so many times before I started losing my sense of humor, so I was grateful when my sensitive vampire ears picked up the sound of two strong cries down the hall.

15

The element of surprise is vastly overrated in any relationship.

—*Love Bites: A Female Vampire's Guide to Less Destructive Relationships*

Jolene had two perfectly healthy babies, in a perfectly normal delivery, in a perfectly normal hospital room.

It was a McClaine family first.

After the inevitable squabble between Mimi and Mama Ginger over who held the babies first (Mama Ginger was lucky she lost the struggle and not, say, a finger) and the pack was allowed to sniff the babies to their hearts' content, I finally made it back to Jolene's recovery room. An exhausted, beaming Zeb handed me a squirming pink bundle, and I fell in love. Little Janelyn, my namesake. The daughter I would never have. The baby I could love and spoil and then immediately hand back to her real mother. Now I knew how Aunt Jettie must have felt, to love a child so completely, to want to be a part of her life, even if you weren't a parent.

When Zeb placed a sleeping baby Joe in my hands, it seemed like an embarrassment of riches.

"They're beautiful," I told Jolene, who was fighting hard not to doze off in her hospital bed. Jolene smiled, her contentment so complete that she didn't have to respond. My eyes pricked with hot, happy tears as Janelyn studied me with her big blue eyes. Her little hand crept out from under the blanket and wrapped around my finger.

"Hello, little baby," I cooed. "I'm Auntie Jane. When your mama says it's OK, I'm going to take you guys to the library and museums and movies. I'll feed you food that'll make you hyper and nauseous, and then I'll bring you straight home. I'll help you hide your first tattoo. We're going to have a great time."

"Nice," Jolene muttered, her mouth quirked into a tired smile. I snickered.

I stroked a finger along the curve of Joe's downy-soft cheek, and for a moment, I felt a keen sense of loss for not being able to have a baby of my own.

Janelyn, who seemed incredibly strong for a newborn, even in my limited experience with babies, pulled my finger to her mouth. *Chomp!*

The moment passed.

"Ow!" I exclaimed. I gently pulled the baby's lip back to find a full set of perfect, tiny white teeth with particularly sharp-looking canines. "What the?"

"It's a wolf thing," Zeb said, looking completely unperturbed by his babies' having more teeth than their paternal grandfather.

Jolene, whose eyes were still closed, raised her hand and waggled her finger at me. "Let that be a lesson on what happens when you plan on interferin' with responsible parentin'."

"No biting the namesake, kid," I told the unrepentant infant. "Especially when the namesake has fangs."

Jolene yawned. "That just means she's happy to see you."

"I hope she's never happy to see you when you're nursing," I muttered. Jolene opened her mouth to protest. "If you launch into some story about the miracle of werewolf nipples, I will leave."

Jolene rolled her eyes and snuggled into Zeb's side. He wrapped his arm around her and cleared his throat. "So, we wanted to talk to you about something. We wanted to wait until the babies were here safely, because we didn't want to jinx ourselves."

I noted with pride how right it seemed now for Zeb to use the word *we* when it came to him and Jolene. And now he had two more little people to add to that unit. When he'd first found Jolene, it bothered me. I'd felt left out, abandoned. Zeb and I used to be a we. We were *the* we. But now, Zeb had the we he was meant to have. And I had my own we with Gabriel. This was the way it was supposed to be; growing, changing, finding your own we.

I really needed some sleep.

"We would like you to be godmother to the twins," Zeb said. "We've thought this over very carefully. And we can't imagine asking anyone else . . . so, no pressure."

"But I'm not all that religious, Zeb. You should probably appoint someone who, you know, hasn't been tossed out of their church for being an unholy monster, to head the kids' spiritual development."

"It's more of a guardianship thing," Zeb assured me. "If anything ever happened to me or Jolene, we would want to know that you would be there for the kids. No one would take care of them like you, love them like you would."

"And you're the least crazy person available for the job," the barely conscious Jolene added.

"Well, that's sort of sad," I told them.

"We know," Zeb admitted. "Doesn't make it untrue."

I peered down at the sleeping bundles in my arms. The burden of their weight seemed just a little bit heavier. Could I accept this kind of responsibility? Despite working with children for most of my adult life, I'd never really taken care of any. I didn't have the kind of life that was conducive to child-rearing. I slept all day. There was rarely solid food in my house. There were lots of pointy, breakable objects down at child-eye level. I wanted to travel, to spend time with Gabriel, to run my shop. Was I really willing to turn all of that upside down if something happened to Zeb and Jolene? Could I raise two kids?

Baby Joe wrapped his little fingers around another of mine, mirroring his twin. I stared down at them.

Yes, I could.

I placed the babies on either side of Jolene and threw my arms around Zeb. "I will do everything I can to give the kids the kind of childhood we never had, Zeb," I promised. "Unconditional love, holidays without drunken nudity, and birthday parties where they don't end up crying. Of course, we'll have to go underground to get away from your families. But I'm sure Dick can forge the necessary paperwork."

Zeb squeezed me back. "You know, when I pictured us having this conversation, I didn't think nudity and forgery would come into it."

I sighed heavily. "And you think you know me so well."

I basked in the new parents' happy glow for a few more minutes before I excused myself. I wanted to call Gabriel, to ask why he and Dick and Andrea hadn't made it down to the hospital yet. But when I walked out into the waiting room, Gabriel was waiting for me. I threw myself into his arms, gave him a smacking kiss on the lips. "Hey, I've been wondering where you guys were. You finally dragged yourselves down here to see the babies?"

Gabriel's face was blank, taut. He had that look in his eye, the "I have bad news, and I'm trying to think of a way to break it gently" thing that always sent me into a panic. A nervous bubble of laughter escaped my throat, even as it constricted. "Gabriel, what is it?"

Gabriel swallowed hard, reaching out to take my hand. "It's Andrea."

"What do you mean, it's Andrea? Is she hurt? Did something happen?" I babbled, panic racing through my chest.

My brain reeled through a number of horrible scenarios. Car accident. Robbery at the store. Halloween prank gone awry. The last thing I'd said to her was, "Watch it, or I'll drop a house on you." And she'd laughed. Oh, God, what if she was dead and those were my last words to her?

"Dick was at the store with her, and he went to run an errand right before closing. When he came back, Andrea was gone. Her car was missing. But the cash register was full. And Dick could smell . . ."

By now, tears were streaming down my cheeks. "What? Gabriel, what's going on?"

"Dick could smell blood, Andrea's blood."

I don't remember much about Gabriel driving us to the shop. The darkened streets of downtown passed by in a blur as my mind raced. Where could Andrea be? I tried to convince myself that it was perfectly reasonable to think that she might have simply hurt herself at the shop, that she'd driven herself to get help. It was so much better than the alternative, that someone had taken Andrea, dragged her, bleeding, out of the shop in her silly pink ballgown. What if it was one of us? I'd been so stupid. I put her right in the line of fire, working in a vampire shop when her rare blood type called out to the undead like a fine, irresistible wine. I wiped at my eyes, knowing it was pointless to try to stop the tears from falling.

"Dick called the police," Gabriel said, his voice bleak. "He's waiting at the shop for them."

I moaned softly, leaning my head against the seat. For

Dick to be willing to call the police, the situation had to be desperate.

We would have been better off calling Barney Fife.

Gabriel dropped me off at the shop. He thought his time would be better spent contacting the local Council members and various underworld characters who might have information about Andrea. So far, I had a lot more faith that he might find her than in the combined forces of the Half-Moon Hollow Police Department.

To say that the police were not exactly concerned about finding a woman who worked in an occult shop and lived with her vampire boyfriend would be a grand understatement. Sergeant Russell Lane, whom I'd gone to school with for thirteen years, seemed far more interested in treating us like suspects than in taking down any information about Andrea.

"Didn't your boss die under strange circumstances here last year?" Sergeant Lane asked, as he scribbled notes in his duty notebook. He looked at Dick and me with a gleam of distrust, even malice, in his eyes.

"I don't consider a seventy-nine-year-old man having a heart attack while moving heavy boxes to be strange," I said, struggling to keep calm. I was a giant, exposed, twitching nerve just standing there, waiting for news, trying to keep from flashing my fangs at Lane.

Lane shrugged. "I just think it's kind of a weird coincidence that your boss dies in the store, and a year later, your employee disappears from the store," he said, giving me a long, appraising look. "Andrea Byrne was a registered blood surrogate, wasn't she?"

"What does that have to do with anything?" Dick growled.

"And you would be?" Lane asked.

"Dick Cheney. I live with Ms. Byrne."

"That name sounds familiar," Lane said, scratching it in his little notebook for future reference. "So, let me get this straight. She lives with a vampire, works for a vampire, and spends her free time letting vampires feed from her."

Sergeant Lane closed his little notebook. "Well, we'll keep an eye out for her. But we can't do much until an official missing-person report is filed."

"I thought I was filing a missing-person report. I know a person who is missing, and I'm reporting it to you," I said, placing a restraining hand on Dick when he took a menacing step toward the officer.

"Look, she could have run out to the grocery store for all you know. Or gone to a costume party," Lane said. "It's Halloween. It's a busy night for us. We're not going to be able to do much for you, anyway. Why don't you wait twenty-four hours and come down to the department to file a report if she doesn't turn up?"

"But she could be anywhere!" I cried. "Look, my friends and family members have been abducted before, I know the signs when I see them."

"I'm sure that being associated with you has its problems." He ignored the enormous amount of stink-eye I was sending his way. "But I can't do anything about a woman who just decided to flake out of work. Besides, she's a grown woman; if she wants to take off for a while, she can."

I opened a door into Sergeant Lane's brain and saw three things. One, he seemed to think that Dick and I had drained Andrea dry and stashed the body and were reporting her missing to cover our tracks. Two, if we had killed Andrea, or even if she was legitimately missing, he thought she probably got what she'd deserved. What could a girl expect when she hung out with this kind of crowd? He planned to go back to the station, make a joke about it at roll call, and forget Andrea ever existed. And three, he had been staring at my boobs through the entire interview. At this point, I've come to expect this of human men and realize that it has nothing to do with me. They want to see all women naked. Except for their mothers.

"Andrea doesn't just flake out," I told him. "This is completely out of character for her. If you think we did something to her, then take us to the station and question us so you can get that out of the way and you can start looking for her."

"Well, I can't exactly hook you up to a lie detector when your heart doesn't beat, now, can I?" Sergeant Lane pointed out.

"Pardon me for being blunt, but she's a missing pretty young woman," I told him. "We both know there's going to be a CNN van parked outside any minute. And I'm going to be more than happy to tell the nice reporters all about your lack of interest in finding my friend."

Lane was smug now. "I think once they hear about Ms. Byrne's background, they won't be all that surprised."

I growled. "Is it uncomfortable to have your head jammed that far up your—"

"Jane!" Dick said, locking his fingers around my wrist, to keep me in place.

"You two have a Happy Halloween, now." Lane sneered and ambled out of the shop.

I let loose a stunning string of profanities and chucked the pewter fairies across the room, shattering one of the little tableside reading lamps. I expected Dick to be having the same reaction, but when I turned, he was sitting on the floor, rubbing a hand over his chest.

"I can't take this," he said, his sea-green eyes round and wet. "I can't—I can't take not knowing. What if she's hurt? What if she's scared? What if this is my fault? What if someone I made one of my stupid back-alley deals with came here and took her to get back at me? I shouldn't have left her alone. But I wanted to—it seemed so important to surprise her."

His hands shaking, Dick took a little blue velvet box out of his back pocket and opened it. Inside was a simple white gold band set with a little heart-shaped ruby. It was obviously old and worn but had recently been cleaned. "I went to pick this up. I thought I'd go the whole traditional, down-on-one-knee route. I thought she'd think it was funny, getting a proposal while she was all dressed up like a princess. When I got back, she was gone.

"She's my happy ever after, Jane," he said quietly. "What am I going to do without her?"

"You won't have to worry about that," I told him. I

was trying so hard to keep my voice upbeat, hopeful, that my throat seemed to burn. "We'll find her."

Dick's face crumpled in on itself, for the briefest of moments. He sniffed and pushed to his feet. "I have to go somewhere, do something, or I'm going to go crazy. You just stay here, OK? In case she calls or the police . . . Wait for me or Gabriel to call you. You call me if you hear *anything*. Got it?"

I nodded. "Dick . . ."

He kissed my forehead and disappeared out the shop door.

Sitting at the counter staring at the phone was making me crazy. I needed to do something with my hands. I cleaned up the mess I'd made of the broken lamp and put the damaged fairies in my office. I wiped down shelves, restocked the coffee bar. I found a pile of unclaimed special orders under the counter with a note from Andrea: "For Jane, reshelve using your 'crazy system.'"

Caught between laughing and bursting into tears, I hauled the books to the shelves, replacing them in the stock one by one. *Zombies: Fact vs. Fiction, On the Hunt for the Wendigo, Chupacabra and Other Demons of the Southern Hemisphere,* and finally, *Rituals and Love Customs of the Were.* I ran a finger down the worn spine of the final title.

"Oh, crap." I sighed, thinking of the box of Mr. Wainwright's books I'd culled from my personal library all those months ago. With everything that was going on, I'd put them in my trunk and forgotten about them. I grabbed my keys and retrieved the box from Big Bertha, finally realizing how early it was when I saw the pink streaks of dawn creeping across the horizon. There was no time to make it home, and I didn't want to leave the shop at this point, anyway. I wondered idly how sun-safe the storage room was, flipping through the book covers on my way back into the shop.

I shelved *Rituals and Love Customs of the Were* with our other copy and took *The Spectrum of Vampirism* over to the special-collections display case. When he'd given it to me, Mr. Wainwright had said it was a particularly rare volume, written by a respected Harvard academic, meaning that I felt even worse about leaving it in my trunk for so long. I carefully wiped off the cover with a soft cloth and unlocked the display case.

The sheer violent force of the blow to my back sent me crashing into the case, splintering the glass. I landed with a thump on the carpet, razor-sharp shards jutting from my arms. One of them must have hit an artery, because my blood was forming a rather large pool on the carpet.

Ow.

"So, you've had it the whole time?" an indignant voice above me growled.

Through the gray haze of pain, I looked up and tried to focus on Emery's face. He sneered down at me, just as pasty as ever but not quite as sweaty. In fact, there was a subtle radiance to his pale, round face. His eyes were no longer dusty brown but a clear, liquid amber color. And his teeth were brilliant, white, and . . . pointy.

Shit.

I shouted, "Emery, who the hell was dumb enough to turn you into a vampire?"

I tried to push up from the floor, but the itching torment of my skin expelling thousands of tiny glass slivers left my arms weak. I glared up at him. I knew that eventually, the shock of Emery's betrayal would catch up with me, but for now, keeping up a sarcastic, condescending front seemed for the best.

"My mistress, Jeanine, only granted me the gift a few short days ago. First, I had to prove I was worthy." Emery sighed. "She found me. She showed me the truth about the world, about vampires. She gave me answers I'd been looking for all my life. She saved me. And she asked so little of me. And I failed!"

Emery kicked out like a preschooler having a tantrum at Wal-Mart. His foot caught me in the ribs, knocking me back against the counter. Dazed, I followed his line of sight to the book still clutched in my hand. Even through the sharp throb of pain, my brain spun. The break-in. Emery's overzealous interest in the inventory. His need to search through every single title. He'd been looking for one specific book all this time. And I'd had it in my trunk. If I hadn't been bleeding profusely, I might have laughed.

"You're an evil henchman, Emery? Seriously? *You* broke into the shop while I was out of town? Why would you do that? And why the big charade with arriving weeks later all scruffy and jet-lagged? I would have given you anything you asked for. Why are you doing this?" I asked.

I wasn't sure what made this situation worse, my stupidity or the choking regret over my stupidity. I'd felt sorry for this doorknob, guilty for not being nicer to him. And he'd been working for Jeanine since the moment I'd met him. He'd deceived us all, turned on his only family to help that crazy bitch terrorize me. I felt my fangs extend over my lips as I ground my teeth together. The anger felt good. It felt clear compared with a muzzy confusion of pain and worry.

Emery smiled down at me. In a patient voice, he said, "I need that book, Jane. I need *The Spectrum of Vampirism* to restore Mistress Jeanine to her full health."

"Anything except that," I spat, rising to my feet. Glass tinkled to the floor from my sleeves. "Now, tell me where Andrea is."

Emery shoved me back down onto the floor, which, given the woozy feeling in my head, was probably where I needed to be anyway. Still holding on to the book, I crawled behind the bar to the fridge. Emery followed, seemingly undisturbed by the blood trail I was leaving.

"I'm a new man, Jane. Capable of things I never dreamed of," he intoned with a faraway expression. "Mistress Jeanine touched me with her dark wisdom. I worship at her feet. I lick the ground where she treads."

I took three bottles of Faux Type O from the fridge and poured one after another down my throat. Wiping my mouth, I peered up at him. My vision was starting to clear. My wounds closed. I was able to flex my arms. My legs felt stronger. I was practically Popeye the freaking Sailor. I hefted myself to my feet. "Adolescence left deep,

deep scars on you, didn't it? I think you need to meet this guy I went to high school with. Name's Adam. I think you'd get along,"

The dreamy note vanished from Emery's face. He'd just realized his mistake, not taking the book from me immediately. Being so new, he didn't realize how quickly we recovered with the help of an infusion. He took a menacing step toward me; my hands tightened around the cover. "I need that book. The mistress demands it. If I don't bring it to her, she will plant her heel on my—"

"I do not want to hear about your sexcapades with Crazy Jeanine," I told him.

"Oh, no, I am not worthy of the mistress's attentions," he said in a hushed, reverent tone.

"Then why do you keep calling her 'mistress'?"

"Because she controls everything I do," he said. "What I eat, when I sleep, how long I'm allowed to go without—"

"I get the picture, Emery. Please don't give me details. And stop talking about her feet, it's icking me out."

"I'm finally coming into my own, Jane," he growled. "Do you know what it's like, living your whole life, waiting for it to start? Knowing that there's something out there for you, something that will complete you, but not knowing what it is?"

"All I'm is hearing is 'blah, blah, blah, I'm a loony tune enjoying my moment,'" I told him. "Now, tell me where Andrea is."

"If you don't give me that book, Jane, I'm going to have to take it," Emery said, drawing himself up before rushing at me. Fully charged from my bloody snack, I punched him in the forehead with all the force I had. And now that he'd lost the element of surprise, Emery wasn't that much of a fighter.

"Ow!" he cried, collapsing in a heap on the floor.

"Emery, please don't do this. You're Mr. Wainwright's family. As much as I hate what you've done, I don't want to—dang it." I sighed as he charged me again, and I punched him in the forehead. Again. "Stay down, Emery."

"Give me that book," Emery demanded.

"Hmmm . . . *No*," I roared.

"Jane, you leave me no choice." Emery pulled a large wooden crucifix out of his jacket.

I gave him an acidic smile. "Sorry, I'm kind of at peace with the whole Christianity thing."

"I thought you might say that." Emery pressed the center of the crucifix, and a stake snicked out. He raised the stake and charged me again. And I punched him in the forehead. Again.

"Why aren't you learning from this?" I grunted, staring down at Emery's crumpled body.

I almost felt bad about the whole thing, right up until I got knocked unconscious. One minute, I was looking down at Emery, and the next, white-hot pain sliced through the back of my neck, paralyzing every muscle in my body. My legs folded under me, and I crashed to the floor, my breath wheezing out in a weak "uhhf" just before my eyelids slid shut.

And for the record, yes, my own stun gun was used to incapacitate me.

16

Change is inevitable. It's necessary for the growth of a relationship. But most of the time, it just plain sucks.

—*Love Bites: A Female Vampire's Guide to Less Destructive Relationships*

When I came to, I was tied up in the basement of a very old home. My mouth tasted like old pennies. And the back of my neck was stinging like crazy. I sat up. But the swishing sensation in my head made me flop back to the stone floor. The ceiling above was solidly constructed and oddly familiar. I looked around, recognizing several of the old boxes and crates.

"Crap," I groaned.

I'd been abducted and taken to River Oaks. This was just embarrassing.

I made another attempt at sitting up, wincing at the raw hemp rope binding my wrists and ankles. Double crap. I leaned against a box of old Christmas decorations and squinted toward the low, small cellar window. It was dark outside. What time was it? Had I been out all day?

Where was Emery? Where was Gabriel? He had to be frantic by now.

Through the fuzzy sensations lingering in my head, I tried to remember if I kept anything down here that could cut through the ropes. I scanned the room for the outline of gardening tools or a saw. In the dark, I could make out the faint pink glow of a polyester Halloween costume.

"Andrea!" I whispered at her prone form. "Andrea, are you OK? Please, answer me. Andrea?"

Andrea was clothed, thank goodness, and lying on an old table of my grandpa's. Her clothes were stained with old blood. She looked as if she was sleeping, but there was no breath, no pulse that I could hear. She was so pale and small. My heart caught in my throat, the edges of my vision tinged a bright, angry crimson. Something was cutting into my lip. It took me a few seconds to recognize that it was my fangs and the blood welling into my mouth was my own, stoking an already scorching hatred for Emery.

"I'm afraid our Andrea is indisposed," Emery said fondly, emerging from a corner to sit at Andrea's shoulders. "She's so beautiful, like a princess in a fairy tale." He chuckled, stroking her hair. "Only, the prince's kiss is what put her to sleep." Emery's smile was sudden, sharp, and vicious. "She was delicious, your Andrea. Well, she's my Andrea now."

"I'm going to kill you," I promised.

Emery's cool, calm Lestat demeanor changed at my harsh tone. "I did it for her!" he hissed. "For my mistress! To prove that I am worthy of her dark gift." He seemed to compose himself. "To hurt you. Oh, how she loves to hurt you." He smiled to himself. "Andrea was my very first kill. It was so much easier than I thought it would be. After drinking that horrible bottled blood, it was a pleasure. You must know. You have to have tasted her, at least once. Giving her my own blood wasn't as easy, though. The mistress is right, it's quite exhausting."

"You turned her?" The division of my feelings tore a hole through my chest, shock and horror that Andrea had been forced out of her human life, relief that she wasn't entirely gone, grief for Dick.

"The mistress promised her to me," he said, running his hand along her still, white cheek. He smiled up at me. "And she said I could have you, as well. I have needs, Jane, needs I've denied for far too long. And since I'm not worthy of the mistress's attentions . . ."

"Oh, just back up the crazy truck, there, Foot Boy. There will be no *having*. Got it?"

"You have such a . . . unique way with words, Jane." A soft, feminine voice chuckled in the darkness. Cindy, our latte-loving teen good-luck charm, stepped into the dim light. The green was washed out of her now-dark hair. It was drawn back into a high, Victorian style, oddly in sync with her ornately embroidered black skirt and white silk blouse. She wasn't wearing makeup, and her black nail polish had been removed. My instinct to protect the girl I'd grown so fond of jumped ahead of my logical thinking skills.

"Cindy, get out of here!" I cried. "You could get hur— oh, for God's sake, you're one of them, aren't you?"

She *tsk*ed and shook her head sympathetically. "Poor Jane."

"I trusted you. I was nice to you. I gave you free coffee!"

She smiled and pinched my cheek. "Yes, and it gave me time to watch you, to listen to you whine and complain to your friends when you thought I was reading. It's amazing what people will say when they think no one's listening. It made writing those letters so much easier."

"Wait a minute, you're Jeanine?" I gasped. "But I saw inside your head. You're a newborn!"

Jeanine took out a vial of rewetting drops and moistened her eyes. She dabbed delicately with a lacy handkerchief. She flashed a simpering smile my way as Emery reverently lowered a red velvet ceremonial cape onto her shoulders. "I'm a very talented actress. I could have been one of the great ladies of the theater, if Grandmama had allowed me to pursue it. But theater people were barely better than circus folk at the time, you see. Really, you were disappointingly easy to fool. I knew you'd try to read my mind, so I came up with that story about poor little Cindy, the misunderstood, lonely newborn, looking for a place to belong. I let you see that much. I knew you wouldn't be able to turn me away. You never even suspected me. Of course, at the end of the day, I had to flush the toxins from your wretched coffee out of my system, but it was worth it. I learned so much about you, Jane, and it helped me direct Emery in how to best . . . instruct you."

"Where exactly did you two meet up, psychoticsingles .com?"

Jeanine's hand snaked out from under her cape, forcing the stun gun against my arm. The quick metallic sting of the current locked my jaw muscles. "Ow!" I grunted.

"There's no reason to be rude, Jane. I don't see why the two of us can't be friends," Jeanine said, smiling guilelessly. "I mean, honestly, we have so much in common. A love of reading, complicated relationships with our mothers, loving the same man. With Gabriel as a sire, we're practically sisters. So let's talk, the two of us. Just a couple of girlfriends."

"I am not braiding your hair," I growled.

In a cheerful voice, she said, "I'm just a good Catholic girl at heart, Jane. I'm very comfortable in churches, convents, monasteries. After Gabriel had so callously rejected my latest round of calls and letters, I traveled all the way to Guatemala, to rest in a little seminary high in the Sierra Madre de Chiapas. And one day, I wandered into the chapel to find Emery."

"She was an answer to my prayers. I thought she was an angel." He sighed. "My dark angel."

"I think I just threw up a little bit in my mouth," I muttered, wincing when Jeanine gave me a light zap with the stun gun.

"Emery was so eager to please," she said, stroking her fingers along the curve of his face. He leaned into her caress like an adoring spaniel. "So considerate. He promised to do anything he could to restore my health, even when it meant bringing me the blood of every student in the seminary. Imagine my shock when I found out he was from Half-Moon Hollow, the birthplace of my dear sire. Emery told me about his uncle's bookshop, about a book he remembered from his boyhood, which described a ritual to 'revampirize' an ailing immortal." She lifted the copy of *The Spectrum of Vampirism*, stained with my blood. "It was fate, you see, the book, Emery, Gabriel, all circling this silly little town. I wanted to leave immediately, but then he got a message from you, saying that his uncle had died. And he learned that you'd been given the store and all of its contents. That complicated matters for us. So, we waited and we watched."

Her lip curled. "And I saw you with him, with my Gabriel. How could I help but reach out to him? You took my sire away. He stopped thinking about me when you came along."

I narrowed my eyes, thinking of all the stress she'd put Gabriel through. "He stopped thinking about you a long time before that." I let out a loud "Gah!" when she shocked me again. "OK, I will admit that was not a constructive thing to say."

"I don't suppose you've guessed what my special ability is, have you, Jane?" She preened, as if she hadn't just sent thousands of volts into my body. "You might call it having a 'one-track mind.' If I focus on someone hard enough, I can find them anywhere. No matter where they are, no matter how hard they try to hide, I just have a knack for guessing where they'll turn up next."

"Your special power is you're a supernaturally gifted stalker?" I panted. "Gabriel really *did* screw up by turning you."

She ignored me, possibly because the stun gun still

had to recharge after the last round. "I'll admit Gabriel's given me a challenge over the last few decades. He's become very skilled at keeping his plans vague, at bouncing between this horrible little shanty town and the rest of civilization. I was always guessing with him. But you, oh, Jane, you were very easy to follow. You were a considerable help to me while Gabriel dragged you from city to city, hotel to hotel. You were practically a homing beacon. I didn't even have to try, which was fortunate for me. I find travel to be so draining. It was all I could do to write those notes and leave them at your hotels before collapsing into a tea-tree and eucalyptus bath. They're very restorative, you know. You might try it sometime, Jane. You're looking a bit tired."

"I'm not tired, I'm concussed."

She chuckled, making calf-eyes at Emery as he lit several oil hurricane lamps I'd kept in storage for power outages. "Meanwhile, Emery stayed here. He wasn't very happy with you either, Jane. You took over the store. You were handed everything his uncle had left in this world. He wanted to punish you. It's another interest we share. So, I let my Emery indulge his need for petty revenge. I helped him learn to guard his thoughts around you. I let him play his little games with you. I even fed him a few ideas. Rifling through your purse and finding that silly little can of vampire mace was particularly inspiring."

Suddenly, the disappearance of my mace made a lot more sense, though I had to wonder what sort of evil vampire ninja skills Jeanine had employed to get at my purse without anyone seeing. I grunted, wanting to smack myself on the forehead. I'd told her to help herself to coffee whenever she needed a refill. My purse was under the counter.

No more trusting teenagers, ever.

I smiled nastily. "Well, it backfired, because sending me a box full of silver is what brought Gabriel and me back together. So . . . thanks for that."

A black sneer flickered across her features before she forced them back into her mask of serene control. I waited for her to shock me again, but the sting didn't come. When I opened my eyes, Jeanine was holding the book in her hand, poring over whatever ritual she was convinced would turn her into a real girl.

"Are you sure this is the right book?" she demanded as Emery cowered before her.

"Of course, mistress," he simpered.

She growled. "But there's hardly anything in here. There's no special ceremony for re-turning a vampire, just a footnote about whether it's possible. The footnote says, 'Highly unlikely.'"

Emery blanched at her tone, spluttering, "B-but-but I didn't make any guarantees, mistress, I said I vaguely remember reading something as a child—"

"You said a little more than that, Emery. As I recall, you seemed sure that you knew how to cure me. You promised!" She stamped her foot.

I hissed out a hoarse laugh. "Emery is your go-to guy in this scenario? You're the worst nemesis I've ever had. *Mama Ginger* has better plotting skills."

"Emery," she said absentmindedly. Emery reached out and backhanded me, his fingers striking my jaw with bone-buckling force.

Ow.

As I stretched my aching jaw, I realized Jeanine was trying to prevent hurting me too badly. The stun gun was enough to keep me in line, but she didn't trust herself to really lash out. She needed me. And the only reason I could think of for keeping me alive would be to—

"Gabriel," I groaned. "You want Gabriel here for whatever weirdo ritual you have planned. I've been relegated to bait. This is insulting."

"Don't be insulted, Jane," she said, her lip drawn up into a bewildered pout. "It's a compliment, really. Gabriel cares for you. He's almost obsessed with your safety and happiness. As soon as he realizes you're not at the shop, he'll come running here looking for you. And your . . . predicament is just the incentive he needs to cooperate. Do you realize that I've been trying to contact him for decades, but the first time he ever responded in any way was when I told him I was going to talk to you, to hurt you? Personally, I don't see the attraction." Her rosebud features grew dark, petulant. "It's not fair. He cared enough to turn you completely, to make sure you could take care of yourself, fend for yourself. He turned me into less. He made me into a ghoul."

"You are not a ghoul. You're a hypochondriac. You travel with a humidifier, for goodness sake." When a lightning-quick flash of insane fury crossed Jeanine's features, I had an idea. If there was no bait, there was no trap, no reason for Gabriel to be here. Jeanine would be left with no big evil plan. She wouldn't be able to hurt him. And with me gone, Jenny would finally get the house. Now that my life seemed to be finally, truly coming to a close, I found I didn't mind so much. Annoying her didn't seem so important now. It really sucked that I was reaching some level of emotional maturity moments before imminent death.

I snickered loudly, making my voice as condescending and Courtney-like as possible. "You don't even have the guts to come after me yourself. You had Foot Boy do your dirty work for you."

Jeanine rolled her eyes but didn't respond. I dug deeper into the bitchy-insult well, lowering my voice to a sly, sneering tone. "You know, Gabriel told me all about your little crush on him, when you were human. Following him around like a little puppy dog, making a nuisance of yourself. I pointed out that not much has changed, since you're still doing pretty much the same thing. And we laaaaaaaughed. Did I mention we were lying in my bed, naked, at the time?"

Jeanine's teeth ground together as she barked out, "Emery!"

Emery turned and really walloped me. Unfortunately, he did it at just the right angle, so that my temple barreled into the corner of a china crate. I slumped to the ground, my head spinning, blood seeping through the neck of my sweatshirt. I was vaguely aware of my arms being pinned under my back, the ropes biting into my wrists. So, instead of dying to protect my beloved, I was going to wake up with a headache and a serious case of pins-and-needles in my arms.

Overall, not my most well-thought-out plan.

As unconsciousness tinged the edge of my vision, I glared up at Jeanine. "I don't like you."

Jeanine grinned, patting my cheek. "I'm glad we've got that out in the open."

From the dark, bottomless pit of oblivion, I heard shouting. I blinked a few times. I heard Dick's pained howl and his voice moaning, "No, baby, no," over and over. When my eyes could focus, I saw him in the corner, Andrea's body pressed against his chest, his face buried in her neck.

Gabriel's voice was louder, stern. "Stay down, Emery!"

I sat up, wincing at the numbness in my arms. I shook my head, trying to fling away the last fuzzy spots in my head.

"Gabriel?" I peered up, seeing Gabriel choking Emery against a wall as Jeanine stood nearby, wringing her hands. She looked so helpless and panicked. It seemed that faced with the object of her obsession and fury, our mutual sire, all of her high-flown evil plans had evaporated, and she was reduced to dithering like a flustered schoolgirl. I almost felt sorry for her.

But not really.

Gabriel dropped a barely conscious Emery at the sound of my hoarse whisper. Emery slumped against a stack of crates, toppling them over. I heard Jeanine gasp as one of the unlit hurricane lamps shattered near her feet, soaking her cloak in the lamp oil.

"Jane?" he murmured, probing my temple gently with his fingertips. Between the barely healed cuts on my arms, the head wound, and the drying maroon blood soaked into my sweatshirt, I imagined I wouldn't be winning any beauty contests soon. Sadly, at this point, I think Gabriel was used to seeing me this way.

"I'm really sorry about this. Emery got me from behind." I groaned. "That's not what it sounds like."

"Are you all right?" he asked.

"Bored and annoyed, a little worried about Emery's mental state. But yeah, I'm fine," I grumbled, trying to push to my feet. "Nope, I was wrong, my head really hurts."

"Come upstairs," he said, taking my arm and supporting my weight. "Jeanine, I've called the Council here. You've gone too far this time. When they see . . ." Gabriel's voice broke as he took in the sight of Dick huddled protectively over Andrea. "There's nothing I can do to help you."

"That's not true," Jeanine mewled. "You and I have a long-owed debt to settle, Gabriel."

"I don't owe you anything," he growled, pushing past her and dragging me with him.

"All of this is your doing! *Your* fault. You made me what I am!"

The pitiful voice, the sight of Jeanine's twisted baby-doll visage, were playing Gabriel's guilt strings like a virtuoso. I could see the conflict play out on his face. After everything, he wanted to try to find a way to help her. He turned, leaving me to stand as my sense of equilibrium returned. "I shouldn't have left you alone, Jeanine," he said. "And I'm sorry for that. But I was afraid of you, afraid of the things you would do. I was ashamed of you. I thought that you would listen to Violette, that she could teach you."

"She didn't teach me anything!" Jeanine pouted. "It was just more rules! More rules than my Grandmama had. Don't feed from the weak. Don't kill for the sake of killing," she said, mimicking a heavy French accent. "It was so much worse than my life. You left me with that. I didn't have anyone to turn to. Please, just give me more of your blood. Make me whole. The Council will understand that I was sick and not in my right mind, that I had no choice but to do what I've done, especially when you talk to them."

He took a deep breath. "I won't do that, Jeanine. I won't speak for you and I won't give you another drop of my blood. There's no such thing as a re-turning."

"Yes, there is!" Jeanine screamed.

"Jeanine," he growled.

I cleared my throat. "Gabriel, let's not antagonize the crazy with the stun gun."

"Jane, don't help. Wait—she has your stun gun?"

I shrugged my shoulders, my expression apologetic.

"I can make you happy, Gabriel, if you just give me the chance. But now that you have *her*, you don't even think of me," Jeanine begged, her voice reedy and desperate. "Can't you see what she's done to me, by coming between us? I need you."

Oh, Lord, it was Gabriel's kryptonite, a lady in distress. But instead of reaching out to Jeanine, he simply shook his head.

"I can't keep living like this," Jeanine cried, real tears of blood streaming down her cheeks now. "I won't keep living this half-life. I want the gift of immortality or no life at all!"

"I gave you the gift of immortality," Gabriel said, his voice cold now. "And you've wasted it."

With a mad cry, Jeanine sparked the stun gun and moved it to the hem of her cloak. "I'll end it now. I'll take you all with me."

"You won't do it. You're terrified of death," I told her. I thought reminding her of the immediate dusty consequences would make her drop the stun gun, but Jeanine seemed to take my words as a challenge. She sneered and pressed it down, the arc of electrical energy combusting the lamp-oil-soaked cloth with a bright orange glow. Within seconds, her clothes were engulfed. Gabriel threw me behind him. But Jeanine stood perfectly still, a shocked look freezing her face in a mask of horrified regret, as if she couldn't believe what she had done in a toddler's fit of temper. Her panicked hands beat at the flames as they licked up her clothes, toward her face. There was a horrible scream as Jeanine's body seemed to disintegrate before our eyes. Her face turned gray, then black, then crumbled into dust. The flaming cloak crumpled to the floor.

I watched as the puddle of oil caught, the fire inching toward the piles of boxes and wooden crates. The flames speared higher and higher, until I thought they might be brushing against the ceiling. We would be trapped. River Oaks would burn. The cellar was going to catch like a Roman candle if—

I shrieked as a blue-white cloud exploded in my face. Dick was standing over Jeanine's remains with the fire extinguisher I kept near the cellar steps. With tears streaking down his deadened, inanimate face, he sprayed foam over the remaining hot spots, dropped the red tank with a clang, and shuffled back to Andrea without a word.

The cold blast from the fire extinguisher seemed to revive Emery, who slowly pushed himself up from the floor. Gabriel sprang to his feet, putting himself between Emery and me.

"Mistress?" Emery mumbled. His dull, unfocused eyes caught sight of the pile of ashes and the red cape, absorbing what it meant. He howled, "No! *No!*"

Emery scanned the room for signs of Jeanine, for an explanation of what had happened. Seeing Dick crouched over Andrea, Emery cried, "That is my mate!" When he advanced on them, Dick looked up with what can only be called a predatory snarl and roared. Even I jumped back. Gabriel's grip tightened around my arm.

"Emery, I think you should back away and sit still until the Council gets here," Gabriel seethed.

Emery's brow furrowed, even as he circled Andrea, trying to find a weakness in Dick's defenses. "What council?"

"The Council for the Equal Treatment of the Undead. The governing body of vampires who are going to lower the boom on you after what you've done," I said.

Emery snorted derisively. "We're vampires, Jane. We're above the law, the constraints of human society. There are no rules for us anymore. It's why I wanted to be a vampire in the first place."

"Actually, there's a whole butt-load of rules, Emery. The Council has rules for everything, especially when it comes to abducting and forcibly turning humans. It's bad for our public image. All those months at the bookshop, and you never bothered reading anything, did you? You bought into Jeanine's promise of a 'dark gift' without even thinking about it. And now, you're going to get the Trial."

"What's the Trial?" Emery asked, his bravado suddenly gone.

"What you've done to Andrea is going to pale in comparison."

As if on cue, Ophelia arrived at the top of the cellar with her Council posse: gaunt and grumpy Peter Crown, a Colonel Sanders lookalike improbably named Waco Marchand, and cool blond Sophie. I was never so glad to see bureaucrats in all my life. It was like a pale, elegant cavalry. Emery had lost all nerve at this point and was cowering behind a junk pile.

Ophelia, a 300-year-old teenager who was wearing skinny dark-wash jeans and a Jonas Brothers T-shirt, took in the sight of Andrea's crumpled body, the pile of ashes on the floor, and my bloodied, chainsaw-massacre-survivor look.

"What did you do this time, Jane?" she demanded, rolling her eyes.

"This time, it really wasn't me," I protested.

"You always say that," she pointed out.

"It was this newborn, Emery Mueller," Gabriel said, dragging Emery up by the collar and pushing him toward Peter. "He kidnapped Andrea Byrne and turned her against her will. Under the direction of his sire, Jeanine, he also attempted to kill Jane with aerosol silver weeks ago, then assaulted and kidnapped her tonight."

"That's quite the rap sheet for a newborn," Ophelia said, nudging Jeanine's remains with her toe.

Gabriel cleared his throat. "When Dick . . . when he's able to speak, he will corroborate my story."

"I see," she said, mulling that over as she scraped the ashes from her hot-pink Converse sneakers. "And I take it this is Jeanine?" Gabriel nodded curtly. "When I told you to take care of the matter, Gabriel, I didn't mean to set her on fire."

I raised my hand for permission to speak. "Actually, she did that to herself."

"You've said that before, too," Ophelia noted. I groaned, hoping Ophelia wasn't going to sic Sophie on me. I'd just gotten over Sophie's brain-scraping brand of interrogation from our last encounter at a Cracker Barrel.

Mr. Marchand nudged her with his elbow. "She's never lied to us before, Ophelia. She's no good at it."

Ophelia sighed, "Fine. Emery Mueller, I hereby take you into the custody of this tribunal on the charge of forcibly creating a vampire. Your Trial is scheduled in two days."

"Like a hearing?" Emery whispered. He seemed caught between being terrified of Ophelia and wanting to kiss *her* feet.

Peter smiled nastily. "No."

Emery whimpered as Peter and Sophie dragged him away.

"I'd like to say I hope I don't see you for a while, Jane, but somehow, I don't think it will work out that way," Ophelia said.

"That seems fair," I grumbled.

Ophelia cast a long glance at Dick, a puzzled expression marring her beautiful face. "Let me know if you need . . . help over the next few days."

With that, the Council swept out of the room in silence. I honestly didn't care whether I ever saw Emery or Ophelia again. Gabriel and I slowly approached Dick. I laid a hand on his shoulder. Dick inhaled sharply, but he didn't snap at us when we gently pried Andrea away from him. Dick allowed Gabriel to carry Andrea upstairs to one of the guest rooms. I washed her neck and face, trying to remove any traces that Emery might have left behind. When she woke, I didn't want her to smell him. I cut the bloodied costume from her body and slipped a soft cotton nightgown over her head. Even though I knew I would be talking to her, laughing with her again soon, it still felt like funeral preparations.

I went downstairs and found Dick and Gabriel in my kitchen, an open bottle of Faux Type O between them. I had to try to swallow the lump in my throat twice before I could manage, "Dick, I'm sorry. It's my fault. If I'd just—I didn't even suspect Emery. I was so self-centered. I thought Jeanine was focused on me. It didn't occur to me that she would go after my friends like this."

Dick's voice was raw, a harsh whisper between sips. "You couldn't have guessed, Jane. None of us did. We're going to lay blame at Emery's feet, where it belongs."

"Um, I was dead drunk when I was turned," Dick said quietly, staring into his glass. "I can't remember a thing. I just woke up, and there I was—no pulse, no breath. I, um, I need to know, Jane, does it hurt? To die, I mean? Does it hurt? Did she suffer?"

His eyes pinned me, tears slipping down his cheeks.

"No, it's just like falling asleep," I told him, tucking his hair behind his ear and giving him a sisterly kiss on the cheek. "It doesn't hurt at all."

"I'm going to stay here for a few days if that's OK," Dick said. "I don't want to move her again."

"You're more than welcome," I said. "I'll lay out some sheets and some towels for you."

I pushed away from the counter to do just that, but my arms and legs were suddenly so tired. I stumbled against the kitchen table and felt Gabriel's hands on my arms, steadying me. "Sorry, I think the blood loss and head injuries are catching up with me."

"I can take care of myself, Stretch," Dick said. "Gabe, take her upstairs, and make her get some sleep. I don't care what you have to do to convince her, I just don't want to hear anything."

I smiled at the half-hearted insinuation. To joke about my sex life, Dick must be feeling a little better. I let Gabriel lift me bridal-style and carry me up the stairs. Now it was my turn to be undressed and tucked into bed. When he slid under the sheets behind me, pulling me to his chest, I turned to him and buried my face against his skin.

"I lied," I told Gabriel, wiping at my eyes. "When I said it doesn't hurt to die. I lied. It's agony. It was like drowning on dry land, being crushed, not being able to breathe. It hurts. But I couldn't tell Dick that. I lied."

"I know, sweetheart," he said, brushing his lips along my brow. "I remember. Even without the added pain of being shot, taking that last breath, it hurts. But sometimes we have to lie to protect the ones we love." I narrowed my eyes at him. He cleared his throat. "Though obviously, I will never be doing that again. But you did the right thing."

"How will this affect Dick?" I asked him. "Will it be weird for him to be with a vampire he hasn't sired?"

He shrugged. "It's not a requirement. There are lots of vampires in very successful relationships."

"Are they going to be OK or not?"

"It's a violation," Gabriel agreed. "Dick will be reminded of it every day. He'll feel he failed her somehow, that he didn't protect her. But he loves her. He will set it all aside to be with her."

"It seems my life is just as uncertain and out of control as when I was human. I thought I'd changed, learned. I thought I was more in control. I'm scared of what's to come, what I don't understand yet."

I closed my eyes as Gabriel murmured, "Jane, you can't worry about the future so much that you miss out on the present. And I'll be with you. No matter what."

I slept that deep sleep that requires that you wake up with a patch of drool drying on your face. Vaguely, I remembered falling asleep with Gabriel, waking at one point when it was dark outside, and finding him awake next to me. I was hungry but far too tired to leave the bed, so he held his wrist to my lips and let me drink from him. There were a few more "sleepy patches," in which I woke, fed, and went back to sleep. But now I was just confused and had serious bed hair.

"What time is it?" I asked, squinting in the twilight.

Gabriel stroked a thumb down my temple, where the flesh was smooth and unmarred now. "Six P.M. On Thursday."

I bolted out of bed. "Holy crap, I slept for three days?"

"You were exhausted," he said. "And you had a lot of healing to do."

"Andrea?" I asked, slipping into some clean jeans.

"Rose late last night," he said, smiling. "She was ravenous. She went through your entire supply of synthetic blood and the Hershey's syrup. Dick says he owes you."

"I think I'll let it slide this once." I snorted. "Just pry Dick off of my couch before tomorrow morning. I don't want him getting too comfortable."

Gabriel followed, laughing, as I tore out of bed and down the stairs. Andrea was standing in my living room, balancing my coffee table on one hand. There was a huge grin on her pale, angelic face. Dick looked like a human who'd been staring at the sun for too long, dazzled and dazed. I launched myself at her, knocking the table right onto Dick's head as I hugged her. Dick was still smiling, even as he threw the wreckage over his shoulder.

"Hey!" She giggled, punching me on the arm. Gabriel, who had followed at a less frantic pace, snickered at Andrea's display of newfound strength.

"Ow." I rubbed my arm and glared at her. "I don't think I'm going to like you having superstrength . . . or being all giddy. It's disconcerting."

"Don't be sorry," she said. "I mean, let's be honest. My entire life was leading to this. I'm lucky it didn't happen long before. Of course, I would have much rather that you or Dick turned me when I had, you know, a choice in the matter. But when I think about it, what was I staying human for, anyway? Emery made the choice I should have made a while ago. My family doesn't speak to me. Everyone I love is going to live forever. And how would my relationship with Dick work out in the long term without a change?"

"You're really OK with this?" I asked, giving her a long, appraising look. She'd been merely beautiful in life. She was stunning now. Her skin was a perfect creamy pearl color that set off the fiery red of her hair. Her lips were soft and pink and full, curving over glistening white teeth. I searched her face for some sign of regret, of sorrow, but found nothing. There was a new exuberance to Andrea. It was if she'd finally figured out what she'd been missing all these years: fangs. "Because I had some . . . adjustment issues that you don't seem to be having."

Andrea shuddered delicately. "Well, the blood thing is gross. Even after spending so much time with you, I have to admit it's weird drinking it myself. But look at all the pros. I can climb walls and lift tables, and, frankly, my ass has never looked better."

"Ew."

"I'm looking forward to eternity, Jane," she said, sliding onto Dick's lap. "Besides, at least now, vampires won't see me as a snack."

"I never saw you as a snack, baby doll." Dick chuckled, kissing her neck.

"I love you so much," she cooed, crushing him to her.

"Me, too, honey. Me, too." Dick stroked his fingers over Andrea's. I noticed that she was wearing the little ruby engagement ring he'd shown me on Halloween night. I felt a rush of relief for both of them. Emery may have turned Andrea, but Dick had marked her forever. She was his. It was that simple. And I felt sorry for whoever said otherwise.

But instead of giving voice to these emotionally mature thoughts, I took the "disgusted teenager" route. I groaned. "Ugh, are you two going to go through some sort of gross honeymoon phase? Because you're going to have to do that somewhere else."

"Maybe we should consider another trip," Gabriel suggested. "The Southern Hemisphere should be far enough away."

"Oh, calm down, both of you," Andrea said, smirking. "You might as well get used to it."

"Remind me to write a 'PDA in the workplace' policy for the shop," I muttered to Gabriel.

"Now that all the newborn angst is settled"—Andrea shot me a stern look—"can we talk about why you don't need a stun gun?"

I put up my hands in a defensive stance. "OK, in hindsight, it was not my wisest purchase."

17

Love is about facing fear. The fear of rejection, the fear of intimacy, the fear of being hurt. With vampire relationships, the fear quotient tends to be a little higher.

—*Love Bites: A Female Vampire's Guide to Less Destructive Relationships*

When Gabriel helped me out of his car, I fussed with his tie, straightening the blue-gray silk before giving his bottom lip a nipping kiss.

"What was that for?" he asked.

I kissed him again and adjusted the straps of my own blood-red silk party dress. "For guaranteeing that I will no longer be remembered as 'Planed Jane' by my classmates."

"Why do I get the feeling that I'm being used for my pretty face?" he asked as we passed under a white and blue balloon arch and a banner that read, "Welcome Back, Howlers! Class of 1998!"

"Hush up, arm candy," I muttered.

Half-Moon Hollow High School's gym smelled exactly the same, like BO and anxiety. The reunion committee had tried valiantly to transform the gym into an Enchanted Paradise using the same props they used at our prom ten years before. Let's see, transparent plastic palm trees lined with twinkle lights? Check. Giant papier-mâché volcano with fake flame streamers blowing out? Check. Giant parachute billowing artfully from the ceiling to give the impression that we were extremely well-dressed castaways under an impromptu shelter? Check. Ignoring the fact that said parachute's storage closet was rumored to be the conception site of Coach Kelly's love child with Mindy Noonan? Check.

"This is a rite of passage?" Gabriel asked, eyeing the faux volcano. "What exactly does this signify?"

"Nothing, let's go," I said, turning on my heel and making what would have been a brilliant dash for the door if Gabriel hadn't caught my arm.

"We agreed this was an important part of your emotional development."

"When did we agree to that?" I demanded as he dragged me toward the registration table.

"You said it, I agreed to it. It's similar to a verbal contract."

"You're not a nice man," I told him.

"I think we've established that," he said as he planted me firmly in front of the table, where a brunette in a cantaloupe-colored suit turned to me with pasted-on smile. I searched her face. Huh. I was expecting to be confronted with someone who'd tortured me in the cafeteria or mocked me in math. But I had no idea who this person was.

"Jane!" she cried. "It's so good to see you!"

"Hey . . ." I zeroed in on her name tag. I didn't even recognize the little senior photo that was laminated next to her name. Like so many of us who graduated from HHHS in the 1990s, she suffered from poufy bangs combined with the horrid plaid flannel of the grunge period. (Pop-culture influence had only so much sway over Hollow girls. We could not be persuaded to put away our curling irons.) I scanned the name. "Mary Beth. How are you?"

"Oh, you know me." She chuckled as she handed me my name tag. I winced, because, no, I didn't. "I'm always busy. I'm just so glad to see you here. You look great. And who is this?"

"This is my boyfriend, Gabriel," I said as she scribbled out a guest name tag with a Sharpie.

Mary Beth winked broadly at him. "Well, you better watch her, Gabriel. She was always one of the sassiest girls in the class."

"Not much has changed," Gabriel informed her.

"I can't wait to find the two of you later so we can catch up," she cooed.

"See? That woman seemed very happy that you're here," he said as we walked away. "She said you were sassy and seemed to think it was a good thing."

"I have no idea who that woman is," I told him.

"It still counts. So, that's what you looked like in high school?" he asked, staring at the tiny yearbook photo embossed on my name tag.

I pinched his arm. "I went through an unfortunate-hair era. Don't judge me. You used to wear stockings."

"They were in fashion at the time," he protested.

"So were the permed bangs. Thank God for cruel college girls and a roommate who read *Cosmo*."

He snorted.

I hadn't seen most of my classmates in a while. Some of them had actually managed to escape the Hollow and establish life on the outside. And the ones who did live in town had daytime schedules, so our paths didn't cross often. Everybody looked . . . smaller. Not weightwise, because a few people had packed on some pounds. But somehow I remember these people as giants, looming over me. Most of them were smiling, making polite conversation. And the social boundaries that had defined us ten years ago seemed to have melted away. The former jocks were mixing with the AV club, the Homecoming queen had an affectionate arm around the softball captain. We ambled past a display of photos, surrounded by white votive candles. In glittery silver letters, it said, "We Remember Fondly . . ."

"I'm on the memorial board!" I gasped. "I thought I took care of that! I RSVP'd, for goodness sake. Dead people don't RSVP!"

"Well, at least they remembered you fondly," Gabriel said, trying to find a silver lining.

"Gah!" I huffed.

"It says fondly!" he said again.

"Oh, Jane, it's so nice to see you back from the dead," I heard Jolene drawl from behind me. Jolene was dressed in a simple sleeveless red dress, backlit by the low votives on the tables. Even with a baby tucked in her arms, her hotness was undeniable. She was smirking, obviously enjoying the premature reports of my demise.

"You brought the kids?" I asked, taking Janelyn from her.

"Zeb sort of insisted on it," she said, rolling her eyes. She nodded to where Zeb stood with Joe, surrounded by girls who wouldn't have given him the time of day in school. They were all cooing and making funny faces at the baby. I couldn't help but think he was trying to show them what they had missed by turning him down as a prom date.

"Something about proving to the jerks from wood shop that his 'boys swim.' And we weren't the only ones." She gestured to several other couples bouncing uncomfortable-looking babies in their Sunday best.

I scoffed. "Well, the twins are obviously the best-looking babies here."

She smiled adoringly at Janelyn. "Obviously."

"Having a good time?" I asked a grinning Zeb as he hefted the baby on one hip.

"This is awesome!" he cried as another group of women flocked around his beautiful children, cooing and ahhing. He handed Joe to me, taking Jolene's arm and dragging her toward Adam Morrow, Rick Mullen, and most of the former baseball team. "I think some of the guys over there haven't seen Jolene yet."

Adam spotted me from across the room, and a smile lit up his perfect, even features. He straightened his tie and was two steps toward me when Gabriel slid his arm around my waist and commented on how fetching I looked with babies in my arms. Adam blanched, seeming to size Gabriel up in one long look, and took two steps back toward safety. I snickered.

"What's funny?" Gabriel asked.

I considered telling him, but I remembered Gabriel had threatened to literally put a boot up Adam's ass the previous year. I didn't think an introduction would go over very well.

"Not a thing. Here, can you take one?" I said, awkwardly shifting both babies in my arms.

"Er, I don't think I'm qualified—OK, then." Gabriel grimaced as I tucked Janelyn into the crook of his elbow. He looked into her little face and cleared his throat. "Um, how do you do?" He seemed offended when I laughed at him. "I've never held a baby before! It's not something men did in my time. Even if they were your own."

"No, you're doing beautifully," I promised, kissing him.

"Hey, cut that out, there are impressionable children present," Dick said, taking Joe from my arms and making silly faces. Joe, who thought Dick was the funniest person alive—in his limited worldview—gurgled hysterically.

Dick had been in high spirits for the last week or so. With Andrea's almost seamless transition into vampirism and his renewed friendship with Gabriel, the only thorn in his side was Emery's sentencing. Of course, Ophelia had lifted that burden a few days before, when she arrived at the shop, looking for a copy of the latest Michele Bardsley novel. Dick had asked her what the Council had decided to do with Emery. She gave him a razor-thin smile and said, "There is no Emery." And then she flounced out of the shop in her usual unsettling manner. Knowing that Emery had suffered hideously at the hands of the Council had given Dick and Andrea some measure of closure. Dick and Mr. Wainwright mourned the end of their bloodline but, given Emery's example, agreed it was probably for the best.

"I don't think you qualify as impressionable anymore, Dick," Gabriel said dryly. "But the child label certainly fits."

Dick responded with a hand gesture that was also inappropriate for underage viewing.

"What are you doing here?" I asked. Dick had a tag on his chest declaring that he was Martin Gruber, president of the Chess Club and the Latin Society. Even in the short-sleeved plaid shirt and Clark Kent glasses (complete with white tape around the nose piece), Dick looked nothing like poor, gangly, bespectacled Martin. "And what are you going to do if Martin actually shows up?"

"Claim identity theft. There was no way I was going to miss this." Dick snickered. "Zeb said there was a distinct possibility you might freak out and smack some people around. Maybe even a cheerleader. You know how I love it when you do that!"

I rolled my eyes and focused on Janelyn, who was spitting up on Gabriel's jacket. The twins giggled and drooled, oblivious to the fact that they were surrounded by monsters. Seriously, werewolves on one side of the family, vampires on the other. What were these kids going to be afraid of?

"There's always clowns," I muttered to myself, shuddering.

Jolene swooped in as I struggled to keep Janelyn still and mop up the mess on Gabriel's shoulder.

"Um, something's leaking from somewhere," I said, holding Janelyn at arm's length as she dribbled from her tiny rosebud mouth.

"Come here, baby," Jolene cooed, tucking the baby into her arms and producing a wet wipe from her purse.

"That is the best part. I can give them back," I told Gabriel quietly.

Gabriel asked, "Where's Andrea?"

Dick nodded to the stunning pale redhead standing by the punchbowl, chatting with Hector Gonzalez and a girl I used to take French with. Andrea was pretending to be Dora Grady. Overweight, cursed with bad skin and a shock of unruly red frizz, Dora was our very own Carrie White, without the telekinetic revenge. While I didn't exactly participate in the locker-room abuse of Dora, my social paralysis, my failure to do anything to help her, still haunted me years later. If anyone deserved to reemerge as slim, beautiful Andrea, it was Dora. I wondered where she was and hoped that she'd found some measure of happiness, that she wasn't here tonight because she'd decided her former classmates weren't worth her time.

And that she wasn't lurking in the eaves of the gym, waiting to trap us inside and kill us in a well-deserved inferno.

I shook off these thoughts. Andrea was adjusting to vampire life far faster than I had. She was already used to nighttime hours. She didn't have the moral confusion I did about feeding from donors, having been in their shoes. And she and her vampire boyfriend, now fiancé, had settled most of their issues before she was turned. I could only hope that she wouldn't ask me to be a bridesmaid.

I thought back to my plan for a Brave New Jane. Andrea would never need one, but so far, I'd made impressive headway on mine.

Normal, healthy relationship? As normal and healthy as I was ever going to get, so: Check.

Fulfilling career? Check.

Loving, nonjudgmental family? I'd created my own and managed to include a few blood relatives, so: Check.

Plan for world peace? I'd get right on it.

I was standing there, admiring my friend, when Gabriel tapped me on the shoulder.

"Can I talk to you for a minute?" he asked, leading me away from the punchbowl, oozing infants, and our friends.

"Where are we going?" I asked as we quietly left the gym and headed for the electives building.

"To sneak around the campus for a little bit in the dark. Isn't this what couples do in the movies?" Gabriel asked as we passed the metal shop.

"Yeah. The horror movies where loving couples are killed by maniacs wielding farm implements. Please don't tell me that after all this, you're leading me to my death."

"Well, you're already dead, and I've gotten used to having you around."

I laughed. "Right back atcha, sweetheart. But seriously, what are we doing out here?"

"I gave your sister a present today," he said, slipping his hand into mine.

"You're dragging me out in the hall to tell me you gave my sister a present? This is just like my sixteenth birthday."

"I'm bringing you out here to tell you that I went to your sister earlier tonight and offered her the deed to my house."

I arched a brow. "You mean the deed to one of your nicer rental properties?"

"To my house on Silver Ridge Road. I asked if she would like to have it, and she accepted. Actually, I'd barely uttered the word 'deed,' and she'd accepted. She'd like to move in as soon as possible."

I found that didn't bother me as much as I thought it would. Our muddy catharsis seemed to have exorcised the old, almost instinctual resentments toward Jenny, though it was sort of weird to be around her now that we'd called an unofficial truce. I was so used to automatically rejecting any invitation to family gatherings that I stumbled over telling Mama that, yes, I'd come to Thanksgiving and to tell Jenny that I'd bring my own dessert blood. When we talked, Jenny couldn't figure out where to put her hands. It was like a bad commercial audition. Also, now that she wasn't openly knocking me to Grandma Ruthie anymore, I don't think they were spending as much time together as they used to. Mama was beside herself with joy, even though I still turned down half her invitations.

I said that Jenny and I had reconciled, not that I'd gone crazy.

"But that's a huge part of your family history. Why would you give it up?" I exclaimed.

Gabriel shrugged. "Eh, I've lived there for a hundred and fifty years. I was getting bored with it. Besides, nobody will take better care of the place than Jenny. And I suspect she'll let your mother put the house on the Historical Society's Spring Tour of Homes, which will indirectly cement your mother's affections for me even further."

"So, you're basically homeless now?"

"No, I still have the houses in—" Gabriel caught himself. "Yes, yes, I am."

I crossed my arms. "So, where do you plan on living?"

"Well, I was thinking I might move in with you."

"Why don't you wait to be asked?"

"Because I'd be waiting forever," he muttered. In a very deliberate motion, he squared my shoulders in front of his and clasped my arms. "I know I could never ask you to leave River Oaks. It means a lot more to you than my family's house means to me. Your aunt Jettie is there. It's your home. I would like it to be my home, too. I want to make a life with you, and for most people, that means living in the same house."

Gabriel kissed me, as gentle as an angel's wing brushing across my lips. "You're my bloodmate in every sense of the word, the person I choose to spend the rest of my immortal life with, if you can stand me that long."

"That's what that means?" My forehead wrinkled in concentration, and I tried to remember the first time I'd hear that word. "Wait, you told Missy the crazy Realtor that she'd suffer dire consequences if she hurt your 'bloodmate.' That was more than a year ago."

"I knew even then. You're it for me, Jane. You're my eternity."

"Well, why couldn't you have told me?" I exclaimed.

Gabriel shrugged. "You—"

"I wasn't ready to hear it yet," I finished for him. "I'm sorry." But as the enormity of what Gabriel had just said sunk in, a huge grin split my face. I brought it under control, so I could narrow my eyes at him. "So, you're saying you will tell me everything now. You won't try to protect me or keep me in the dark. You'll trust me to make a rational decision about bad news after I have my inevitable, initial panic attack?"

He nodded solemnly. "I will."

"And when I have my spastic fits of insecurity, when I make inappropriate jokes and wonder aloud why you love me, you'll understand that this has nothing to do with you but years and years of conditioning by my mother?"

He smirked. "I will."

"Will you agree never to accept invitations issued by my family unless you check with me first?"

He nodded. "Absolutely."

I giggled, throwing my arms around him and kissing him deeply. "I love you."

"Wait, it's my turn," he said, cupping my face so I was locked in that bottomless gray gaze of his. "Do you promise to trust that I want to be with you and no one else? That I'm not going anywhere? Will you promise to stop trying to find problems in our relationship where there are none, to give us time to work on the problems we do have?"

"What problems?"

Gabriel huffed out a breath. "Jane."

"I will," I promised.

"Will you quit trying to push me away?"

"I will."

"Will you promise never to let Dick move into our house?"

I snickered. "I will . . . but, um, there's one last thing."

Gabriel frowned. "What's that?"

"Can we wait on telling my mother that you're moving in? As much as she likes you, she has this thing about 'living in sin.' The minute she finds out, the pressure for you to make an honest woman of me will start. She's already making noises about us getting engaged. I think this would just fuel her fire."

"I could always propose," he suggested, kissing my cheek.

Suddenly, my mouth went dry. As much as I couldn't imagine my life without Gabriel, I knew that neither one of us was ready for the rice-and-veil route just yet. We'd only reconciled a few weeks before. As sure as I was of his love, I needed more time before I could accept a ring from him.

What can I say? I'm a contrary soul.

"Thank you, but I'm not ready yet," I told him. Gabriel tried and failed to tamp down the flash of disappointment on his face. "I won't marry anyone but you, Gabriel Nightengale. But for now, let's just see if we can live together without anyone getting hurt. And the family thing, it won't be that big of a deal. It just means you can't leave any evidence of you living there lying around where my family can see it, like clothes or personal items or your car. It's just for the next few decades, until, you know, they die."

"Let me get this straight. You can face down psychotic vampires and legions of anal-retentive entrepreneurs, but you're afraid to tell your parents that I'll be living with you before marriage?"

I nodded. "Yes, that's exactly it."

"We'll have to talk about this," Gabriel said dryly.

"But hey, between Jenny's new attitude and having you present at Christmas, I may be able to escape the holidays unscathed."

Gabriel blanched, his face even paler in the moonlight filtering through the window. "Christmas? With your relatives?"

I smiled, my fangs nicking my lip. "Welcome to the family, honey."

Gabriel smiled back and kissed me, long and deep. "I can live with that."